GAVIN BALLER BOOK 3: GALACTIC KINGPIN

Printed in the United States of America

First Printing, 2019

ISBN 9781077443822

www.superheumann.com

TABLE OF CONTENTS

CHAPTER 1

OVERBURST

Gavin's boots smacked against the floor of the spacecraft's main hallway as he ran far faster than needed. White walls flew by in the fringes of his vision along with crew members on their way to jobs or meals in different parts of the Silver Hammer. Dark strands of shoulder-length hair swung in front of his eyes, sticking to the sweat on his forehead. The gray and white military jumpsuit hugging his muscles had an uncanny ability to whisk away the perspiration under his armpits but did nothing to cool him during extended periods of exertion. His heart pounded, though admittedly as much from embarrassment as exercise.

The massive silver vessel acted as a giant cage, holding him in place with no exits or means of escape. Physically confined, emotionally frustrated, it seemed he had no options for release.

Smells of purple alien Cytemore flowers filled his lungs as he plunged into the arboretum at the ship's center. Twenty and thirty-foot tall trees reached for a ceiling shining with artificial sunlight and blue skies. Yellow and orange blossoms wafted on the warm breeze from air ducts overhead; one deep red bloom spitting pollen like wisps of pink smoke. Moist, humid air reminded Gavin of summers in Brazil with his grandparents. An insect about the size of a large bee buzzed in front of Gavin's face as he jogged through the garden. Waving his hand, Gavin shooed the bug away, wishing he could do the same to his current feelings of stupidity and inadequacy.

"Those things have a nasty sting, from what I understand."

Gavin stopped in his tracks, turning to see who had spoken. His best friend Seth sat on a bench, reclined like an old man about to play chess in Central Park. His brown hair, recently trimmed, fluttered on the draft from above; tight white shirt clinging to his chest and accenting the muscles slowly forming beneath.

Gavin had to admit the past four months had done wonders for his friend. Where Gavin balked under Zaire's tutelage, Seth excelled. Everything from language to combat training had been absorbed by the man like water on thirsty soil. Where once a thin comic book geek had sat, now a commanding presence resided. A year in solitary confinement will push a man to his breaking point, but in Seth's case, no cracks remained — only the firm resolve of tempered steel.

Releasing a tired breath, Gavin placed his hands on his knees and nodded at his friend. "I saw a gardener get stung by one a few weeks ago. Her hand swelled up to the size of a grapefruit."

"Yeah, so it's not a good idea to piss them off." Seth patted his hand on the bench next to him as an invitation for Gavin to sit.

"I'm surprised Zaire let you out of class early." Gavin walked slowly toward his friend. He sat down, looking up at the trees and shrubs filling the pleasant five-acre wide space. A greenskeeper trimmed a series of vines encroaching on the path with a pair of silver scissors. The snipping of pruning shears reminded Gavin of his dad working in his garden in São Paolo.

"She's not as big of a hard-ass with me as she is with you because she knows I'll study on my own." Seth sniffed the pollinated air.

Gavin stretched his legs, a burning sensation rippling from his calves to his thighs. "Still, she's pretty strict when it comes to punctuality. You've got to be at least a half hour late to class at this point."

"I've been tutoring Ashton the last few days," Seth said. "Even after spending five years in that zoo on the Gadabout, he didn't really pick up any of the language. He's having a hard time and Zaire thought it would be good for me to help push him along. He and I finished up about ten minutes ago. Plus, as I was walking toward the control deck, I saw Isla in one of the training rooms and she looked ready to kill the next person who spoke to her. I assumed by her rage that it had something to do with you."

"I'm not always a jerk, you know." Gavin's head dropped slightly; eyes focused on the dirt at their feet.

Seth placed his hand on his friend's shoulder. "No, only most of the time. What happened?"

"I'm, you know…" Gavin began, face smirking in annoyance. "It's, just…frustrating."

"You want to get laid," Seth replied with a nod.

"Holy crap, yes!" Gavin sat back, hand running through his long black hair. "It's been four months since we left Kr'thotok and I'd hoped that during that time, our relationship would progress past the kissing and hand-holding stage. There's only so many times you can read *Oh the Places You'll Go!* before you actually want to go somewhere."

"Dude, you know how sacred physical relationships are to the Dubaku," Seth said, swiping at a tiny purple butterfly attempting to land on his nose. "They won't even talk about their husbands or wives except with the closest and most trusted of peers. I mean, Zaire didn't even tell us she was married until after you guys were rescued by her husband. I know it's not ideal, and for us it's weird, but you have to respect that."

"I know. I do. And she wants to get married first, and that's fine, it's just I'm having a hard time pulling the trigger on that aspect of my life. We got in a fight because I asked her to stay in my room overnight again."

"Why?" Seth asked. "You know where she stands. Why are you pushing it? Isla is the best woman you're ever going to find, Gavin Baller, out in space or back on Earth. Don't screw it up because you can't keep it in your pants."

Gavin's head tilted back, neck cracking with the movement. "I know, okay. I know. It's stupid and I wasn't thinking. I'm embarrassed about it. Marriage is just a bit too much for me to think about right now. I mean, we're flying through space in what looks like a giant silver wasp, trying to find a warlord who I was cloned from, and we just fought in a war on a planet with blue lava where I killed a bunch of alien soldiers. It's a lot to deal with. Two years ago, my biggest worry was what would Armond White say about me in his next movie review. That guy hated me."

"We've all been through a lot, I'll admit, but I'm surprised it's the marriage question that's giving you trouble," Seth said, placing his elbows on his knees and leaning forward. "You asked her to marry you after you'd only known her for four days."

"That wasn't, like, an official proposal. It was more a, 'Hey, I intend to marry you one day,' sort of thing."

"You've wanted to get married since we were kids. What's holding you back now?"

Gavin's forehead crinkled. His feelings of inadequacy had grown exponentially each day they traveled closer to Abraxas-Mon, the amazing warlord that everyone loved, who also happened to be Gavin's 'genetic donor'. Since his early childhood, Gavin had always been the strongest and most handsome guy in the room. Faced with the disappointment of his cloned status, everything had changed. Questions filled his brain, most of which had become too painful to think about.

What would happen when the two men, original and copy, stood face to face? How could Gavin possibly compare with a man known throughout the Galactic Commonwealth as the Great Hero and Wealth-Bringer? Would Isla realize she could do so much better and leave Gavin for his superior self?

He didn't want to think about it, let alone talk about it.

Lucky for him, he wouldn't have to. The Thought-Mech bracelet on Seth's right wrist began flashing purple in alert. Seth's eyes watched each blink intently, like a doctor reading a patient chart.

"Zaire wants all of us in the command center immediately." He stood up from the bench.

"You've gotten really good at reading those things," Gavin admitted, pushing himself from the comfort of his seat.

"It's not too far from Morse Code, though the ebbing and flowing of the light adds different meaning. If you'd spend more time studying with me and less time arguing with your girlfriend, you'd be able to pick it up too."

Stretching his back, Gavin followed Seth toward the main briefing room on the upper deck. They exited the garden, fragrant flowers giving way to sanitary hallways. The air became less humid, sucking the moisture from Gavin's skin like a leech.

"A drink of water would be nice," he mumbled.

"If you need me to talk to Isla, I'll do it," Seth offered, waving at a passing soldier. "You just need to be more understanding."

Seth approached an elevator on their right, pressing his hand against the door to summon the lift. The entrance folded open, and the two men stepped inside the white-walled conveyance with its smooth glowing surfaces. Gavin licked his dry lips and decided to change the subject.

"And how are you doing so well through all of this?" he asked. "You look like you've put on 15 pounds of muscle in the last two months."

"I probably have," Seth admitted, flexing his left bicep. "Detrius has been training me an hour a day. I've really started to enjoy the workouts, and it's beginning to show. After almost a year in a prison cell, I figured life was short and I needed to do more with it."

"What are Bomb and the ladies up to?"

"Mainly studying, too," Seth said, eyes forward. "Bomb has been progressing incredibly fast. Rolatok has been giving her more and more advanced lessons and she eats them up. Her language is still a bit stilted and caveman like, but I'm sure that will pass soon enough too as she grasps higher grammatical principles. When was the last time you talked to her?"

"I don't know, probably two or three weeks. I don't even know where they're staying on the ship."

"Well, you'll be surprised at how far she's come in that time. Bray and Merida too. Seuss still has some socialization issues, but we're working through them. Those are some tough women, that's for sure."

"You and Bomb are spending a lot of time together, according to Ashton," Gavin smiled.

"Concentrate on your own relationship and then you can focus on whether I'm pursuing one or not," Seth said, lips pulling up at the edges.

"So, you're saying you're pursuing a relationship then?" Gavin prodded.

The elevator door pleated open like a flower, revealing the spacious command center beyond. Seth stepped forward and motioned for Gavin to follow. "I think we have more important things to worry about currently then whether or not I'm interested in a woman."

Gavin followed his friend into the round, four-storied control deck. As always, the walls rippled with blue energy on a white background; glowing Luminaries flittering on the air like swarms of insects. Crew members worked along the elevated walkway above, performing their tasks and controlling various aspects of the ship, a din of conversation filling the spherical space. Cleanser smells mixed with the fragrance of ripe peach and invaded Gavin's nose, reminding him of the contrasting elements of the Silver Hammer that he still couldn't quite reconcile.

"You received my message. Good," Zaire said, waving the two men toward the center table. She stood regally in her Hierarchy robes, white fabric tumbling to the floor in elegant waves of silk. A golden clasp held her black hair back in a bun, brown skin glowing softly against the blueish light. Decade's worth of worry and responsibility lined her eyes and mouth, but even at her age she would be considered beautiful by any estimation.

Standing across from her, equally as magnificent, and even more lovely, her daughter Isla glared at Gavin, arms crossed. A standard white and red uniform conformed to her body snuggly, revealing every stiff muscle and ounce of frustration. Even in her irritation, she took Gavin's breath away, ebony curls falling across her shoulder, bronze lips contrasting against dark flesh.

Zaire's husband Ogpog, the New Zealander Ashton, former zoo resident Bomb, and the seven-foot tall, gray-skinned alien captain of Gavin's Silverback Guard, Brek the Phylónethese, filled out the remainder of space around the conference table.

Blinking his four eyes one after the other, Brek snorted like an animal in greeting to Gavin. The others stood stoically while a collection of Luminaries swirled in the air above them.

"Brek, where's Rolatok?" Gavin asked. "He told me he'd make some of those sweet roll things that are so good."

"Fraptaps," Seth interjected.

"Yeah, those," Gavin continued. "We should have him bring some to us."

Ogpog pressed his hand to the table and illuminated what looked like a star map. "I do not like the Cádavrite coming onto the bridge for unofficial business."

"Hey," Gavin said a bit more harshly than intended. "We've talked about this. Just because the guy almost died and was put through some artificial process that turned his skin kind of gray doesn't make him less than the rest of us. Cádavrite are no different than you or me, and it's not their fault anyway. You guys need to deal with it."

"I do not wish to continue that conversation at the present," Ogpog replied.

Gavin stood, hands on his hips. "Well apparently we still need to if you guys can't treat him like a human being."

"We came as soon as we got your message, Matriarch," Seth said, cutting the argument short. He approached Zaire with a bow.

Zaire nodded in reply, eyebrows raising slightly. "I have told you many times that I am no longer Matriarch. The Hierarchy has dictated it so."

"And we've told *you* many times that the Hierarchy can shove their dictates right up their asses," Gavin said with a smile. "You're the Matriarch on this ship, and as far as I'm concerned, anywhere else you go."

"Gavin, it's good to see you." Zaire motioned for him to take his place next to her.

"Good to see you, Zaire," Gavin greeted with a nod.

"We missed you at the Rylok Festival Dinner last week," Zaire said.

"Sorry about that," he said. "I'll be at the next one, I promise."

In truth, Gavin had avoided most of the social gatherings over the last month. It seemed the closer they drew to Abraxas-Mon, the more isolated Gavin felt; the more isolated he felt the more likely it became for him to avoid people. He realized the cycle needed to stop before he eventually pushed everyone away, but even so, Gavin found the task a difficult one.

"Gavin," Ashton whispered in his New Zealand accent while sidling up to the actor. His blond hair, always perfectly combed, bounced with each movement, as if the man's energetic nature extended to his very follicles. "I have those…items you requested."

"Those 'items' better not be contraband meat packets from the Athelbrath Flesh Harvest," Zaire said, never looking away from the Luminaries.

"You have excellent hearing," Ashton said, scurrying back to his place next to the table and adjusting the buttons on his cream-colored dress shirt.

"You are not to become a trafficker aboard this vessel, Ashton Pingree," Zaire stated flatly.

"It's not that big a deal," Gavin shrugged.

Zaire took a moderating breath. "It is a big deal when you smuggle prohibited materials aboard this ship. Those rations are not processed correctly and may contain bacteria that can contaminate one's bowels. Plus, the hunting practices at the Athelbrath Flesh Harvest are barbaric and should not be supported."

"Ashton didn't smuggle them onboard," Gavin countered. "It's not his fault your crew enjoys a bit of meat now and then."

Zaire motioned for Ogpog to begin the briefing. "We can discuss your little trafficking ring later. Let us continue with why we are meeting in the first place."

"I am glad you are all here," Ogpog said in a deep and powerful voice. His towering frame, draped in a colorful bandolier signifying his rank as Prelate, shifted to the right as his muscular arms waved through the Luminaries like a prophet calling down fire from heaven. The tiny lights shifted and formed into a man's face; a face Gavin recognized: Raymond Halford of Earth.

"You found him," Seth breathed.

"I found him," Bomb said with a nod. "Only one place would take man like Halford: Gadabout." She practically spat the word. Gavin understood her hatred of the scummy city-state; she had been a captive in a zoo there since childhood and forced to be little more than an animal used for breeding.

"How did you find him?" Gavin asked, unaware Bomb possessed any tracking skills, let alone the base of knowledge needed to use the ship's thought-interface.

Everything about the woman had evolved over the roughly five months since they had rescued her, Ashton, the late Malory, and the three other zoo prisoners. Her long blonde hair, originally course and tangled, now billowed over her shoulder from a ponytail, shining in the lights of the floating Luminaries. By any standard, Gavin would consider her attractive, but so much more than mere good looks surged deep within her core. Bomb could eventually rival Isla in terms of leadership and capability given the chance, easily eclipsing Gavin in every way.

"Bomb has proven herself an excellent sleuth when it comes to movement and instinct," Ogpog said. "She naturally sees past many of the preconceptions the rest of us have regarding logic and problem solving. Simply put: her view of the universe is pure. She sees what others miss and is almost as good at uncovering a lie as a Nythensus. All she needed to do was spend a few hours studying gravity river traffic and the movements of Hierarchy vessels. Once she narrowed things down a bit, she ran a search for Kr'thotok space vessels which led her to some well-hidden landing logs signed by Fralt Randok on the Gadabout. Bomb is quite impressive; I trust her conclusions."

"Fralt Randok?" Gavin mused. "Isn't that they guy who Zaire shot in the knee when we escaped from that crap-hole?"

Zaire smiled slightly. "The same."

"Okay, so if we know where this Halford guy is, do we go get him now and arrest him or something?" Ashton questioned.

"Not yet," Zaire said. "We have much bigger problems. Watch the Speculates."

Again, the glowing Luminaries spiraled and reformed into a series of hundreds of spaceships. An entire fleet.

"As you can see here," Ogpog continued, "our intelligence has informed us that the Hierarchy armada has been amassed near the asteroid cluster Ganymede. Conversely, what remains of the Rebirth Militia after the battle of Kr'thotok has coalesced less than a four-cycle journey from there on a 45-degree y-axis. They will likely not commence a pitched battle for some months, but speed is now our only ally. War is a forgone conclusion at this point. Militia raiding parties have already attacked several colonies on adjacent planets."

"Alright." Gavin watched the Luminaries twinkle and move to show both armadas. "We race to Abraxas-Mon and get him on our side as quickly as possible."

"There is one more problem," Isla said, waving her hand through the Speculates. The tiny lights transformed into a spherical shape; a planet covered in large landmasses, smaller oceans, and heavy cloud-cover.

"Thank you, Isla'a. This is the sacred planet Asha'asethol," Zaire began. "Home to the Perennial forefathers, the Asha'andasa."

"I thought Abraxas-Mon was on the desert planet Granthus," Gavin said, confident in his intel.

"I see you have been studying the military documents I provided," Zaire said.

Gavin nodded. "I have. Brek, Detrius and I go over them every morning. According to my calculations we still have another month before we reach Granthus. 30 days, 16 hours, 12 minutes."

"That is correct," Ogpog said. "The problem is that we will not make it to Granthus before our supplies run out. Our last clandestine restock was cut short by that Hierarchy patrol. They are less than a day behind us at this point and riding the gravity streams at full speed. Since the battle on Kr'thotok, my beautiful Konti'ikont has not been at full strength or velocity. Even now, the Hierarchy cruisers are within striking distance. We needed a location to rest and recoup."

Gavin waved his hand through the Luminaries, reforming them into the shape of an alien bust, large head tapering to a thin chin, intelligent and kind eyes staring out from deeply set sockets. "Correct me if I'm wrong but coming to Asha'asethol uninvited is considered a sacrilegious act."

"Very true," Zaire confirmed. "But since we are outlaws anyway, and the Hierarchy is currently undermining millennia of the Perennial's work, we realized holding to such restrictions would only aid in galactic death. And the Plenipotentiary would never authorize their fleet to come within a day's journey of the sacred planet, giving us a chance to breathe and reevaluate."

The Luminaries churned and billowed, whirling from the shape of the Asha'andasa into what appeared to be an alien city built around a temple complex with a flat-topped pyramid in the center.

"This is the capital city Æstork, and the holy temple Othpethoth," Ogpog said. "We are approaching the planet now and will set our course toward the outskirts. Have any of our messages been answered, Isla'a?"

"No, Father," she replied. "Communications are being relayed from the capitol telling of recent vessels landing and departing, but we have received no responses thus far. It is possible they are unhappy with our proximity to the planet without an official overture from the Asha'andasa Grand Council."

"Have you guys ever been here before?" Ashton asked.

"Yes," Zaire admitted. "But it has been over 20 years."

"It'll be so cool to meet actual Perennials," Seth prattled.

"What about you, Isla?" Gavin asked, looking her in the eyes for the first time since entering the command center. "You ever been here?"

"I have not," she answered, a sad smile crossing her lips. "I have not seen a member of the Elder Race since my childhood."

"It has been rare for them to venture beyond the sacred planet for many years now," Zaire informed. "Few Dubaku have been called here in the last few cycles."

"Their inattention has cost many lives," Brek said, scratching his shoulder.

Gavin clapped his hands. "Well, I'm all for setting down and getting some help before we find Abraxas---"

An explosion rocked the ship, throwing Gavin against the table and tossing Seth and Zaire to the floor. The Silver Hammer pitched to the right 15 degrees and knocked a crew member from the upper walkway two stories above. The Dubaku crashed to the ground in a lump and didn't move. Luminaries scattered like gazelle from a predator. Brek leaped into the air in surprise, landing on his large feet before pulling a knife from his belt.

The ship slowly righted itself, but not before two more people fell from the elevated workstations, one of them screaming as her ankles shattered on impact. Alarms blared, walls flashing red in shock and fear.

"Holy shit!" Ashton cried, planting his feet so he wouldn't fall over.

"An Overburst!" Brek howled.

Gavin ran over to Isla as she held firmly to the table. "Are you alright?" he asked, heart pounding like a boxer in an unexpected fight.

"I am," she said, touching his face, anger and resentment fleeing her eyes in worry and apprehension's wake.

"I'm sorry," Gavin began.

Isla cut him off. "Now is not the time."

Bomb growled as she pulled Seth back on his feet. Ogpog rushed to Zaire, who stood with no need for assistance.

"What was that?" Gavin asked, looking around the command center. His mind quickly calculated the Silver Hammer's mass. Any force powerful enough to upset the inertia of the immense ship, let alone rock it back and forth, would need to be as forceful and destructive as a nuclear explosion.

"Gavin Baller!" Brek bellowed, unharnessing a rifle out of a leather pouch across his back. "We are under attack! We're lucky the Overburst didn't crack the ship in two. It's a blatant attempt to intimidate us."

"What's an 'Overburst'?" Ashton asked, wiping sweat from his upper lip.

"Think of a Gravity Bomb at a much larger scale and far more destructive," Seth said. "Like a nuke in space with gravity instead of fire."

"Sir! Matriarch!" a crewmate shouted from above. "The Hierarchy advanced fleet has arrived."

"The entire advanced fleet?" Ogpog questioned, yelling over the blaring alarm.

"Yes, Prelate! They have been riding our wake and pushed forward unexpectedly in the last hundredth roused-cycle. The blast damaged our---"

A second detonation tossed Gavin and Isla backward, vibrations rattling their teeth. Gavin rolled onto his side, holding Isla close. They tumbled end over end for several feet before slowing to a stop and suddenly rocking back in the opposite direction as the ship shifted again. The limp form of the unconscious crewman who had fallen to the lower level flopped past them on his way across the tilting room.

"Gravity buffers are shifting!" Zaire shouted as she grabbed the table for support. Gavin tried to stand but found he and Isla plunging instead toward the far wall as if the entire Silver Hammer tilted on a giant gimbal.

"Seth!" Bomb yelled, reaching for the man as he tripped and fell next to Ashton.

Settling at 20 degrees off axis, the ship remained steady at that harsh angle, allowing Gavin to plant his feet enough to keep from sliding all the way across the massive command center. His inner ear throbbed as the gravity around him continued to undulate in uncomfortable waves, twisting his stomach into knots. A group of Luminaries flew by, stopping next to him and forming the shape of a vomiting emoji face.

"Is everyone alright?" Zaire asked, holding fast to the table.

"We're okay," Seth said as he grabbed Bomb's hand and pulled himself up the fresh incline toward the center of the room. Brek picked up Ashton under his arm like a three-year-old child and stomped loudly with each step.

"You don't have to carry me, Brek," the New Zealander barked.

"We need to right Konti'ikont and return fire!" Ogpog cried as he scrambled to his feet. Walking up the steep slope toward the table, he grasped Zaire's hand. "My Matriarch, we must prepare for battle."

"We're not going to have much luck if we don't fix the gravity in here," Gavin said, pulling himself and Isla from the angled floor.

Zaire's mouth opened to answer, but before words could pass her lips, the ceiling and walls flickered; the purplish red of the alarm dissipating in favor of a three-story-tall image of a woman. Gavin looked up at the ceiling into angry eyes and a scowling face. All the Luminaries in the command center shifted as well, transforming into three dimensional holograms of the woman, each moving in concert with the screen above.

"Lady Zaire." The woman's voice echoed loudly as if the entire ship shouted her words. Her face, young, smooth as granite but equally as hard, looked familiar, as if Gavin had seen her before but couldn't quite place exactly where. Black hair pulled back tightly into a bun, a streak of yellow running from her forehead all the way up to the pinnacle of her opulent beehive in one twisting swirl. Gold hoop earrings, needlessly large and ornate, dangled from her lobes and accented a choker of pure silver around her neck. Whoever she was, Gavin could tell, despite her dramatic ornamentation, she was not a woman to trifle with.

"Mistress Brendant," Zaire said, a bite to her voice. "I have not seen you since our dinner prior to the battle of Kr'thotok."

That's where Gavin had seen her. This Brendant had been one of the Plenipotentiary representatives at the party their first night aboard the Silver Hammer after they'd escaped the Gadabout. He remembered her sneering at his bare feet, as if Gavin had broken some unassailable rule of decorum. She walked through the banquet talking down to Zaire and looking at Bomb and the other women like they were nothing more than stray animals. The memory certainly colored his opinion of the Mistress beyond her attack on their ship.

"Prelate Ogpog," Brendant continued, volume almost too loud to endure. "The vessel Konti'ikont has been disabled and will be returned to the Hierarchy upon your surrender. The fact you have come to the Sacred World shows how far you and the former Matriarch have fallen in your heresy."

"She will always be my Matriarch," Ogpog responded.

"Tell me, Brendant," Zaire said, holding firmly to the table to keep her feet from sliding out from under her. "Are you aware of the Hierarchy's betrayal of the Asha'andasa? Has your new Matriarch sent you here blindly, or are you an accomplice to their crimes?"

"I *am* the new Matriarch," Brendant stated firmly.

"That's bullshit," Gavin shouted, stumbling against the

slanting ground. Isla came up beside him, rage evident on her face.

Brendant smiled broadly. "Ah, Mr. Baller. The man who has thrown the entire Commonwealth into disarray. I must admit when I first saw you aboard that very ship, I doubted your basic intelligence. Now I see I was only half wrong."

"Shut up, lady," Gavin said, waving his hand dismissively toward the ceiling. "Let me tell you how this is going to go, okay? You're going to fight us and loose. Zaire is going to kill you because obviously you're kind of a bitch; she's going to reclaim her place as Matriarch, and everything will be the way it should be."

"I am glad you are so confident, Mr. Baller," Brendant replied. "Particularly as I could burn that great vessel to cinders at this very moment and kill all of you."

"You know what?" Gavin yelled through grit teeth.

"We surrender," Zaire said, stepping in front of Gavin and squeezing his wrist tightly. "We surrender to your grace and seek mercy from our superiors."

"Like hell we do!" Gavin protested.

Zaire's fingers dug into the flesh on the back of Gavin's hand painfully. "We surrender, my Matriarch," she repeated without looking away from the imposing image above them. "We only require enough time to reassert our gravity and we can be boarded and taken into custody."

"We agree to your terms, Lady Zaire," Brendant said, eyes tapering to suspicious slits. "But if there are any surprises once my strike team boards, I promise I will not hesitate to sacrifice you and every living soul on that ship in the very shadow of the Sacred World of the Asha'andasa."

"There will be no stratagem employed, I promise on my Matriarchal oath."

"Very well. Prepare for our arrival." The image of Brendant rippled like the surface of a lake and disappeared, returning the ceiling to its previous shade of red and purple.

"I will shoot that woman in the face," Brek grunted, cocking his rifle with his mouth while still holding Ashton under his arm.

Gavin pulled his wrist from Zaire's grasp and rubbed his scratched skin. "I'm with Brek. What the hell was that? And where does she get off calling herself the Matriarch? We can't just give up!"

"And we will not," Zaire said, nodding to Isla. "You know what to do, Isla'a."

"I will prepare, Mother," Isla said, letting go of the table and sliding down the sloping floor toward the closest exit.

"Where are you going?" Gavin called after her. "Why can't you to just tell me what's going on before you run off all the time?"

Gravity began to shift back, ground slowly leveling out. Gavin's equilibrium wavered, giving him the feeling of still standing at an angle even though the ground beneath him centered under his feet.

"Whoa, I'm dizzy," Seth said, wobbling up to Gavin while Bomb supported him from under his armpit.

"Put me down!" Ashton yelled, thumping his fists against Brek's thick leg. The Phylónethese blinked the two sets of eyes on his asymmetrical face and grimaced, dropping the blond man to the floor unceremoniously. "Bugger! You could have warned me!"

"I followed your directive," Brek replied.

"Where is Isla going, Zaire?" Gavin asked.

Zaire rushed to Ogpog as if Gavin hadn't spoken. "Order the Fra'aklob to ready for departure now!"

"Yes, my Matriarch," Ogpog said, turning toward the hallway on their left and running at full speed.

"What the hell is going on?!" Gavin shouted. "And what is a Fra'aklob?"

"Aklob means to shoot," Seth answered.

"I know what Aklob means, Seth" Gavin said, smacking his hand against the table. "What's Fra'aklob?"

"Slingshot," Zaire answered. She grabbed Gavin's arm and pulled him toward the elevator he and Seth had exited earlier. "Isla'a and I prepared for this eventuality. I knew the fleet would be ordered to pursue us at all costs so as not to tip the balance of power back toward the Perennials. We readied a small ship known as a Slingshot for you and a small crew to use for escape. We are close enough to the planet now to launch."

"Why does nobody tell me these things?" Gavin asked, hands flying over his head.

"We did not think it would be needed," Zaire soothed. "It was merely a precaution."

Seth ran up beside them, Bomb hovering close by. "They'll shoot us down or destroy the Silver Hammer if we try to escape now."

"Brek!" Zaire called over her shoulder. "Follow Gavin and myself to the tertiary landing bay. Isla'a awaits our arrival."

"Yes, Matriarch," Brek replied, beating his fist against his chest in recognition of the order.

"What is going on?!" Gavin shouted, veins bulging along his forearms.

"The Slingshot rides gravity much more quickly than a standard vessel," Zaire answered. "The Hierarchy fleet will not know it took off until after they search the data logs, leaving the Silver Hammer safe from assault. It only seats four individuals and can outrun any pursuit over a limited distance. The ship has the capability to run at excessive speeds for mere moments before its engines falter, but as I said, we are close enough to the planet to allow our escape."

Gavin began to understand. "They won't come after us once

they find out we ran?"

"No member of the Hierarchy would set foot on Asha'asethol without the proper invitation. They see it as desecration. In truth, I feel arriving unbidden is a deep dishonor to the Elder Race as well, but we will have to risk the Perennial's displeasure nonetheless if we are to thwart galactic genocide."

Gavin nodded. "Alright, let's go."

"If Gavin's going, then I'm going," Seth said, hands on his hips.

"I goes where Seth and Gavin goes," Bomb agreed.

Zaire grabbed Seth's face like a kind mother. "I am sorry Mr. Kemp, but this is one journey where you must stay behind."

"No," Seth protested. "No! We've been through too much to all get separated now."

"Seth, we must argue our case directly to the Perennials," Zaire said, sadness in her eyes. "Gavin, Brek, Isla'a and I will go. The rest must remain with my husband on Konti'ikont."

"Zaire, what will happen to everybody left on the ship once it's captured?" Gavin asked.

"Ogpog will claim everyone onboard was merely following our orders," Zaire replied, pressing her hand against the elevator door to activate the transport. "He will be arrested while everyone else remains here on the ship, performing their duties under new command. They will be safe."

Seth shook his head. "I'm not staying behind."

"Not I as well," Bomb said.

Gavin stepped between Zaire and Seth, looking his friend in the eyes. "We'll get this worked out; I promise."

"You don't know that," Seth replied. He grabbed Gavin's shoulders. "We've been through a lot, but the bad stuff only happens when we're all not together."

"It'll be okay; I promise," Gavin repeated. Looking to Bomb's determined face, he smiled. "Keep this guy safe, okay, Bomb? He's going to need you to take care of him."

"I will, Gavin Baller," she said, thumping her fist against her chest in the same way Brek would.

"Gavin, we need to stick together," Seth pleaded.

"I need you way more than you need me, buddy," Gavin admitted, hand resting firmly on Seth's shoulder. "It's been that way since we were kids. You'll be more than fine until we meet up again. Plus, I'll have three of the best warriors in the universe with me. Even I can't screw that up."

Seth chuckled, eyes moist. "I wouldn't be so sure of that."

The elevator opened and Zaire pulled Gavin and Brek inside. As the doors closed, Gavin took one last look at his best friend. If anything happened to Seth — the slightest injury or second of captivity — Gavin would never forgive himself.

CHAPTER 2

OH, SO THAT'S AN AXELROTH!

"Prepare for gravity displacement," Isla said from the seat above Gavin.

"I love that you use technical terms when you should just say, 'Gavin, get ready to throw up!'" he yelled, holding tightly to the vines that had grown from his chair and acted as a harness. The donut-shaped Slingshot rumbled like a freight train, tilting toward the open bay door and an expanse of stars surrounding a tennis ball-sized planet far in the distance. He looked up at Isla's boot-covered feet dangling less than twelve inches above his head.

"We are prepared!" Brek said from somewhere below and slightly behind Gavin.

"How bad is this 'gravity displacement' going to be?!" Gavin asked, feet kicking at the window in front of him. Unlike any spacecraft he'd ever seen, the Slingshot stood on its end like someone about to roll a bagel down a hill. Cramped quarters gave little room for movement. The front glass almost touched Gavin's knees, all four seats stacked on top of each other like chairs on a Ferris wheel.

"The lead Hierarchy vessel is about to board the Silver Hammer. We must leave now," Zaire ordered.

"Understood," Isla said.

"How bad will the gravity displacement be?" Gavin asked again, hoping to get an answer that sounded something like, 'it's gonna feel real good,' but expecting a response more along the lines of, 'you're going to pass out and puke all over yourself and wish you were dead.'

With an unexpected jolt, the Slingshot rocketed forward, leaving behind the Silver Hammer's landing bay before Gavin could register they'd taken off. Gravity pulled with merciless force, pinning his head against the seatback in an attempt to peel his skin from his face.

"I don't like gravity displacement," he said, voice vibrating, eyes shaking like balls of jelly.

"The displacement has not yet begun," Isla informed. "It gets much worse!"

"It's so great to hear that..."

Space itself seemed to morph suddenly, stars pulling in rounded streaks as if being seen through a drop of water. Whether an illusion or an actual effect of the Slingshot's engine, Gavin couldn't be sure, but one thing he did know was that his sinuses did not appreciate the result.

In a flash the world disappeared, all senses blending into one. Thoughts became colors which laughed like smells. Gavin's entire body became taffy stretching across the Grand Canyon. He didn't feel nauseous, thank goodness, but at the same time couldn't be sure he wasn't wetting his pants at that very moment either.

The universe slowed down almost as quickly as it had accelerated. Shapes came into view, first blurry, then focusing as

Gavin's senses recalibrated. A metallic flavor clung to the roof of his mouth, hands quivering uncontrollably. Gavin blinked to refresh his eyes, expecting the view through his window to be similar to what he had witnessed before leaving the landing bay: a field of stars with the Perennial's planet much closer than before. He turned out to be half right.

The planet *was* much closer. Terrifyingly close. Close enough to kiss.

They had entered the atmosphere during their instantaneous and jarring jump and found themselves shooting toward the ground from less than a thousand feet above Asha'asethol's surface. Falling face-first, Gavin pulled against his harness, feet kicking the glass in front of him before realization dawned that whether he freed himself from his seatbelt or not, he had nowhere to go but down. Individual trees stared up at him against a jungle background rushing to meet them. A city basked in morning sunshine on the horizon near the banks of a river, but quickly disappeared from view as the overgrown wilds approached with rocket speed.

A number popped into Gavin's head: six. The number of seconds until they crashed.

"Gravity order restoring!" Isla shouted above the roar of the air buffeting the ship.

Closing his eyes, Gavin hoped this crash would end as successfully as his last, where their ship, Mordecai, had extended a singularity around the crew and saved their lives. As he counted down the seconds, no such force field materialized.

Two seconds. One.

Everything fell perfectly silent, no engine sound, no rush of air, no screaming of strained metal. Had they crashed? Were they dead? Is this what death felt like?

Blood rushed back to Gavin's face, drool trickling from his lower lip. A bird chirped somewhere to his left, the sound of Brek's heavy breathing chorusing the tweets. Opening his eyes, Gavin looked down on his reflection in the glass, a patch of dirt staring back at him through the window. Tufts of yellow grass wafted in a slight breeze less than five feet below his face as a bright blue beetle scampered into a small hole dug in the soil.

"Excellent timing, Isla'a," Zaire groaned, voice hoarse. "We are hovering mere inches from the ground. Is everyone in adequate health?"

"No," Gavin croaked. He pulled at his harness, wanting desperately to stand upright and escape the ship. He reached for the window, feeling the cold glass against his fingers. "Can you stand the ship back up? All the blood in my body is rushing to my eyeballs."

"I am trying," Isla remarked.

"I think I filled my external bladder unit," Brek said from the lower seat.

"Are you saying you just peed yourself?" Gavin asked.

"It is a common after-effect of gravity displacement," the Phylónethese said, not a hint of shame in his voice.

"The Slingshot controls are not responding," Isla said. Gavin looked up, seeing only her boots above him. She continued, "I will pull the cabin chairs back and open the door, but we will need to climb down manually."

"Fine, just get me out of here," Gavin replied, head pounding from the influx of blood to his face.

Servos whirred loudly as Gavin's chair pulled away from the window and locked into the release clasp. His harness unsnapped, almost dropping him from his seat, if not for his quick reflexes. Brek wasn't as agile.

"Akteloth!" the bulbous warrior bellowed as he tumbled from his chair and landed face-first against the glass five feet below. "Warn me you're gonna drop us next time!"

"Sorry," Isla said, waving from above. "The belts

automatically dislodge once re-latched. Do you need any assistance?"

"I'm fine." Brek stood, rubbing his elbow with a growl.

"Let us survey our surroundings," Zaire called from the back of the ship. Light filled the Slingshot along with warm air as she opened the side door. Animal and bird calls echoed outside, reminding Gavin of quiet afternoons with his grandfather in what jungles remained on the outskirts of São Paulo.

He dropped himself next to Brek, light-headedness forcing him to sway back and forth as the blood filtered to the rest of his body. Had they been upright, Gavin would have had no problem exiting the ship, but as they currently floated face-down, several control panels stood in his way. He climbed over each one, eyes focused on the sunlight and smell of wet leaves beyond the door.

"Wow," Gavin said, stepping from the claustrophobic interior into afternoon splendor. A lush jungle surrounded him, colorful butterflies prancing on the air while red and green lizards sat on moss-covered logs spitting out their long tongues in search of a meal. Spongy ground squished under Gavin's feet. He stomped, squirting water in all directions as if he'd stepped on a water balloon.

"This area of the planet receives a great deal of rainfall," Zaire said, grabbing a nearby vine and breaking it open. Liquid poured from the plant like a faucet. "Asha'asethol is a world of either desert or jungle," she continued, taking a drink from the vine. "Ocean and atmospheric currents create a band of desert between the middle latitudes while dense forests dominate elsewhere. It is quite beautiful."

Remembering his thirst, Gavin reached over and took a tentative sip from the vine. Sweet liquid, thicker than water but every bit as refreshing, splashed his tongue and sated his dehydration. Gavin swished the fluid around in his mouth, savoring the flavor and wishing he'd brought a water bottle with him so he could fill it with the pleasant draft.

Brek sloshed next to them, as much from the sopping soil as from the urine that apparently filled his space-colostomy bag. The Phylónethese's heavy feet sank several inches into the sodden ground.

"It feels like home," he said, closing his eyes and breathing deep. "The area of Phylos where I grew up has a similar environment."

"Yeah, I spent a lot of time with my grandparents in a country called Brazil back on Earth," Gavin agreed. "It definitely brings back memories."

"We have a problem," Isla said, poking her head out the door.

"What is it, Isla'a?" Zaire asked.

"The gravity engines have seized. It will be at least a full roused-cycle before they cool enough for us to travel. We pushed our speeds beyond normal operating parameters."

Zaire looked up at the sun overhead. "It should not be a problem. We are currently less than a full Presh from the holy temple complex."

"Okay, so a Presh is about equal to three miles if I remember correctly," Gavin said, allowing a purple butterfly to land on his outstretched index finger. "Which means we better get moving if we're going to get there before dark."

"Gavin is correct," Isla said. "I will grab what few rations we have onboard, and we should head out immediately."

"Agreed," Zaire said, eyes still fixed on the sky above. Isla stepped back in the ship's dark interior.

"I have a better idea, come to think of it," Gavin mused, watching as the butterfly flitted away, only to be plucked from the air by a lizard tongue and quickly devoured. "Why don't we radio for help and have someone come and pick us up?"

Zaire shook her head. "There are no transport ships or vessels of any kind in the capitol city."

"Why not?" Gavin asked.

"Because the Perennials think they're better than us," Brek scoffed.

"That is not the reason, Commander Brek," Zaire chided, finger held up like an unamused professor. "The Elder Race is one of organic simplicity. Within the confines of the temple complex only nature's creatures are allowed."

"What, like horses and stuff?" Gavin questioned.

Isla jumped out of the ship holding a canvas backpack and several foot-long machete-like knives, marked with the intricate ceremonial designs of the Praetorian Guard. "Here," she shouted, tossing the bag to Gavin. "We have enough rations for the night. No more."

"We should not need more than that," Zaire replied. She grabbed the hem of her robes and pulled them over her head, leaving her in a standard form-fitting Matriarch uniform of white and gray, with a red rectangle running from her right shoulder to her hip. "And to answer your question Gavin, yes; there are animals similar to horses here on Asha'asethol, but the Perennials do not ride them. Everything on this planet is in balance with everything else. You shall see. Respect reigns, from the most important magistrate to the minutest insect."

"A fantasy, if you ask me," Brek said, adjusting the rifle across his back and kicking at a lizard scampering by.

Zaire tossed her fine robes inside the ship unceremoniously and stood firm, holding Brek's intimidating gaze without flinching. "It is not a fantasy; and no one asked for your opinion," she replied, eyes darkening. "I have been here before, and you will respect the customs of the Elder Race. As for your weapon: you will leave it behind on the ship."

Brek shuddered angrily like a rhinoceros. "Why?"

"Weapons, particularly rifles and pistols, are not allowed in the temple complex," Zaire answered. "It is a sacred place."

"A Phylónethese is never without his weapon! It is a dishonor to be found unprepared for battle. If I die without my rifle in-hand I will be unworthy to be welcomed into Paradise."

Zaire put her hands on her hips, feet planted firmly. "We are already offending the Asha'andasa by coming here without permission. I will not further insult them by walking fully armed into their temple complex."

"Isla'a has blades with her," Brek protested, pointing at Isla as she strapped one of the machetes to her belt.

"These are for cutting our way through the jungle," Isla defended.

"Is it really necessary that he leaves his gun behind?" Gavin questioned. "I mean, we're about to trek through a jungle on an alien planet. I can't be the only one who's a little worried about that."

"Gavin speaks true, Mother," Isla agreed.

Zaire's hands flew into the air. "Of course, you would say that."

"I am agreeing with him because his concern is warranted," Isla said. "Not because I am in love with him."

Gavin smiled. "You *are* in love with me though, right?"

Isla took a deep breath, lips turning upward slightly. "Yes, despite your best efforts to anger me to the point of killing you."

"I just had to check." Gavin took her hand and squeezed.

"They're sweet," Brek said, nudging Zaire with his massive elbow. "Even though Gavin Baller is completely unworthy of Isla'a, I will shoot any Axelroths that threatens them in the forest."

Gavin's head turned quickly toward his Silverback Guard commander, leaving the 'unworthy' comment behind in favor of a more visceral fear.

"Axelroths live here?" he asked. "Okay, I've been told Axelroths eat people. That dude on the Gadabout said he would feed me to one. I don't imagine they're fluffy kittens."

"They are large and hideous," Brek said. "Terrifying creatures who smell of death and excrete the full skeletons of their prey."

Face turning white, Gavin swallowed. "Thank you for the visual, Brek."

"Fine," Zaire conceded. "You may bring your rifle, but only until we reach the city walkway that leads to the temple. Do you agree?"

Brek grimaced. "I will agree only if I know my weapon will be properly cared for and returned."

"Are we seriously going to run into an Axelroth out here?" Gavin asked, looking around at the trees as if one of them would come to life and rip his flesh off.

"Unlikely," Zaire said, taking one of the knives from Isla and stepping into the trees. "While Axelroths are native to this planet, these forests surrounding the Holy City Æstork are used by the Perennials for sacred contemplation and communing with nature. Thus, dangerous animals are asked to move to other areas. Let us stop talking and start walking."

Gavin crinkled his nose in doubt. "They just ask the Axelroths nicely to leave? 'Hey man-eating animal: get the hell out of here because we're using this forest to pray?'"

"I would not expect you to yet understand the hallowed connection between all forms of life, particularly the life of the Asha'andasa," Zaire said without looking back. "Once in the temple complex, feeling the spirit that there resides, you will gain a more eternal perspective."

Following warily, Gavin looked back toward the Slingshot as it quickly disappeared through the forest behind them. Insects buzzed around the group, trees blocking out the sun and plunging them into deep shadow.

Zaire hacked at creepers and trailing plants, carving a path in front of them. Isla did the same, allowing Brek to point his rifle at anything that moved. At one point a large butterfly fritted in front of them, startling Brek. The Phylónethese almost fired on the colorful bug in his tense vigil.

"How do you know where we're going, Zaire?" Gavin asked, swatting at what looked like a large mosquito, three inches long and covered in tiny hairs. A swarm seemed to follow in their sweaty wake. "If I get bit by these things, will I die, or something?"

"They are not poisonous, though you will get a rash," Zaire informed between machete slicing. "And as for our course: because of the planets ocean and atmospheric system, clouds in the stratosphere almost always move in thin strips from east to west. I gauged our direction easily between that and the sun's position. We are indeed moving north, directly toward the capital and temple complex we saw from the sky during our descent."

Nodding in understanding, Gavin stepped in a puddle of mud, turning his gray boots into a mass of blotchy brownish green.

Time passed slowly in the humid jungle as the group maneuvered around trees and through undergrowth. Animal life abounded in every direction, drawing Gavin's attention to insects, lizards, slimy orange frog-like creatures with claws, and fowls both as small as hummingbirds and as big and majestic as eagles. A deep growl emanated from somewhere on their right, reminding Gavin of potentially bigger dangers lurking in the forest.

"So, we're for sure not going to get chased by an Axelroth, right?" Gavin asked after another half hour of walking.

"You don't even know what one looks like, Gavin," Isla answered. "How do you know they are not beautiful?"

"All life is beautiful," Zaire added.

Brek scoffed. "Axelroths are not beautiful. Their teeth are as long as my arm, with hair thick as rope."

"You are not helping Commander Brek," Zaire said as she cut through a hanging vine.

"Yeah, you're really not," Gavin agreed.

After another hour, the group stopped at a waterfall spilling over a rockface 100 feet high. A pool filled with crystal clear liquid below the cataract, smelling of soggy earth and blossoming florae. Black fish with long feeler-like barbells extending 12 inches from their gills swam along stones on the bottom. Something howled in the trees next to them loud enough to be heard over the waterfall's rumble. Gavin's eyes narrowed on the grove, hoping some giant critter didn't charge out to eat them.

"What was that?" he asked, moving closer to Brek.

A three-foot-tall monkey-like creature with short green hair and eyes like an insect jumped onto a nearby rock. Two long arms scratched at its feet, a third hanging limply from its right armpit. The animal cocked its head, clacking its yellow teeth as if warning the group to stay away.

"An Argyle Ape," Isla breathed in amazement. "I thought they only came out at dusk."

"Do they all have three arms like that?" Gavin asked. Pulling two protein bars from his backpack, he tossed one to Isla. The monkey jumped up and down, scratching at its head furiously.

"They do not," Zaire said, eyeing the animal curiously. "The poor creature must have been infected by a Gangut Parasite during utero. The parasite breads in the stomachs of Axelroths and is excreted in their feces, getting onto fruits and leaves and infecting Argyle females so the parasite is passed onto their unborn children. Birth defects like extra limbs are common and make these infected apes more likely to be eaten by Axelroths and thus continue the cycle."

"That's messed up," Gavin admitted, chewing his sticky,

flavorless excuse for a meal.

"Poor thing," Isla said, taking a bite of her snack.

Gavin leaned forward to look more closely at the deformed creature. "Wait, if the parasite comes from Axelroth poop, and this little guy was infected, wouldn't that mean there's poop, and thus Axelroths nearby?"

"This animal could have come from anywhere along the inner mountain ranges," Zaire answered.

Gavin watched the monkey continue jumping and pawing at its head, until it suddenly stopped and went rigid. All other sounds ceased as well: no birds, no insects, only the roll of cascading water.

"I do not like this beast," Brek growled, lowering his rifle toward the ape.

"Why did it stop moving all of a sudden?" Gavin asked. Without a squawk, the Argyle leaped into the pool and swam clumsily toward the bottom.

Zaire grabbed Gavin's arm and pulled him back toward the trees. "We are in danger!" she cried, feet spattering through puddles of stagnant water.

"What do you mean?" Gavin asked, almost tripping on a root as they ran.

A roar, loud enough to cut off the sound of the waterfall completely, penetrated the jungle from somewhere behind them, followed by the sound of breaking tree limbs.

"What the hell was that?" Gavin shouted without looking back.

"Axelroth!" Brek confirmed, easily running past Zaire and Gavin on his muscular alien legs.

"Shit!" Gavin cried, tossing what remained of his protein bar behind him as if he could scare off whatever approached.

Another howl rocked the jungle. Zaire darted behind a large boulder covered in moss and threw Gavin against the rock. Isla came up beside them.

Gavin looked out quickly to see a gigantic creature, bigger than an elephant, smash through the trees toward them. Large lizard-like legs descended from a rotund body covered in red and gold scales. Black hair ran along its back, thick as cables, leading to a head that seemed disproportionately large compared to its body. A mane of dark fur ringed the Axelroth's neck, while its face, squat like a bull dog's, contorted in hungry rage. Swishing like a whip, an enormous tail knocked leaves from trees and forced small animals to retreat in terror. Confirming Brek's description, the Axelroth's teeth poked out of the creature's mouth, each as long as Gavin's arm. Saliva dripped from its lips; a long, thin, purply tongue licking a canine-like nose.

The Axelroth bounded in their direction, yellow eyes focused on the trio and their protective boulder. Gavin froze, unaware what strategy would work best against a carnivorous alien monster.

"Die, hateful creature!" Brek shouted from above. Gavin looked up to see the Phylónethese standing on top of the rock, firing his rifle. Loud bangs echoed in the forest, bullets penetrating the Axelroth's hide.

"Kill it, Brek!" Gavin cried. "Kill it!"

Like a wild boar being shot by a pellet gun, Brek's assault did little more than anger the Axelroth. Head craning back, the beast bellowed deafeningly before slamming itself into the boulder and launching Brek back to the ground. The rock shifted a few inches, pushing against Gavin and proving their current defensive position would not be sufficient. Brek landed in the mud behind them, scampering through the slime quickly to his feet.

"We are out-matched," the commander shouted. "Flee now!"

An Axelroth paw wrapped around the boulder, long claws gouging into the rock.

"Shit!" Gavin repeated as the four of them charged through the jungle again. Powerful animal legs crashed through the underbrush behind them, quickly gaining.

"This way," Zaire commanded, pointing toward a tight cluster of trees on their left. "Squeeze through the bramble! The beast will be too big to follow."

Brek turned and fired several more shots at their pursuer. Isla leaped forward first, crawling between the branches and thick trunks to a small clearing beyond less than ten feet square.

"Now you," Zaire ordered.

Gavin glanced back as Brek fired again, Axelroth less than 200 feet away. He dove through the vines toward what safety the cluster might provide. Zaire followed, as did Brek, who barely fit between the two main trees.

Without slowing down, the Axelroth slammed its head against the copse, gnawing at branches five feet from Gavin's face. The creature's breath, hot and moist, billowed into the confined space, smelling like all the food in a refrigerator had been left to rot over the summer. Chunks of wood and bark splintered from above, sticking in Gavin's hair as teeth and claws tore at the trees.

"We gotta get out of here," he said, looking around for any chance to escape.

"The problem is that we must get past the Axelroth if we are to reach the city," Zaire said, still holding her machete. "If we continue running in this direction we will retreat farther into the jungle, which is what the beast would prefer. We must get around him and make our way toward the chasm."

"What chasm?" Gavin spat.

"There is a cliff not far from our current position. The Axelroth will not be able to cross."

"How will *we* cross?" Gavin asked, a glob of thick saliva landing on his shoulder. He jumped in shock, shaking his arms as if trying to make the spittle crawl off his body. "It's acid! It just spit acid on me!"

"It is not acid, Gavin," Isla said, grabbing his shoulders and stopping his flailing.

"That thing is trying to eat us!" Gavin shouted, eyes bulging. "For all I know, a smaller alien is going to jump out of his mouth and crawl up my ass!"

"Calm down," Zaire urged, sweat dripping from her lined forehead.

"Don't tell me to calm down!"

The Axelroth's teeth continue gnashing against the hardwood and vines, front paws tearing at the ground as if trying to dig past the roots. Its rough tongue slithered between the trees, waving less than a foot from Gavin's face. Rotten smells intensified, forcing his throat to gag involuntarily.

 Brek swatted at the tongue with his rifle. "My weapon is useless against the creature. He is a full-grown male, hide thicker than my---"

"Step back," Zaire interrupted, pushing Brek aside as the Axelroth's tongue wrapped around a vine next to Isla's face. "Get ready to run."

Raising her knife over her head, Zaire swung the sharp blade down and cut the beast's tongue like a worm severed in two. Deep red blood as thick as molasses splattered on leaves and twigs at their feet. The Axelroth's head shot back, a piercing roar blasting in Gavin's ears.

"Go!" Zaire commanded. She pushed Gavin and Brek through the briers and trees past the enormous animal thrashing around in pain. The Axelroth slammed its mouth against the ground, tongue twisting into the dirt as if seeking a painkiller.

"Shit, shit, shit," Gavin cussed, sprinting at full speed behind Zaire and Brek. He looked back to verify Isla ran behind him, seeing the Axelroth over her shoulder pivoting like an enraged pit bull about to charge. He grabbed Isla's hand and hurled forward, trees blurring to nothing as they passed.

"Down here," Zaire said as they reached a steep decline. A few trees covered the surface of the ravine, vines and ferns filling the space between.

They made their way down as quickly as they could, slipping on the damp earth and mud. The Axelroth's cry drew uncomfortably close behind. Gavin pushed large leaves out of his face, feeling liquid pooling into his boots as he stepped in a shallow pool somewhere beneath the undergrowth.

"How much farther, Mother?" Isla asked, holding tight to Gavin's hand.

"The trees are thinning," she replied between ragged breaths. "We are close."

A branch snapped loudly from the top of the ridge and then tumbled down the ravine. The Axelroth stood above them, lemon eyes protruding from deep-set sockets like a drunk about to vomit.

"Shit!" Gavin cried, feet moving fast beneath him.

"Stop saying that," Isla yelled.

"I'll say 'shit' as many times as I want as long as I'm being chased by a monster!"

Jungle gave way to sunlight as they broke through on the edge of a rocky cliff 100 feet across. A stiff breeze blew from the chasm, the sound of a river thundering below. A wood bridge spanned the expanse 50 yards to their left, though neglect had taken its toll. Weeds sprouted from the seams, pieces of flooring crumbling like termite-infested timbers.

"That does not look safe," Gavin said, running along the precipice edge.

The Axelroth burst through the trees behind them, each step rumbling the ground like a landslide.

"I'll choose the bridge over the beast," Brek bellowed.

"We will be safe once we cross," Zaire said, approaching the wooden walkway.

"That's what you said about the jungle," Gavin breathed.

Close enough to practically nip at their heels, The Axelroth pushed unrelentingly forward as if aware of his quarry's imminent escape. Brek crossed the bridge first, followed by Zaire, and finally Gavin and Isla. Boards groaned under their weight as they charged across, a section of handrail coming loose and spiraling toward the river far below. Gavin wanted to look down and get a better view of the canyon but could hear the Axelroth's grunting close behind.

Reaching the far side, Gavin took a deep breath and turned back toward the wild creature. As Zaire predicted, the Axelroth remained on the far side, pounding its front arms into the ground like a frustrated gorilla. The animal howled in deep baritone, teeth shining in the late afternoon sun.

"I told you," Zaire said, panting like a marathon runner. "We are safe on this side of the canyon."

"Forgive me for having a hard time trusting when we are and are not safe at this point," Gavin said. He leaned forward and placed his hands on his knees, breathing deeply.

"The perimeter walkway is just beyond these trees," Zaire said, pointing toward the north. "Once there, we will be greeted by holy sentinels. At that point you are to leave your gun behind, Commander Brek."

Grunting in perturbed acceptance, Brek nodded. "At least it slowed down the Axelroth. We may have been eaten had I left it aboard the Slingshot."

"*I'm* glad you had it," Gavin said.

Zaire rolled her weary eyes. "Let us continue."

The group headed through the trees, leaving the Axelroth to spit and fume on the other side of the bridge. Passing through an evenly spaced grove filled with tall grass, buildings began to come into view through the thicket.

Gavin ran his hand through the tall turf growing almost waist high. "We're not going to get arrested or something for coming here unannounced, are we? The way you guys worry about Perennial etiquette makes me afraid we'll be executed for using the wrong fork."

Zaire stopped, eyebrows pushing close together in concern. "Something is wrong."

"What is it, mother?" Isla asked.

"This grove should be well manicured; the grass perfectly trimmed; trees pruned. This is a holy site."

"Maybe they gave the gardener the weekend off, or something," Gavin said.

Zaire shook her head. "No. Something is amiss."

They continued walking, leaving the wood, and taking their first steps onto the pale-yellow perimeter walkway. A silent city met their view beyond the stone trail. Gavin kicked a broken cobblestone, noticing that the brick path seemed every bit as abandoned as the garden had been. Small plants, like dandelions, sprouted from between the stones, cracks running in all directions. One section of the walkway to their right appeared to have been hit by some form of explosive years before, leaving behind a crater now filled with weeds, grass, and shattered stones.

"Is it always this quiet?" Gavin asked. "And this…broken?"

Other than a few chirps of unseen birds, no other sounds emanated from the nearby buildings. As Gavin looked closer at the city outskirts before him, signs of battle appeared everywhere. Rubble littered the ground, toppled buildings half-standing against the breeze. Flowers grew between fractured bricks while vines crept along the base of a broken Perennial statue. Reminded of footage he'd seen on the nightly news of war-torn locales in the Middle East, Gavin had the distinct impression they weren't going to be greeted by holy sentinels.

"What happened here?" he asked.

Zaire stepped forward, eyes focusing on the crumbled walls of a demolished home 30 feet away. Tears rolled down her cheeks freely, mouth half open as if words wanted to escape but had been strangled before being uttered.

"These are the scars of war," Brek said, picking up a stone from the walkway and tossing it aside.

"What war?" Gavin asked. Isla squeezed his hand, face drooping in sadness. "Seriously. What war!? When did this happen?"

Wiping a tear from below her eye, Zaire took a deep breath. "I do not know."

CHAPTER 3

ROTTING PARADISE

A white bird with a plume of green feathers on its head pecked at the remnants of a decomposing yellow fruit. Rancid juice dripped from its purple beak onto the crumbling steps of what had once been an impressive municipal building of some type. Gavin looked up at the windowless edifice, stone walls reaching twenty stories high. Cracks and scorch marks marred the façade, rendering what had once been a stately locale into something little better than the decayed produce being consumed by the bird.

Other monuments and marble towers, equally as tall and magnificent, buckled slowly under the weight of neglectful years. Some buildings, either burned or heavily damaged by explosives, appeared on the verge of collapse.

How could this be the famed Holy City Zaire had spoken about so highly? Who had attacked, and where had the Perennials hidden themselves? Had they even survived?

No sounds beyond the wind and their own footsteps greeted

the group. They'd walked for over an hour toward the temple complex in the city center, never seeing another living soul. Zaire had remained completely quiet, pain sucking the life from her face and body.

The sun began to sink low in the sky, casting menacing shadows on every street. Luckily, they'd come across no dead bodies or other gruesome discoveries, but that fact did little to calm Gavin's fraying nerves.

What had happened here? Why had it happened? When?

"How much farther?" Brek asked, rotating his shoulder, and twisting his neck to the side as if stretching a knotted muscle.

Zaire stopped, looking to their right at a set of four pillars supporting part of a wooden roof. She blew out a depressed breath, slow and passionless.

"That was where I lived for my brief time here on Asha'asethol," she said, barely above a whisper. "A center courtyard opened on a crystal pool and garden. I would spend my afternoons bathing and reading, speaking to the other visitors of the future and our duties."

In his imagination, Gavin could picture what the building had looked like a decade before, which brought more sadness at its current state of disrepair.

"Let us continue toward the temple," Isla said, allowing her mother no more time to grieve. "From the maps I studied as a youth, we are close. I believe up here and around the next corner."

"You are correct, Isla'a," Zaire nodded. "We must go."

Turning the corner, an unsavory smell hit Gavin like a putrid wall. A pile of brown soil three feet high filled the pathway in front of them. Gavin realized immediately it wasn't dirt.

He plugged his nose instinctively. "Ah…what is that stuff?"

Brek pulled his rifle from his back and scanned the buildings. "It's Axelroth feces."

"Shit. You gotta be kidding me." Gavin stepped away from the pile of poop, foot smearing against a smaller glob he hadn't noticed. He scraped his boot against the concrete in a vain attempt to clean himself.

"If Axelroths have invaded the city, there is little hope for finding anyone alive," Zaire said, plunging her blade deep into the putrid mass. Twisting the knife, the dung broke into dried pieces and fell to the ground. "Lucky for us, this pile is at least a week old. We should be fine to continue toward the sanctuary."

A few minutes later, they came to their destination. The temple, like Incan towers in the Amazon only much larger, featured a set of stairs leading from the bottom to a plateaued spot on top about thirty stories high. Some sort of stone administrative building graced the pinnacle above, kissed by the setting sun. The temple had not been spared from damage, sections of demolished steps evidencing a brutal fight.

"Let me guess…we have to climb to the top," Gavin said, assuming the answer before he spoke.

"Yes," Zaire replied, eyes focused on the temple apex.

"Brek, you want to carry me?" Gavin asked.

"No, sir."

Gavin looked over at Isla.

"I am not transporting you, that is for sure," she said, taking her first steps up the stairs. "And a gentleman would first ask to carry me."

"I didn't say I *wouldn't* carry you," he called after her, before beginning his ascent. "Nobody trip; it'll be a long fall."

Halfway up the temple face, Gavin's calves burned from the climb. He glanced at Brek tromping behind him, breathing like an ox after a long day under the yoke. Isla continued to lead the way silently.

By the time they reached the peak, the sun had all but set on the horizon. As the tallest building in the entire city, the temple offered an unparalleled view of the metropolis and the jungles beyond. From the final set of steps, Gavin gained a better appreciation for the devastation that had befallen the area. Even in the fading light, it became obvious the city would never be salvaged from the wreck it had become.

"Let us go inside," Zaire said, walking toward the stone building in the center of the temple. "We can stay here for the night and then reevaluate in the morning. Worst case scenario, we will hike back to the Slingshot and pray the engines have released and are functional once again."

"State your purpose at the Holy Temple," a shrill voice cried from the dark recesses of the building.

Brek again pulled his weapon out, ready for battle. Isla brandished her knife like an expert gladiator.

"Who was that?" Gavin asked.

Zaire held up her hand for the group to stop.

"I ask again: state your purpose at the Holy Temple," the voice reiterated.

"I am Zaire, former Dubaku Matriarch," Zaire shouted toward the stone entrance. "I and my attendants have come with foul portent, but now realize far worse has already befallen the Elder City."

Footsteps echoed from the darkness. Pink clouds overhead reflected enough light for Gavin to make out a tall being, slender and graceful, walking in a long white and brown robe. The fabric wrapping the alien's body seemed as light as air, billowing on unseen currents as if winds blew across the temple that Gavin couldn't feel.

Stepping into the evening glow, a Perennial, male by the dark patterns running up his bald and extended cranium, placed his hands together as if greeting a royal delegation. Bright blue eyes, much larger than any Gavin had ever seen, reflected the sky and visible stars like mirrors. A thin nose and mouth rounded out the narrow face, warmth emanating from the ancient man. He looked like one of the famous Easter Island statues come to life, which made Gavin question his elementary school history lessons.

"Welcome," the Perennial greeted. "It has been some time since visitors have entered the temple complex. It is against custom to accept one who has arrived unbidden, but I will forgive your trespass."

"We are unworthy of such grace," Zaire said, head bowed in supplication.

"I am Phrensha'al, caretaker of the Temple of Othpethoth." The Perennial eyed Brek suspiciously, focusing on his rifle. "Weapons are not permitted inside the Holy City."

Visibly bristling like an agitated cat, Brek snorted. "From the looks of your 'Holy City,' you could have used more weapons and less pious judgement."

"Commander Brek!" Zaire shouted; eyes wide at his disrespect.

"What happened here?" Gavin asked, hoping to get a straight answer before matters of etiquette derailed their purpose.

"Burgess," The Perennial said with a wave of his hand.

Gavin raised an eyebrow. "Burgess? Is that some sort of code?"

A small blue-skinned Nythensus man waddled out of the darkness to stand next to Phrensha'al. A scar ran up the left side of the three-foot-tall man's face, ceremonial robes draping to the floor. His hands and fingers moved quickly, communicating to the Perennial in the silent Nythensus language.

"Burgess," the Perennial continued, "Would you please take our guests inside and prepare a meal?"

Burgess nodded and gestured with his left hand.

Phrensha'al bowed in understanding to the short alien. "Yes, I agree, that would be in keeping with protocol."

Brek moved close to Gavin and muttered in his ear. "They speak of protocol and tradition while their civilization lies in ruins at our feet. We must be ready for battle; I am sure of it."

"Let's just get inside and find out what's going on," Gavin whispered. "After that, we can figure out what our plan needs to be."

"Agreed."

"Burgess will show you inside," Phrensha'al said, arms wide in welcome. "Rest and be of good cheer, for here no troubles can reach you."

Gavin nodded, bullet holes along the stone walls staring back at him. *No troubles?* He couldn't quite believe that.

"Thank you for your hospitality," Zaire said with a bow, stepping to follow Burgess into the building. Gavin walked behind her, Isla coming up next to him.

"Are you going to share Brek's conspiracy theories with me, or will I need to eavesdrop?" she asked.

"He just wants to kill stuff, that's all," Gavin answered. "And you have to admit this is really weird."

Isla stepped past him toward Zaire. "I will withhold judgement. I suggest you do the same."

Gavin bit his lip. She was still mad.

Candles lit a large room in dancing flickers of orange light. A long table sat low to the floor in a conversation pit surrounded by pillows. Four pillars, one on each corner of the table, supported a stone roof overhead. Several ornamental chairs lined the walls, but it appeared the group would be lying on the pillows during their meal. The door remained open to their right, allowing a light breeze to blow from the temple plateau and flutter the candles.

"Please, enjoy our comforts while Burgess cooks something for us to eat," Phrensha'al said, motioning for the group to sit. "The capitol city Æstork is well known for growing ripe Galbrath fruit. Even in its current disheveled state, Burgess has procured many succulent examples, along with rare Zonron Weeds. I hope you will enjoy."

Gavin, stomach growling at the thought of a good meal, stepped down toward the table and brushed his palm against one of the pillows. Soft fur, finer than anything he'd ever touched, tickled his fingers, and smelled of rich earth and summer meadows. He sat back, feeling the large cushion conform perfectly to his body. Tingles radiated from his spine as if comfort had suddenly evolved from an abstract idea into something he could touch. Closing his eyes, Gavin let out a sigh and worried he might fall asleep then and there.

Brek kneeled like a lumbering giant, bumping into the table and knocking over one of the candles.

"Sorry," he said, wiping at the spilled wax with his thick fingers.

"You must have many questions," Phrensha'al began, pouring hot liquid into a cup in front of Zaire.

"We do, Elder Phrensha'al," Zaire said, blowing the steam from the drink before taking a sip.

The Perennial placed a cup in front of Gavin and filled it to the brim. "I will answer what I can, but our laws are strict here in the temple. This sacred place must not be defiled."

"Just tell us what happened here," Gavin said, grabbing his drink and taking a whiff of what he assumed to be tea. A fragrance of lemon mixed with grass clippings made his mouth turn down in disappointment. He would give anything for a hot chocolate or shot of Brazilian pinga.

"Yes, Lord Phrensha'al," Zaire agreed. "What my brusque companion is trying to say is how did the Holy City come to this state?"

Phrensha'al sat gracefully down at the head of the table as if being lowered into place. He closed his eyes. "Five annular-cycles ago, an unknown army descended on Asha'asethol, decimating the planet in a single day."

Gavin put down his cup. "Five years ago? They attacked five years ago?"

"That is impossible," Isla said, eyes wide. "Why would anyone attack this planet?"

"I do not know," Phrensha'al continued. "The army slaughtered the majority of our people and then fled, leaving behind few survivors. What remained slowly dispersed to search for other populations. Only I endured to care for the temple. I would not abandon our sacred shrine. None have since returned."

"How did word of this attack not reach the rest of the Commonwealth?" Zaire asked. "We have been receiving transmissions and reports of visitors for those five annular cycles. We had no reason to believe anything amiss transpired here."

"Again, All the Gods have given for me to know is that an unknown force rained fire and drove my race to the edge of extinction. Where these signals you speak of are originating, I cannot guess, but they could not have been sent from anywhere in this city. What few technologies we allowed here were destroyed on that tragic day. Would you care for more tea?"

This being the first Perennial Gavin had ever met, he didn't know whether to judge the entire species on this one man. Phrensha'al's calm demeanor and pleasant cadence did little to put Gavin at ease. An entire civilization, the oldest in the galaxy, wiped out overnight and hidden from the rest of the Commonwealth for half a decade, and this guy only cares about being a proper host?

"We don't need more tea," Gavin said. "What can you tell us about the attack? Why didn't you try to contact anyone?"

"My place is here protecting the sacred Temple Othpethoth, not solving riddles," Phrensha'al said, pouring Zaire more drink regardless of Gavin's objection. "I felt it my duty to bury the dead, but beyond that, I have relied on the Gods for their grace."

"You've gotta be kidding me," Gavin murmured, rubbing his forehead.

Isla grabbed his hand and squeezed. "His was a sacred duty, Gavin. Protecting the Temple is of utmost importance."

"So is letting the rest of the Commonwealth know that they've been completely undermined for five years," Gavin said, standing up and pulling his hand away from Isla. "I don't pretend to understand all the cultural baggage you guys bring with you, but I don't think I'm overstating that this is a huge deal."

"You are the clone, are you not?" Phrensha'al inquired calmly. He placed his teapot on the table and lay his hands slowly next to the silver kettle.

"…How do you know that?" Gavin stuttered.

"My race is long in knowing. There are few things that cannot be gleaned from every movement and blink of a living being."

"Yes, I'm the clone," Gavin confirmed, sitting back down next to Isla. "We were on our way to see Abraxas-Mon and let him know that the Hierarchy is trying to take full control of the galaxy behind the Perennial's backs, but I guess it doesn't matter anymore since you're the only one left."

"There are others," Phrensha'al said. "They do their duty as I. Even now many search the Cordenu'lun Galaxy for signs of more intelligent life, not knowing what has befallen our people."

"Mother," Isla interrupted. "Could this attack have been perpetrated by the Hierarchy?"

Zaire shook her head. "I do not think it possible. While they kept many things from me as Matriarch, something of this scale would be beyond their means to inflict and suppress. They do not wish to destroy the Asha'andasa, merely exert their own control."

"Then who did it?" Brek asked.

"Phrensha'al," Zaire said, turning toward the Perennial. "You stated this was an unknown army?"

"Yes, Matriarch of the Dubaku. Their ships were of unique design, with flat wings extending from a cylindrical hull; armor unmarked by clan symbols or other racial distinctions. Many of the ground troops seemed to be of Phylónethese or Athelbrath proportions, but I could not be certain they were indeed of either of those races beneath their bright blue armor and yellow capes."

"Could an unknown alien species have attacked, you think?" Gavin asked.

"The term 'alien' is an offensive one," Phrensha'al said with a raised finger. "It implies disparity of life where none exists."

"Yeah, I've heard this argument before," Gavin muttered.

Zaire nodded silently for a moment. "I remember a report from Abraxas-Mon some years ago about an encounter with an unregistered army that destroyed some of his legions and then fled."

"Could this be the same army that attacked Asha'asethol?" Isla questioned.

"I do not know," Zaire admitted. "It was a single report, the details of which I no longer recall. They could be related or merely my own mind searching for answers wherever I can find them."

"I have a question for all of you," Phrensha'al said, bringing his hands in front of him as if about to pray. "When was the last time you spoke directly with the Great Warlord Abraxas-Mon?"

"It has been several years," Zaire answered. "Though I have received reports from his campaigns detailing their success during that time."

"Just as you have received reports from this very planet?" Phrensha'al asked.

Gavin sat back as best he could against his pillow. "What are you saying?"

Phrensha'al took a sip of his tea. "That Abraxas-Mon may

have already fallen before this enemy."

"You think Abraxas-Mon might be dead?" Gavin asked, throat going dry.

"I have lived a great many annular cycles," Phrensha'al said with a nod of his head. "More than all of you put together. I was already a man of middle growth when the first thousand Idumeans were introduced to the Commonwealth a millennium ago. I spoke with Efua and Kwame, the progenitors of your clan, when they were welcomed to this very temple. With time comes understanding. The puzzle pieces do not yet form a complete whole, but evidence suggests that if Abraxas-Mon indeed met these marauders and since then has made no personal contact with members of the Hierarchy..."

"Then he may be dead already," Gavin answered before the Perennial could finish.

"Precisely, young clone."

"If that is true," Isla said, head shaking slowly, "then our entire plan to oppose the Hierarchy has failed before it even began."

"Worse," Gavin interrupted. "There may be an entire new species out there waiting to destroy all of us. And if Abraxas-Mon has been beaten, we're really screwed."

"We do not know Abraxas-Mon has fallen," Zaire assured. "Until we have evidence of that fact, we must press forward."

Brek took a drink of his tea and spit it back into his cup. "That is disgusting urine."

"It is not urine," Isla said.

"It tastes like urine," Brek affirmed. "And we may have greater worries than Abraxas-Mon."

"What do you mean?" Gavin asked.

"Let's say Abraxas-Mon was somehow destroyed by this mystery army that decimated the Asha'andasa. Does the Hierarchy have any chance of standing against them? Does any

Commonwealth army?"

Everyone at the table fell silent as Burgess entered the room holding a platter of food covered in a white cloth. With so much to digest already, Gavin suddenly didn't feel hungry anymore.

"Well, all this throws a monkey wrench into everything we had planned," Gavin said. "Maybe we'd be better off---"

A bright white light shot through the entrance next to them, filling the space with a blinding brilliance. Burgess dropped his metal dish in surprise, a loud clang adding to the spotlight's shocking emergence. Gavin turned, hand shielding his eyes while the rumble of gravity engines vibrated the stone walls of the temple building.

"It is a Hierarchy drop ship!" Isla shouted, bolting to her feet. "Their engine pulsation is very distinct!"

Brek followed her lead, practically knocking the table over as he stood and readied his weapon.

"I thought you said they wouldn't come here without express permission," Gavin yelled to Zaire as he pushed himself up.

She pulled the machete from her belt. "Apparently nothing I believed is true anymore."

"What's the plan?" Gavin asked Brek, running to his commander's side.

"We kick their asses," Brek bellowed.

CHAPTER 4

SACRED BLOOD

"This is a holy place! No lives can be taken here!" Phrensha'al said, arms waving about like a worried butler. The bright light streaming in through the open door amplified wrinkles on the Perennial's face, showing care and worry that had seemed completely absent from the man during their discussion. "I command you to dispose of your weapons out of respect for this holy edifice!"

Brek pointed his rife at Phrensha'al and snorted. "You can try and take my weapon from me, if you want."

"Brek!" Zaire shouted. "Show the proper respect!"

Burgess, the short Nythensus, scurried to a dark corner and hid behind a three-foot-tall ceramic vase, as if the plant urn would protect him.

Isla ran to one of the entrance pillars and peered into the light. Gavin did the same, pressing his back to the column across from her. Outside, a dark silver beetle-like vessel hovered near the steps. The chrome transport ship, as big as a C-17 bomber Gavin had seen at an airshow as a teenager, shifted slightly from right to left as if compensating for fluctuating air currents. The bottom ramp sat open, revealing a small section of the interior.

Two shadows moved across the lighted stones between Gavin and the dropship as soldiers walked back and forth. Warm wind continued to blow through the darkness, amplified by the pulsating resonance of the craft's gravity engines.

"I see two of them," Gavin whispered to Isla.

"There are four," she corrected. "Two have already made their way around the Temple Hall."

"Let me charge out there and kill them," Brek bellowed, cocking his rifle in punctuation.

"There must be no violence here," Phrensha'al pleaded once again.

Gavin turned to Zaire. "What do we do?"

"We must talk to them," she said. "They need to be made aware of the situation here on Asha'asethol and the possible danger facing the Commonwealth. If we avoid a pitched battle now, we may be able to get word to Brendant and the rest of the Hierarchy."

"Or the drop-team may be under orders to execute us on sight," Brek growled.

"That goes against everything the Hierarchy stands for," Isla said, glancing from the nearby ship, to Brek, and back. "Life is sacred."

"Many claim such things before killing the innocent," Brek scoffed. "My experience is the Hierarchy says one thing and does another."

"That is not true," Phrensha'al said. "Honor is all we have. The Hierarchy was established to solidify that principle."

Brek glowered at the tall, lean alien. "Maybe if you stepped out of your broken temple, you would see the universe as it really is."

"Alright," Gavin interrupted. "Do we wave a white flag or something? Beg them not to shoot us?"

Zaire stepped into the light without a word.

"I guess we just walk out then," Gavin said, rubbing his eyes.

Before he could follow her into the penetrating glare, Zaire waved her hand subtly for the rest of them to stay behind.

"She doesn't trust them," Gavin said.

"After what I have seen today, I am not sure I trust anyone outside of the four of us," Isla agreed.

Zaire walked toward the soldiers, tossing her knife to the ground.

"I am Zaire, former Matriarch," she pronounced as the warriors raised their weapons. "We are not your enemies."

Phrensha'al ran after her, more frazzled than he had been upon their initial encounter. "This is a holy place," he said, voice almost cracking. "There should be no violence here."

"Lady Zaire," the lead warrior shouted, never pulling his gaze from the disgraced Matriarch. Gavin couldn't be sure through the glare, but the man appeared to be wearing the uniform of a Praetorian, sacred guards to the Matriarchy. "You are under arrest, as are your consorts," the soldier continued.

Zaire walked forward confidently. "There is much we need to discuss."

"Stand down!" the Praetorian commanded, rifle never wavering.

"Come inside and we can discuss your grievances over tea," Phrensha'al said, motioning for the men to enter the building.

"I have my orders, Elder," the lead warrior said. "It is an honor to meet a member of the Asha'andasa, but my reverence cannot overcome my duty; so it is written."

"You speak well, Praetorian," Phrensha'al said with a slight bow.

Brek nudged Gavin. "Let me go out there and tear their arms off."

"We trust Zaire," Gavin urged, practically hugging the pillar. "Be patient."

Watching through the bright spotlight, Gavin's brain fed him data. Since the Battle on Kr'thotok his ability to process numbers had increased. Somehow, he could now understand the velocity of the wind along with how many bricks made up the exterior platform.

Pushing those needless details aside, Gavin focused on the potential dangers floating fifty feet away. The ship carried at least twenty soldiers. Four had exited already. Each warrior held their weapon confidently, thumbs poised to switch their rifles from stun to kill at the slightest need.

"What is your name, Praetorian?" Zaire asked. "You must be new to the Guard if we have never met before. I was Matriarch for several decades and made it a point to get to know all warriors in my service."

Gavin's eyes narrowed. Zaire didn't know this guy. Over the past five months, Gavin had watched her interact with every officer on the Silver Hammer. They all knew her well and would have died for her even after the Hierarchy stripped her mantle. If she had never met a member of the Praetorian Guard, it meant they had been appointed by someone else and likely had no loyalty to Zaire at all. That made the situation more dangerous, in Gavin's opinion.

"Lady Zaire," the soldier said, eyes focused along his rifle barrel. "You will command your daughter, Commander Brek, and the clone to come out of the temple."

"If that would curtail the possibility of violence, I would do as the Praetorian orders," Phrensha'al said, turning to Zaire.

The flood light slowly dimmed to a less blinding radiance. Gavin's eyes adjusted, seeing more detail. Indeed, the soldier wore the armor of a Praetorian; complete with blue decorative accents and ceremonial blade hanging from his belt. A green rectangle tattoo glowed palely beneath the man's left eye, signifying his elevated station. The three warriors flanking the Praetorian also wore the proper garb of ranking Prelates, though their orange color scheme designated them as infantry warriors only.

"Before I do that, allow me to ask you a question, Praetorian," Zaire said, a light bounce to her voice as if they spoke over hors d'oeuvres instead of weapons. "Why did the new Matriarch order you to come down to the planet uninvited? Would that not be the utmost insult to the Elder Race?"

"Permission was granted to our vessel through the proper channels," the soldier answered. "Unlike your offensive incursion."

"Who sent the invitation?" Phrensha'al asked, fingers twitching in excitement. "What clearance phrase was given?"

"Erita'alosh, Epsinsoth, Ganolok."

Phrensha'al bowed deeply. "You have indeed been given clearance. It is a joy to speak with one who enters when properly bidden."

What the hell? Gavin thought, body still pressed tightly to the interior pillar. *Is the dude lying? How did they get permission if the planet is in ruins?*

Zaire seemed to share his doubt. "How is that possible?" she asked. "Look on the destruction around you. Even in the dark of night it is evident something is terribly wrong here on Asha'asethol. Where are the sacred city lights? The fires of the Eternal Watch? Where are the sounds of music and the smells of grateful feasting?"

Her words framed the scene perfectly. From the top of the temple the soldiers couldn't miss the darkness of the deserted city. No candles burned, no flames warming meals in any of the vacant buildings. In fact, the only flicker of light Gavin could see anywhere on the horizon glowed many miles to the south, deep in the jungle. He hadn't noticed it before the spotlight had dimmed, but now it drew his eye unescapably. What burned so far to the south? It must be near where they had first landed...

Gavin's eyes widened. "They destroyed the Slingshot," he whispered to Isla.

"How do you know?" she asked.

"There's a fire in the forest in the distance near where we landed."

Her forehead creased. "Destroying the ship would be against protocol."

"They're here to kill us," Brek said with a nod.

"The engines could have overheated," Isla theorized.

"How likely is that?" Gavin asked.

Isla didn't answer. She blinked rapidly as if processing the information.

Zaire continued. "I must speak to Brendant. You yourselves can attest to the disaster that has struck the Commonwealth without us even knowing. You must realize this."

"Lady Zaire," the soldier continued, ignoring her plea. "You are to command your daughter, Commander Brek, and the clone---"

"Look around you!" she screamed, cutting off his order. "This planet, the holiest and most sacred, is in ruins and has been for years! Does that not prick your heart and call you to your duty?"

"My duty is to the Hierarchy," the man said, stepping closer to Zaire. "I serve no other master. Forgive me, Elder."

"You are a man of honor," Phrensha'al replied. "I respect your duty."

"Surrender and come aboard my ship and you will be taken for judgement," The Praetorian said, refocusing on Zaire.

Gavin's brain shouted at him to act. Somehow, he knew they would execute all of them, probably Phrensha'al too if needed. Gavin couldn't let that happen. Stepping out from behind the column, he smiled and sauntered over to Zaire.

The Praetorian shifted his aim quickly. "Elevate your hands to show you hold no weapon!"

"Guys, come on," Gavin said with a broad grin. "There's no need for any shooting or anything. I mean, honestly, this Perennial here will literally slash his own wrists if any of us even talk about desecrating the temple, okay?"

"Arrest him," the lead soldier nodded to one of his lieutenants.

Gavin stepped past Zaire and stood directly in front of the Praetorian. "Let me introduce myself: I'm Gavin Baller."

The guards looked at each other blankly.

"It's a lot to take in, I know," Gavin continued, pacing casually back and forth. "Now, I know what you're thinking: 'Gavin, you haven't done any movies in the past year-plus. Should we still consider you famous, or are you a has-been now?' Honestly, time will tell."

The Praetorian lowered his weapon slightly. "What are you talking about?"

"This one is the clone," Phrensha'al offered. "His manners are appalling, even for an Idumean."

"You just don't like anybody, do you?" Gavin asked. He walked back over to face the lead soldier, eye to eye. "It doesn't matter. I'll surrender, no problem, but first I want to ask you one more question. It's a simple one."

"Fine," the guard stated. "Last question."

"If we surrender now, will my friends and I make it back to the Matriarch's ship unharmed?"

"Yes," the Praetorian replied without hesitation.

Despite the confidence of the response, Gavin knew the man lied. He couldn't consciously know exactly how he could be so sure, but a combination of eye-twitch, sweat excretion, capillary blush, and a thousand other nonverbal cues gave Gavin a precise picture of their future. He and the rest of the team would in fact be executed once they set foot on that ship.

Gavin clapped his hands. "Alright, that's all I need to know."

Bridging the distance between himself and the Praetorian in an instant, Gavin grabbed his rifle and tried to pull it from the man's hands. Jumping to support their assaulted commander, the other guards prepared to fire. The Praetorian struggled against Gavin's strong arm, but before he could fight back Gavin had placed his finger over the trigger and squeezed. The orange blast struck the infantry soldier on their right in the thigh and sent him screaming toward the stone ground.

"Taste death!" Brek cried, jumping out from the temple entrance and shooting one of the soldiers on Gavin's left in the face. Blood sprayed the air, smearing the temple stones in a deep red spatter.

Phrensha'al screamed, as did the guard Gavin had shot in the leg.

Zaire picked her knife up off the ground and kicked the injured soldier in the head, silencing his protracted whimpering.

"No violence!" Phrensha'al cried, backing away from the impromptu battle.

"We need back-up!" the remaining warrior shouted into his wrist communicator as he backed toward the Hierarchy vessel. He fired randomly, narrowly missing Gavin and the Praetorian as they wrestled for the rifle, hitting Brek in the right bicep. The rotund Phylónethese roared and thundered toward the wide-eyed soldier.

A silver blade spiraled, end over end through the air, passing Brek as if he stood still. The ceremonial knife hit the retreating guard in the chest, eliciting a shocked gasp of air from the man. He dropped his gun and stood frozen, staring down at the knife imbedded six inches in his sternum.

"That was my kill!" Brek yelled, pointing at the grayish-red blood dripping from his arm.

Isla ran forward and pulled her knife from the soldier's chest. "This isn't a competition," she said to Brek.

"A little help here, guys," Gavin called to his comrades.

"You will die!" the Praetorian spat at Gavin through grit teeth.

The actor held firmly to the rifle, easily strong enough to keep the guard from gaining the upper hand. "I'd worry about yourself, dude."

Brek grabbed the man by the neck and tossed him down the steps. Armor crashed against stone as the Praetorian tumbled end over end down the thirty-story staircase. Gavin could tell exactly how far the soldier had fallen by how many steps he impacted.

"Thanks," Gavin said, holding the officer's silver rifle. "You okay?"

Blood seeped from Brek's right bicep and dripped onto the temple stones. "I'll be fine. Just another scar."

The dropship swerved suddenly, almost knocking Zaire over as she attempted to grab hold of the still-open ramp. Cannons on the port and starboard side lit up and fired, obliterating one of the statues next to the administration building. Gavin and Brek dove for cover as chunks of stone rained down on them like summer hail.

Phrensha'al stumbled drunkenly, mouth hanging open in aghast unbelief. "They're firing on the temple!"

"Mother!" Isla called to Zaire while pointing toward the swerving ship. "I will follow the Grav-Twist Protocol!"

Zaire nodded and charged toward the wavering vessel. Stepping onto a broken stone block, she propelled herself toward the open ramp and landed with the agility of a lemur. Isla followed suit, leaping through the air with legs kicking under her as if using unseen steps. She touched down next to her mother and without a word spoken, the two women charged into the bowels of the ship.

"Stop this now!" Phrensha'al pleaded. "You are desecrating the holy site!"

The ship veered farther from the temple plateau and back over the open city. An unconscious soldier toppled down the ramp and fell into the darkness below, evidence of Zaire and Isla's progression inside the vessel.

"Leave this place!" Phrensha'al shrieked over the continued buzzing of the gravity engines. "This temple is not a house of blood!"

Brek grabbed the Perennial by his robes and lifted him a foot off the ground. "You are the first Asha'andasa I have met in my entire life. If they are all cowards like you, I would be eternally disappointed."

Stones cracked loudly like two semi-trucks smashing into each other as the dropship pivoted and crashed against the stairs. Pieces of masonry clattered against ancient brick as the vessel lifted again, tilting slightly to the right.

"Don't kill him," Gavin shouted to Brek as he ran toward the cantering vessel. "I need to help Isla and Zaire!"

His boots barely touched the large temple bricks as he propelled himself forward, ready to jump toward the transport's ramp. Numbers computed in his brain, telling Gavin the ship sat approximately five feet from the edge of the stairs and three feet up, moving away from the temple plateau at four feet per second. It would take him three more seconds to reach the spacecraft and cover an almost 20-foot jump. Top speed would be required to make the leap and reach the ramp without falling to his death. Flashes of jumping out of an airplane over the jungles of Brazil came to mind. He didn't need a parachute then, and he wouldn't now.

Pushing off with all his strength, Gavin soared through the air, confident in his math. With a foot to go however, the ship rocked backward, pulling just out of reach.

Realization dawned, slowing time to a crawl. He would miss the ramp by a mere three inches.

Three inches.

When people told stories of Gavin Baller they would say, 'Yeah, he was a great actor, and showed a lot of courage, but in the end, he missed the ramp by three inches, and that was it.'

Stupid people.

He closed his eyes, not wanting to see the temple stairs rushing up to meet him.

Something grabbed his left wrist and held tight, swinging Gavin under the ramp and then back toward the temple. He looked up to see Isla, teeth grit, muscles straining. Her right arm wrapped around one of the ramp hydraulics while her left extended over space and held Gavin firm.

"I cannot hold you!" she cried, every vein in her body straining against her brown skin.

Gavin kicked at the open air beneath him and reached up to grab the ramp edge with his left hand. Bicep flexing, Gavin lifted himself next to Isla, who slumped over to massage her hyper-extended arm.

"Thanks," Gavin gasped, aware how close he had just come to death.

"You can repay me by helping my mother," Isla said, handing him her ceremonial machete. "Go quickly and I will meet you back here."

"On it!" Gavin left Isla on the ramp, plunging inside the ship. Unlike all the other Dubaku vessels Gavin had seen, this one appeared much less organic. No light or warmth emanated from the walls, no smells of greenery or comforting fragrances. This ship reminded him of Earth vehicles; stark, angular, and lifeless.

Turning a corner from the main loading bay, Gavin stumbled over an unconscious soldier lying in the hall. Blood dripped from the man's nose, but other than that he seemed unharmed. Sounds of laser fire drew his attention to the left, and a steel ladder leading farther into the craft. He climbed quickly, coming upon two more knocked-out warriors at the top.

Every time he saw Zaire in action it scared him a little more than it had before. Her skill and ferocity, unmatched by anything Gavin had ever seen, reminded him that for all the growth he had obtained over the past year-plus, he would never reach a level where he could stand toe-to-toe with the true Matriarch of the Dubaku people.

Voices echoed from around a corner on his right. Gavin slammed his back against the wall and inched his way slowly forward. The closer he drew to the doorway the more he recognized the voice.

"…and that is how we found the temple. You are honor-bound to seek answers with me."

Gavin peered through the doorway to see Zaire, holding a gravity bomb in her right hand, addressing a group of 22 soldiers: 13 men and 11 women. Every single warrior pointed their weapons at the former Matriarch, hesitating to fire. If she detonated the gravity bomb it would disrupt the ship's engines and likely send them crashing to the ground. Gavin had experienced that fact first-hand. From this height the engines wouldn't have time to recalibrate, and they would likely all die or be badly injured.

"Now that we have had a moment to talk," Zaire continued, "I hope you will see that there is more going on here than any of us knew."

Several of the soldiers wavered in their aim, eyes darting around the room as if looking for an excuse to lower their rifles.

"Zaire, you need any help?" Gavin asked, stepping slowly into the room. Half the guns turned toward him, the other half remaining focused on Zaire.

"I am fine Gavin. I have just been explaining our position to these fine soldiers here."

"They paying attention?"

"Unclear." Zaire grasped the gravity bomb tightly, obviously prepared to shatter the devise if necessary. "Where is my daughter?"

"I left her on the ramp. She said she'd meet us back there."

One of the lead soldiers, wearing full armor and the red rank of commander emblazoned across her chest, stepped forward. "You are no longer the Matriarch," the woman said, never lowering her weapon. "You cannot issue orders. We follow Brendant, the true Matriarch. If you wish to kill all of us by detonating that gravity bomb and obstructing our engines, then that is your choice."

"I don't like the sound of that, personally" Gavin said, holding up his knife in preparation for battle. "How about we all just listen to Zaire. Some bad shit went down on this planet. We all need to figure out what happened."

"My duty is not to investigate, but to apprehend," the commander said.

"And what were your orders regarding me and my family?" Zaire asked the soldier. "I am no fool. You would have executed all of us."

"Not all of you," the woman answered, looking at Zaire. "You, your daughter and the clone would be spared. You still will be if you surrender. The Phylónethese is unimportant and is to be executed. Our orders are unequivocal."

"Why?" Gavin asked. "Why not just kill all of us and be done with it?"

"It is not our place to question," another soldier replied.

Zaire's lips compressed tightly. "Where is the Matriarch's ship now?"

"Waiting in orbit before returning to Cartoshí," the female officer answered. "We are to rendezvous once you are captured. Another ship will be dispatched if you damage this one. There is nowhere for you to run, disgraced Zaire."

"I see now that none of you understand the difference between duty and moral obligation," Zaire said, disappointment dripping from her words. "Your training was overseen by Plenipotentiary members who obviously value their rank above all else. You will regret your decision to turn your backs on the greater threat."

"You are the greater threat," the woman said, stepping closer to Zaire.

"At this moment you are correct," Zaire said with a smile. "Isla'a! Do you have command of the bridge?"

"I do, mother," Isla's voice echoed from the intercom.

"You know what to do, daughter."

The ship swerved like a car on a rainy roadway, throwing Gavin to the right and into the wall. Everyone tipped, several soldiers falling over and firing their rifles wildly. Zaire grabbed Gavin's shoulder and pulled him back through the door before any of the warriors had regained their bearings.

"What are we doing?" Gavin cried as they bolted down the hall toward the landing bay.

A terrible jolt ran through the ship as if they had crashed into something. Gavin figured they likely had, feeling vibrations run up his legs and turn them to jelly.

Zaire spun and threw the gravity bomb back down the hallway just as they entered the loading area. A familiar screech tore the air as the bomb detonated behind them. Gravity itself tingled throughout the ship, reminding Gavin of each time he had been pulled into one of the mini singularities. As they turned toward the ramp, movement across the landing bay caught his eye. Isla clamored down a ladder on the other side of the open space one-handed, nodding to her mother.

"Jump now!" Zaire commanded, pushing Gavin toward the

open ramp. The ship had indeed crashed into the temple, but it would not stay there, as the vessel began to tip backward, pushing at the crumbled stones along its hull.

The spacecraft toppled back as if about to roll down a hill. The ramp pitched from negative 45 degrees toward zero. Through the exit, Gavin could see the center temple building slowly disappearing in favor of night sky.

He ran down the ramp, leaping like his life depended on it. Stones rushed up to meet him as Gavin curled in a ball and rolled along the hard surface, elbows smacking rock with painful force. Coming to a stop on his stomach, Gavin turned as Isla and Zaire landed next to him.

With a sickening groan, the dropship continued rolling backward until it spilled over the edge and down the long flight of stairs. A gruesome rumble quickly moved away from them as the ship careened toward the ground below. Gavin imagined the soldiers inside being spun around and around, smashing together as the vessel gyrated and bounced on its way toward an inevitable stop, like a basketball kicked down a mountainside.

"Holy shit," Gavin breathed, pushing himself back to his feet.

"What happened?" Brek asked as he dropped Phrensha'al and ran up to the trio.

"Zaire and Isla happened." Gavin patted dust from his pants, examining a bloody scrape on his right elbow.

Isla kneeled next to Zaire, who lay on her back breathing raggedly. "Mother, are you alright?"

"I hit my head," Zaire answered, eyes closed painfully tight. "I will recover."

Gavin ran over to the now obliterated staircase in time to see the dropship smash onto the street and spin into a derelict building. Walls crumbled around the vessel, sound taking a moment to reach Gavin's ears so high above. Smoke rose and then silence.

"Holy shit," he repeated.

"Indeed," Brek said, standing beside him.

"You think anyone survived?"

Brek nodded. "Likely yes, though I'm sure the living are suffering their own hell at the moment."

"Gavin!" Isla shouted. "My mother needs help!"

The two men turned and rushed to their Matriarch's side. Zaire sat up slowly, eyes still closed. Blood dripped from behind her ear, staining her white shirt.

"She's bleeding," Gavin said.

"More blood!" Phrensha'al wailed from behind them. "More blood to clean!"

Gavin stood and walked over to the tall Perennial as he kneeled hunched over on the cold stones. Long fingers cradled a broken chunk of brick like a sacred relic. Blood stained the stones in front of him.

"Phrensha'al, we didn't mean for this to happen…" Gavin began.

"And yet here we are, surrounded by more death!" the alien cried. "It took me months to bury the dead after we were attacked. The temple grounds were littered with bodies; even children were not spared! And now you bring more! I cannot wash off the blood. It cakes between my fingers. I couldn't wash it clean. Burgess? Where are you Burgess? We need to clean! Bring me scrubbers for cleaning!"

The Perennial continued to sob, wiping at a spot of blood with his robes but only smearing it around on the pale-yellow slab. Gavin realized in that moment that Phrensha'al, far from being a mere slave of tradition, had suffered more than any of them had imagined. Spirit broken, the ancient Perennial had retreated to the safety of the only thing that made sense: his job in the temple. For five years he must have hidden away his pain and now relapsed into a state of complete wreck.

Burgess came running from wherever he had been hiding inside the temple building, holding several rags. He dove next to Phrensha'al and began spitting on the blood and then mopping the gore like a frantic chambermaid.

"Let them be for now," Isla said, leaving her mother in favor of the soldier who Gavin had shot in the leg. He still lay comatose among the cracked bricks. "We do not have time to mourn for the temple or this planet."

"What do you mean?" Gavin asked.

Brek tore the sleeve from his right arm and began wrapping it around his wounded bicep. "The Matriarch's ship will be dispatching more soldiers shortly, without doubt."

"And if you are right about them destroying the Slingshot," Isla continued, "then we need a way off this planet." She reached down and pulled the Thought-Mech communication bracelet from the unconscious soldier.

"I know where we may find a ship," Zaire said, eyes still closed, blood dripping slowly down her neck.

"Where?" Gavin asked.

"The Gardens of Light," she replied.

"Much of the Gardens were burned," Phrensha'al said without lifting his head. "They burned for days and days. The smoke touched the heavens, but the Gods sent no rain." Burgess continued wiping at the blood without looking up.

Zaire opened her eyes, face pale and sweaty. "We will make our way to the Gardens, nonetheless. It is possible something survived or has sprouted since."

"And we must hurry," Isla said, squeezing the Thought-Mech as if crushing a tin can. "I just read the soldiers' orders. Upon putting Brek to death and bringing us back to Cartoshí, we are to be publicly executed…"

"Well, that's not a surprise," Gavin interrupted.

"…along with the entire crew of the Silver Hammer and everyone onboard."

Gavin blinked. "Are you serious? That's like ten thousand people, including Seth, Ashton, and everybody."

"It would be an illegal act, Mother," Isla said, stepping over to help Zaire stand. "The Commonwealth would revolt against the Hierarchy under such circumstances."

Zaire stood wobbly, leaning on Isla for support. "Things are far worse than we ever feared," she said, touching the back of her head and coming away with crimson fingers. "It is possible they could claim some heinous act was performed by the crew to justify their deaths. It is possible the Hierarchy is plotting some act of terror as we speak to enrage the population so they will support the executions. Whatever transpired on this planet is now about to swallow the rest of the Commonwealth."

"Would they really kill all those people?" Gavin asked, feeling sick to his stomach.

Zaire took a deep breath. "Before today, I would have never accepted such an eventuality in a hundred millennia. Now, however, I believe we have been blinded by an unknown force that has slaughtered the Asha'andasa, possibly destroyed Abraxas-Mon, and is about to decimate the galaxy as we know it. And so, I say yes, they will be slaughtered."

CHAPTER 5

GARDENS OF LIGHT AND ASH

Fatigue pressed against the back of Gavin's head, along with a steady ache, as he watched the sun rise through the trees in front of him. They had walked all night, only now arriving at the sacred gardens where the Asha'andasa would apparently grow their spacecraft. Gavin couldn't quite wrap his head around it, but after interacting with several vessels over the past year and feeling their fear and even love, it made an interesting kind of sense.

Tall grasses and overgrown bushes lined what Gavin assumed had once been a well-manicured path through the gardens. Weeds sprouted everywhere, all the smells of life billowing on the morning wind. Temperatures rose steadily with the sun, reminding Gavin how hot the jungle had been the day before as they ran from that Axelroth. Sweat trickled down his back, reminding him of how scared he felt escaping the beast.

He held Isla's right hand tighter than necessary as they pushed through a lush grove. The past 24 hours had reminded him how fleeting life could be and how flippantly he had treated their relationship. Isla's injured left arm, the one she had used to save him from falling to his death, hung limply at her side while the elbow swelled from being hyperextended.

She loved him; of that he had no doubt. But did she know how much he loved her beyond her beautiful body and perfect face?

"Your arm doing okay?" he asked, squeezing Isla's hand.

"It will mend," she answered.

"What can I do for you? You need any food or anything? I can carry you if you get tired or something…or I can have Brek carry you. He's really strong."

The Phylónethese grumbled behind them, boot splashing loudly in a puddle.

Isla smiled and rubbed her thumb lightly along his fingers. "I will be fine, Gavin. We will be fine."

"I know, I just…things are crazy. I'm here for you if you need anything, is all I'm saying."

"I know you are, Gavin," she said, kissing his cheek lightly. "We will rescue our friends and continue with our mission. Together. I have no misgivings of this."

Gavin didn't feel quite so confident. Doubt blossomed in his chest like a black flower, turning his intestines into haphazard braids. Seth. Ashton. Bomb. Ogpog. Rolatok, and so many others; all about to be put to death. Would things have been different if they'd just surrendered or stayed on the Silver Hammer to begin with? He didn't want to doubt Zaire, but at the same time he didn't want to feel responsible for the deaths of his friends. Hopefully, they could find a ship and rescue them.

Of course, his brain fed him their odds of success in that regard, which made him want to dry-heave.

"I will not go with you," Phrensha'al repeated for the tenth time, cutting off Gavin's moment of self-reflection. The Perennial tripped on a broken branch and stumbled into Burgess, walking next to him. Brek following close behind to guarantee the two aliens couldn't flee into the forest. "You cannot force Burgess and I to accompany you off this planet."

"I am not explaining it again," Zaire said, pushing a cluster of branches out of the way for the group. "I am convinced the Hierarchy is unaware of the attack here or the impending doom that awaits them. You must stand before them and share what information you have. At the very least, *some* of them will side with us."

"The temple will be unguarded," Phrensha'al whined. "I will be abandoning my duty!"

"You're not abandoning anything," Brek said, nudging the Perennial with his bulbous elbow. "You're being *forced* to abandon it. Keep walking."

"You will answer to the Gods, you Phylónethese brute," Phrensha'al said.

Brek nodded. "You're damn right I will. And they can kiss my Aktelothing ass when I do."

"That's a visual I could have done without," Gavin smiled.

A rumble overhead forced the group to stop and hide at the base of some of the trees. Gavin looked up, seeing a Hierarchy ship through the leaves as it soared high overhead.

"The patrols are moving farther out from the city," Zaire said, squatting next to a bush. "If they thermal scan the gardens, they will find us."

"Even then, we will still have time," Brek assured. "There are many animals in this area now; certainly, Axelroths and their prey. Military heat scans will be inconclusive. I had the same problem during a forest hunt in my youth. Thermal searches are not as effective unless you already know where to look."

"Even so," Zaire continued, "we must move more quickly."

The group wandered through the trees, eventually coming to a clearing. Enormous black stalks that at one time had been plants of some sort, stood charred in the early morning light. Fresh shrubs had sprung up in the years since the attack, but none of the larger vegetation had recovered. Hundred-foot-tall trunks, easily twenty feet thick, stood as reminders of wonders Gavin couldn't comprehend and now would never see in their full glory.

"It's all burned," Brek said, bowing and picking up a handful of ash.

"No," Zaire said pointing to what looked like an onion the size of a watermelon. "Some of the plants are still sprouting."

"Yes, but we don't have twenty annular cycles to wait around for it to mature," Brek protested.

"So, the ships start out as onions?" Gavin asked.

"They are grown within the fruit and then molded," Isla said. "It is exceptionally beautiful. A full-grown plant will be as big as the ship inside. They continue growing for centuries after as they feed on gravitational energy. The Silver Hammer, for example, is over four hundred years old and reaching the end of its growing period. That is why it is so large."

Zaire knelt next to the plant, digging into the soil at the base. "This is a sprout from a larger growth. If we can find the direction of the root, we may be able to follow it back to a more mature specimen."

"The Gods are not on your side," Phrensha'al spat, kicking at the dirt and ash. "You will not be successful."

Reaching deep into the soil, Zaire smiled. "Here! I have found the root. It is growing toward the east." She stood and dusted off her hand. "Let us move in this direction, toward that burned out hollow."

"You should rest," Gavin said. "At least for a few minutes."

"I am fine, Gavin," Zaire replied, though the fatigue in her voice did little to confirm her words. "Let us find a ship first and then I will rest."

The group wandered through the black forest, weaving between a tight cluster of scorched timber. Walking around one of dead trunks, Gavin saw something that took his breath away.

"What is that?" he asked, looking up at a pale white onion-like plant, 40 feet in diameter sitting at the top of a massive green stalk at least two stories overhead. Several thin growths sprouted near the top and sides of the large orb, reaching for the sky.

"That is a ship," Zaire answered. She stepped close to the root and rubbed her hand across the course green surface.

Brek leaned forward and took a whiff from a cluster of flowers growing along the stalk. "It's wild. This plant hasn't been tended since the attack. Look at the sprouts on top. Those should have been trimmed off years ago."

"It is the best we have, Commander Brek," Zaire said. "Let us get her started. Brek and I will climb up and see if the ship is in viable shape for space travel. It will take a few minutes."

"You should not be climbing, Mother," Isla said, dropping Gavin's hand and stepping next to Brek. "You rest. I will go with Brek and survey the vessel."

Zaire nodded in understanding; a flash of gratitude apparent in her smile. "Thank you, Isla'a. I will stay here and recuperate for a moment."

"You shouldn't be climbing either, Isla," Gavin protested. "Your arm is still hurt from last night and your elbow is swollen. I should do the climbing."

Isla touched his face softly. "You do not know how to help a vessel progress in these early stages. I must go, and I will be fine. I am a good enough climber that I only need one good arm. Trust me, my love."

"I'll go with you guys," Gavin said eagerly. "I can help you climb."

"Stay with my mother, Gavin, in case she needs anything. There is still much danger. Please."

"…Alright," he agreed.

Gavin sat on a dried-out stump, watching as Brek and Isla scaled the stalk like insects straining to reach the nectar from a flower above. Phrensha'al and Burgess took seats as well, turning away from Gavin as if they found his presence offensive.

"Here." Zaire handed Gavin a shiny gray fruit about the size of an apple. "We should eat what we can. I am sure you are hungry. You almost always are."

"What is it?"

"A Kont," she replied. "Some call it Hammer Fruit. It is a high-protein vegetable with a hard outer-shell. They are difficult to come by in the Commonwealth because they only grow in sacred gardens like this one on very few planets. They are actually how the Silver Hammer got it's official name of Konti'ikont."

Gavin sniffed the vegetable, smelling nothing more than dirt and grass. "How do you open it?"

"Smash it against a rock and the shell will crack."

With a strong swing, Gavin split the shell open on the stump next to him. He peeled back the hard surface, revealing a rose-colored and moist interior. A fragrance like bell pepper cleared his head as he took a bite.

"It's good," he said between chews. "It's really good. I like it."

"I thought you might," Zaire said, taking a seat next to him on an overturned log. "How are you doing?"

"I'm fine."

"How are you doing?" Zaire asked again, staring at Gavin with tired eyes.

"I should be asking you that question. I mean, you've got dried blood on your neck, for crap's sake."

Zaire smiled, looking up as Isla and Brek disappeared over a series of leaves at the base of the plant-ship. "Do you remember the first time we met?"

Gavin took another bite from his Kont and chewed slowly. "How could I forget? I was paralyzed and sitting in a chair you guys pulled out of a dumpster."

"You had been unconscious for a while before that, and I remember watching you as you slept."

"That doesn't sound weird or anything," Gavin said.

"You reminded me so much of Abraxas-Mon; every feature, every slight movement."

"It makes sense. I *am* his clone."

Zaire reached over to a bush and plucked a small blue berry, tossing it into her mouth. "I never told you this, but for the first five years of his life, I was one of Abraxas-Mon's chief caretakers."

"What…you were like his nanny, or something?"

"One of several, but yes," Zaire said, eating another berry. "I cared for him deeply. I was his Mala'apand: a loving guardian. Once I gave birth to Isla'a, I was forced to step away. I remember him crying when I left, asking me to remain, but my Matriarchal duties took precedent."

"Why are you telling me this?" Gavin asked, feeling uncomfortable with the conversation's direction. "You're not one for sharing pieces of your past. I've learned that the hard way."

Zaire's head dropped slightly. "Because I do not like thinking that he may be dead. I do not like thinking that I abandoned him and have not spoken face to face with him in almost five years."

"Honestly, I hope he's alive too," Gavin said, picking a small flower and smelling cinnamon and sugar from the pollen. "Not just because we need his army to save the Commonwealth, either. I've been kind of excited to meet him, like, maybe we'll be brothers who haven't seen each other in a long time. Maybe we'll laugh and be best friends. I hope so, anyway. I'm afraid I'll be a huge disappointment to him."

"I do not think you have to worry about that," Zaire soothed. "I, on the other hand, feel the shame of my desertion."

"You didn't desert him. You had a duty. I'm sure he didn't hold a grudge or anything," Gavin said.

"I know he did not. It was not his way. Even so, the memory stings. His death would be a terrible burden for all of us and would rob me of my chance to truly apologize. I wanted he and Isla'a to meet finally and perhaps…" her words trailed off; eyes focused on the ground.

Gavin took the last bite of his Kont and threw the seed core into the bushes. He knew what she wanted. The thought pained him.

He swallowed his bite and spoke. "I'm not Abraxas-Mon. I'll never be Abraxas-Mon. If I'm not a good enough match for your daughter---"

"That is not what I am saying," Zaire interrupted.

"It certainly sounds like what you're saying."

"I am not." Zaire placed her hand on Gavin's knee and looked him in the eye. "You have proven to be more than I could have hoped after that first meeting. At that point, I assumed our entire plan had come crashing down and that I would have to kill you to keep you from falling into Halford's grasp. I felt hatred and disappointment and I longed for some solution that would keep war from erupting. You have saved more lives at this point than I ever could have guessed, and yet war like I never imagined now lies crouched to strike. So much of what I believed to be immutable has proven to be lies and cunning duplicity. I am a ship in search of a harbor that never existed. I only pray I will be strong enough to endure to the end."

"You will," Gavin assured. "Sometimes life doesn't turn out the way we thought it would. I mean, I thought everything in the Commonwealth was going to be like a paradise where everybody sang stupid songs all the rime, but it certainly didn't turn out to be that way. And that reminds me of something else that's been bothering me."

"What is that?"

"All you've ever talked about is how life is sacred and how we all need to work together, and yet here in the Commonwealth, you have the Cádavrites that are basically slaves through no fault of their own. They, what? Get mortally wounded and you guys save them and then they're suddenly less than human and you enslave them? Ogpog always treats Rolatok like a dog trying to hump his leg; and you don't do anything about it, even when I point it out."

Zaire picked at her fingernails. "It is hypocritical, I am aware."

"Then let's stop it!"

"It is not that simple," Zaire continued. "I know that it is not right, and yet my entire life I have been taught that Cádavrite are unholy creatures, resuscitated after death through unnatural means and thus losing part of their humanity. It has been this way since the process was discovered over a century ago. Becoming a member of the Cádavrite Guild is worse than a death sentence for us. Many would take their own lives afterward if they did not believe worse things awaited beings who commit suicide. That pattern of social conditioning cannot be broken overnight. I know Rolatok is a good man, but I still see him as an abomination. I am trying, believe me."

"I guess we all have things to learn," Gavin said, nudging Zaire.

"We do." She nodded. "Over the last few years, I feel like my education has accelerated. The mistakes I have *almost* made would have been some of the worst in my life. The mistakes I *did* make, have set us on our current path."

Gavin reached over and pulled a leaf from a vine growing along the desiccated stump. "I wish I could go back and change things. I really do."

"As do I, but not when it comes to you." Zaire smiled, a true, joyful grin. "I see in you a future I could not have guessed. My daughter is blessed to have you, despite your stupidity and carnal lusts."

"I knew that was going to come up," Gavin said, eyes rolling like a teenager being reprimanded by his mother.

"She is lucky to have you," Zaire reiterated, reaching over and squeezing Gavin's hand. "And you are lucky to have her. Relationships like that are destined for greatness. No, you are not Abraxas-Mon, and I am glad. I pray he is not dead, but if he is, at least we have a Gavin Baller to light up the galaxy."

"Mother! Gavin!" Isla shouted from above. "The ship is wild, but space-worthy. Brek is molding the interior now. We should be able to set off within a few hours."

"Excellent, Isla'a!" Zaire called back. "We will pick some fruit and vegetables for everyone to eat and then climb aboard."

Gavin watched as Isla smiled and crawled back over to the ship. "You sure she's lucky to have me?" he asked.

"As sure as I am that you do not deserve her," Zaire replied with a smile. "But do not worry; we never truly deserve the people we love. We are merely blessed to be accepted into their presence. Now, pick as many Konts as you can find and then get Phrensha'al and Burgess ready to climb."

"It smells like aloe in here...like really bad," Gavin said, touching the white interior wall of the ship and coming away with a sticky film adhering to his palm. "Ah, that's gross."

"Normally ships take several months to dry out," Isla said, ushering Gavin into a rounded center room with a lopsided table and no windows. "We do not have that time. As you can see, the surfaces are still soft and very moist. The hallways and walls are not perfectly straight yet either. It will take some time for the craft to become accustomed to our presence and to anticipate our needs. It is wild and thus not fully prepared to accommodate us, nor will it understand the difference between friend and foe. We will need to be vigilant while the craft learns and grows."

"So, what do we do until it's dry? Not touch anything?"

"We will all likely have sticky clothes for the next few days," Isla said, pulling a Kont out of Gavin's backpack. "Luckily the showers should be working by this evening, and the ship is already producing limited supplies of food, so we will not starve."

"Thank heavens for small favors," Gavin said. He looked around the room, surveying the rippled walls and uneven floor. "Alright Mordecai 2.0; keep us alive and I'll be your best friend."

"Gavin," Brek growled, walking into the room from one of the two side hallways. "The ship can't talk."

"I know that, Brek."

"Then why were you talking to it?"

Gavin looked at Isla, who smiled and raised her shoulders.

Zaire walked in, Phrensha'al and Burgess behind her. "I understand your protests, Lord Phrensha'al, but I will ask you one more time: what is more important, the lives of people we can save by thwarting war, or the Temple?"

"The Temple represents our link to the eternities," Phrensha'al answered.

Burgess twisted his fingers and waved his hands in communication.

"Exactly Burgess!" Phrensha'al continued. "Lives are sacred, but it is only through the Temple that they are brought to true enlightenment. What is a life spent wallowing without true knowledge?"

Gavin leaned against the wall, instantly regretting it as moisture seeped into the fabric of his shirt. "Look, Frenchie, the Temple is never going to be rebuilt and refurbished if nobody knows it's been blown up a couple times, right?"

"My name is Phrensha'al, not Frenchie."

"Whatever. Look, you want the Temple to be fixed, right?"

"I do, clone."

"Then going and telling everyone it needs to be fixed is the fastest way to do that, right?"

Phrensha'al's mouth formed an even deeper frown than usual. "I suppose you are correct."

"Awesome," Gavin clapped, peeling his shirt from against the sticky wall. "Let's get the hell out of here then."

"Indeed," Zaire said. "Since this is an unregistered vessel, it will be a bit easier to avoid detection during our journey, but it will still take three to four Earth weeks to reach Cartoshí."

"What are you talking about, three to four weeks?" Gavin fussed. "Seth, Ogpog and everybody else will be long dead by then!"

"No," Zaire corrected. "I have been monitoring the Thought-Mech Isla'a took from the soldier earlier. A public trial has been announced upon the arrival of Brendant's ship on Cartoshí. There, evidence will be presented, and judgment pronounced. I have no idea what charges they will bring, but obviously execution is a foregone conclusion already, according to this data."

"So, we need to get to Cartoshí and rescue Seth and the crew," Gavin said with conviction.

"No," Zaire corrected again. "We need to get in front of the Plenipotentiary Council first and present our findings. They need to hear from Phrensha'al about the destruction of Asha'asethol and the unknown threat that may have destroyed Abraxas-Mon as well. Attempting a rescue with these limited resources would be foolhardy when we have another course of action."

"So, even though it's going to take a stupid long time to get there, we still have a good chance of saving everybody?" Gavin asked.

"I pray so, yes," Zaire answered.

A shudder ran through the ship, followed by a clumsy lurch, like a baby falling over after trying to stand. Brek stumbled, slipping on the moist floor, and pressing his face against the gooey wall.

"What was that?" Brek grumbled, strands of syrupy liquid sticking to his lopsided nose. His four eyes blinked rapidly, a disgusted sneer spreading across his lips.

The ship shook again, this time as if trying to pull free of the stalk still attached beneath.

"We have been discovered," Isla said, looking at Zaire.

"Are you sure?" Gavin asked.

"All of us, to the bridge," Zaire ordered. "Only there will we find harnesses to secure us in place."

They rushed down the hall behind Zaire, irregular floor undulating under their feet. Gavin slipped in a small puddle and caught himself against the wall before he face-planted.

Four pilot chairs greeted them as they entered the bridge. Unlike the seats Gavin had seen on other ships, these seemed to be little more than growths protruding out of the floor at strange angles.

"Morph to screen," Zaire yelled.

Nothing happened.

"Vessel: morph to screen!" she commanded again.

Slowly the front end of the room rippled like water, turning translucent and revealing two Hierarchy spacecrafts floating in the air directly in front of them.

"Akteloth!" Brek cursed.

"Everyone, strap in!" Zaire ordered.

"With what?" Gavin asked. "These lumps aren't even really

chairs yet. And there's only four of them."

Isla pushed Gavin toward one of the seats. "It will conform to your body. Just sit."

Zaire pointed at Phrensha'al. "You and Burgess share a seat. I will stand while piloting for now."

Gavin pressed his butt into the growth as the ship continued to heave back and forth. The seat morphed around him, coating his back and shoulders in a warm wet embrace.

"This is weird," he whispered to himself.

Pasty tendrils grew from the floor at Zaire's feet, reaching up and encasing both her hands. "I am trying to communicate with the Hierarchy vessels but getting no response."

"I didn't have time to calibrate the communication array," Brek said, watching with a concerned look as his chair slithered up his arms.

"A brisk escape is our only option," Zaire concluded. "Is everyone strapped in?"

"We are prepared, Mother," Isla said.

"Then hold on!"

Zaire pushed her hands down deeper into their strange white cocoons and the ship plunged forward. Still held in place by the stem below, the craft vibrated wildly, tugging with full force. The vessels in front of them stood firm, cannons glowing in preparation to fire.

"They're going to shoot us," Gavin said, squishing the soft armrest between his fingers like playdough.

"I am aware," Zaire replied without looking back.

With a surprising jerk, the ship shot forward, finally free of its stalk. Moving far faster than Gavin had anticipated, the craft slammed into one of the Hierarchy vessels and bounced off like a pinball. They rocked side to side for a second before Zaire pulled back on the control vines and they pointed up toward the sky above.

"Prepare for full velocity," she shouted. "This will not be pleasant!"

Gravity engines roared, sending a wave of rippling air along Gavin's forearm. His hair seemed to stand on end slightly as if completing an electrical current. Weightlessness prevailed for a fraction of a second before a crushing weight pressed down on his chest.

Gavin's vision went suddenly red as his head pinned painfully against the headrest. Calculating their speed would be impossible without some frame of reference, but Gavin knew they must be traveling recklessly fast. Clouds blew by them through the clear screen, ship shaking like a withdrawing drug addict. He tried to close his eyes but found gravity holding them open. The chair seemed to encompass him. Moist fingers wrapped his shoulders and arms to hold him in place. Red vision dimmed toward black as all the blood in his face pooled in the back of his brain.

On the verge of passing out, Gavin felt the ship suddenly slow down, giving him a chance to clear his head and breathe.

"Wow," he said, pulling his right arm from its sticky indentation on the armrest. "Everybody okay?"

"The Perennial and Nythensus are unconscious," Brek said from behind Gavin's chair.

"Mother!" Isla shouted, jumping from her seat.

Zaire slumped against the controls; hands still encased in the creamy tendrils.

Gavin detached himself from his lumpy chair and rushed over behind Isla as she pulled her mother from the vines. Kneeling next to Zaire, Gavin could tell by the color of her skin that she needed to lie down immediately.

"Is she okay?" he asked helplessly. "What do we do?"

"I will be alright…" Zaire said weakly. "My head was not prepared for such a…potent gravity push. The ship also pulled a great deal…of energy from me."

Through the front window, Gavin saw faint stars against dark blue. They hadn't made it out of the atmosphere yet. "Those ships have to be right on our tail," he said. "We need to keep going."

"I will pilot the ship," Isla replied, still cradling her mother's neck.

"No," Zaire said with a meager shake of the head. "The ship is young and does not have access to the gravity streams while still on this planet. It is siphoning energy from the pilot. Once we reach the…main rivers it will have sufficient power, but until then it needs to…draw from a host. Gavin is the only one strong enough to withstand the strain."

"I am strong," Brek protested, towering over the crouched trio.

"Trust me, Commander," Zaire continued with closed eyes. "Gavin is stronger than you. Not physically, but energetically."

"What does that mean?" Brek asked.

Isla touched Gavin's shoulder. "My mother is correct. Gavin is a genetically perfect specimen. He has the best chance of withstanding the strain."

Gavin stood, looking over at the tentacles sticking out of the floor. Their tips writhed slightly like worms searching for lunch.

"I don't know how to fly this thing," he said.

"Allow yourself to feel the energy of the ship," Zaire answered. "From there just…take us away from here as fast as possible. Stay to the starboard side of the system's sun and we should start out more or less on-course."

Doubt filled Gavin's chest. He reached over and touched one of the vines, bleached plant squishing between his forefinger and thumb.

As he slipped his hands between the tendrils, slime covered Gavin's skin. The vines grew up his forearms and slithered all the way to his elbow. A warm feeling tingled along his arm hair as if his skin merged with the ship and extended along the floor.

Gavin closed his eyes, allowing his thoughts to ebb to nothing. He felt Brek's heavy feet pressing against the ground; could smell Isla's scent on the air; liquid dripped from the ceiling in an adjacent room. He perceived all of it. The ship quivered in confusion, so suddenly thrown from the safety if its garden into a terrifying chase through the stratosphere. Gavin calmed himself and felt the ship calm. He breathed and felt the ship breathe.

"Alright, let's go," he whispered.

The ship took off like a shot, breaking through the atmosphere. The vines tightened around Gavin's wrists, almost pleading for strength.

Take mine, he murmured. *Take what you need.*

Cold space bit at the hull as they left the planet behind. Every surface in the ship communicated with Gavin, feeding him temperatures, stress levels, energy needs. He and the ship were one in a beautiful merging of consciousness. Quickly, fatigue set in as the vessel pulled nutrients and willpower from his body and mind, but Gavin knew he needed to fight past his tiredness and endure. Keeping the sun on their starboard, the ship and Gavin surged through the nothingness, leaving behind the Hierarchy and anyone else looking to do them harm.

Gavin glanced back at Isla. "Alright, point me in the right direction. Next stop, Cartoshí…in three to four weeks."

CHAPTER 6

DEATH BECOMES HER

"That is not an embarrassing story at all," Gavin laughed between bites of his salad. "That's like saying, 'I'm embarrassed to be so good at everything.'"

Isla smiled, poking what looked like a cherry tomato with her fork and tossing into her mouth. "I was very embarrassed! Do you know how my instructor reacted?"

"I'm sure he was thrilled to be shown up by a ten-year-old," Gavin said.

"He was not." Isla shook her head, blissfully chewing her food.

For the past 23 days, Gavin, Isla, and the rest of their tiny crew, had hunkered down and prepared for their Cartoshí incursion. Once she had rested and recovered from her head injury, Zaire spent her days training them on what would happen when they landed at the Citadel on Cartoshí. Every possible eventuality had been discussed, from escaping capture, to infiltration, to surrender.

Gavin had paid attention to every lesson but concentrated more on Isla than any plans they had formulated. He realized he had not given their courtship the attention it deserved back on the Silver Hammer.

Most of his "relationships" back on Earth had consisted of little more than sex and photo-ops. That fact had not prepared him for the reality of loving and caring for someone other than himself in a meaningful and long-term way. Comprehension had finally cracked through his thick skull and Gavin wanted to make sure he showed his affections in ways other than the physical.

He found he enjoyed it far more than expected.

They spent a great deal of time together talking and laughing. He had learned much about her childhood and things he had never thought to ask. In turn, he had shared stories of his movie career and why he had chosen some roles before others; things the two of them had never discussed. They had said more meaningful words to each other over the past three weeks than they had during the five-month journey aboard the Silver Hammer after the Battle of Kr'thotok. Conversations grew naturally, and for the first time, Gavin felt he knew the woman he had fallen in love with.

Hopefully, she knew him, too.

"Who fixed the table?" Gavin asked, tapping the white surface with his finger. He pulled a round yellow vegetable from his plate and placed it on the flat surface. The vegetable sat perfectly still, not shifting to one side or the other. "See? Things don't roll off anymore."

Isla smiled. "Brek did a good job forming the hallways and such, but Phylónethese are not known for their subtlety. I have been doing my best to smooth the surfaces and level out some of the other features."

"That's good. Those first few days, I kept rolling out of my bed because it was so lopsided."

"Hopefully, things are more to your liking now," Isla said.

Gavin took her hand. "They are, indeed."

The walls rippled suddenly, like a stone hitting the surface of a quiet pond. Zaire's voice resonated from every surface.

"We have arrived at Cartoshí," she said. "We have already been asked to identify ourselves by two different ships in the vicinity. I need Gavin, Isla, and Brek on the bridge immediately."

"Let's go." Gavin stood.

Gavin and Isla made their way down the hall toward the bridge. Brek stepped out of his bedroom and blocked their way.

"I was in the middle of a nap," the gray brute grumbled as he threw on his jacket.

"You going to be awake enough if things go south once we get down there?" Gavin asked.

Brek puffed breath from his large lopsided nose. "Could I kill you with my bare hand?"

"I'd put up a fight," Gavin said, slapping the Phylónethese on his shoulder.

Zaire sat in the lead pilot's chair as they entered the bridge. She pivoted her seat and motioned for the three friends to sit. Through the front screen Gavin could see other ships whizzing by them on a field of stars like the 405 Freeway during rush hour. A beautiful blue planet, kissed with white clouds and small green landmasses, filled the view in front of them.

"There is a great deal of traffic along the registered gravity belts around Cartoshí," Zaire informed, head nodding toward the view screen. "Since we had to bypass that Hierarchy checkpoint three days ago, it is possible Matriarch Brendant's ship has beaten us here by at least a few hours."

"I have been monitoring the communications," Brek said as he took his seat. "No announcements have been made of her arrival."

"I know," Zaire replied. "Which worries me. The last time I visited Cartoshí was right before we set off on our journey to retrieve Gavin from Earth. There was much pomp and circumstance involved in that visit. The regents celebrated for several days. If Brendant is traveling in secret, or avoiding attention, it does not bode well for us. I am not trusting anything or anyone until we are safely in the council chambers and are able to call for a Sanctuary Vote. That will, by law, give us the audience we require."

"How long until we land?" Gavin asked.

Zaire stood, pointing toward Cartoshí's horizon. "If you look there near the planet's equator you will see the city Mantatol and the citadel. Even from orbit the tower is visible.

Gavin had been taught about the Capital Citadel on Cartoshí and had wondered if he would ever see it. Following Zaire's finger, he saw a thin point poking out from the surface of the planet. The tower had been built ten centuries before with the formation of the Hierarchy. It reached over 30 miles into the stratosphere, more than five miles square at the base. Even from space, Gavin had to admit the structure inspired.

"I see it," Gavin said, a touch of awe to his voice.

Zaire turned back toward the group. "We will be entering planetary gravity momentarily. Our ideal landing point will place us next to the citadel textile factory. There are no guards in the facility and as long as we don't draw undue attention to ourselves, we should be able to get to the service elevators that lead into the Citadel itself."

"What do we expect upon our arrival?" Brek asked.

Zaire sat back down. "At this point, our only option is to outrun any pursuers and hope we can get as close to our target as possible. I am receiving more requests for identification every thousandth cycle. By the time we enter the atmosphere we will likely have several law enforcement ships following us."

"Mordecai Jr. has grown us several weapons over the past

two weeks," Isla said. "I will have them ready."

"Why did you name the vessel?" Brek questioned.

"We talked about this already," Gavin said, not wanting to explain himself again to the hulking Phylónethese.

"I still do not understand."

"In any case," Zaire interrupted. "Our final approach starts now. Strap in. I have confined Burgess and Phrensha'al to their quarters for the remainder of the voyage."

"Smart move," Gavin said.

The ship walls shifted from their customary white and blue color to a deep orange. Gravity shifted like a tide pulling out on the California ocean.

"What's happening?" Gavin asked, clutching at his chair instinctively.

"Unidentified vessel," a female voice rang through the ship. "You will answer our hails or be escorted to a holding facility to verify your cargo. If you do not comply, we will tether you, as required by law."

Gavin's eyebrow raised. "What does 'tether you' mean?"

Turning in her chair, Zaire placed her hands back inside the control tendrils. "I am sure you can figure it out. We will not be giving them the chance."

The ship shot toward the planet below, atmosphere approaching at uncomfortable velocity. Gravity compensated aboard the vessel, though Gavin could still feel the tug of their speed in his bones. A harness grew over Gavin's shoulders and around his legs to hold him safe.

Within 30 seconds, they passed through a cloud cover over a turquoise ocean and pulled up to run parallel with the horizon.

Water sped by beneath them, no land apparent except for a tower on the skyline barely visible through hundreds of miles worth of atmosphere and haze.

Gavin pointed toward the distant column. "Is that the citadel?"

"It is," Isla informed.

"Holy crap, it's huge!"

"Wait until you see it up-close."

As she spoke the words, a landmass came into view in front of them, racing toward the ship.

"I am coming in at incredible speed," Zaire warned. "Our instrumentation is fighting against me. The ship is afraid we will crash and is trying to slow us down. Gavin, I need you to gauge our distance to the citadel. Can you do that?"

He looked out the window as the tower grew in size with each passing second. A beach blew by beneath them, followed by houses and eventually skyscrapers. Judging from the building's sizes and locations relative to one another, Gavin quickly calculated their speed. They would reach the citadel in 47 seconds.

"I got it," Gavin shouted to Zaire.

"Very good! I will need you to tell me precisely when to stop so we do not crash into the citadel."

"What?!" Gavin gasped. "At the speed we're going that doesn't give me any room for error!"

"I understand. If we slow down, we will be stopped by military forces within moments of landing. This way we should have enough time to get inside the building before security is alerted to our presence. You will need to be incredibly precise, so we stop within landing distance."

"Are you serious?!"

"Just tell me, Gavin!"

"Fine! Ten seconds."

The tower filled the screen, blocking out the sun as they

entered its elongated shadow. Gavin did his best to formulate every variable, knowing if he under-shot they would be captured, and if he over-shot they would be dead. Or if Zaire hesitated when he told her to stop, they'd be dead. Should he give her a second, or trust her reaction time?

Closing his eyes, Gavin counted. 3…2…1.

"Now!"

Zaire reversed the engines, throwing everyone forward in their seats. Blood rushed to Gavin's face as they came to an almost dead stop. The harness thankfully held him in place; otherwise, he figured his head would have gone through the view screen.

Gavin opened his eyes, seeing the walls of the citadel less than 200 feet away.

"Good work, Gavin," Zaire said. "Prepare for drop."

"What do you---" The ship plummeted to the ground before Gavin could finish his sentence. The tower flew past them as they reached terminal velocity.

"Gravity is coming back online," Zaire shouted.

Arms going weightless, stomach fluttering like a flock of sparrows trying to escape, Gavin lifted against the harness before being slammed back into the seat. His spine compressed, chin smacking his chest. The experience reminded him of a particularly rough rollercoaster at the L.A. County Fair. Twelve-year-old Seth had gotten motion-sick; Gavin thought his brain had been jiggled to mush and vowed never to return to the event.

Eyelids half-open, lips twitching, Gavin slumped forward like a jellyfish on the beach.

"I think you shattered my skeleton."

"I am setting us down," Zaire informed, voice seemingly unaffected by the forceful jostling. "Grab your weapons and make for the exit. I am sending a message to Phrensha'al and Burgess now to meet us at the door."

"Gavin, are you okay?" Isla asked, concern in her eyes.

"Did you throw up?" Brek questioned.

"I'm fine," Gavin groaned.

"There is no dishonor in vomiting on a mission," Brek comforted.

Gavin's harness released as the ship came to a rocky landing. A yelp sound, like a child yelling 'ow', resounded from the walls on impact. Mordecai squealed in discomfort. Shifting slightly to the left, the vessel settled and went quiet.

"Go!" Zaire commanded.

Feet unsteady beneath him, Gavin stumbled from his chair. Isla grabbed his arm and helped him wobble down the hall. Brek ran toward his room, opening the door and reaching to grab four silver rifles with their familiar tree-limb appearance that accented the natural contours of the ship.

"Here," he said as he handed Gavin one of the weapons.

Shaking the lingering blood from his sinuses, Gavin took the rifle and led the way toward the side ramp.

"You Dubaku pilots!" Phrensha'al shouted as they neared the exit. Gavin turned to see the Perennial limping next to Burgess, ceremonial robes more wrinkled than the alien probably cared for. "I almost broke my leg during your clumsy flying."

"Shut up and let's go," Gavin said as he waved the pretentious duo to follow them.

The ramp lowered, letting in a smell that reminded Gavin more of home than anything he had inhaled since leaving Earth: smog. Exhaust mixed with saltwater and a twist of ozone. Running down the ramp, Gavin smiled in spite of himself.

The ship had landed on what Gavin assumed to be some sort of elevated parking garage. Polished cement covered the area like a high-end auto dealership. Flying vehicles of every shape, size, and color soared overhead. A city at least twice the size of Los Angeles spread out toward the horizon below them, full of buildings, space craft, and the sound of millions of aliens and humans living their lives. For a moment, Gavin imagined himself standing next to the pool on his back porch, hearing the distant roar of the freeway. If L.A. had been built on an alien planet, this is what it would have looked like.

Turning around, Gavin saw the citadel up-close for the first time. Golden-brown walls stretched for miles on his right and left, ornate sculptures and text lining the ramparts in scenes of warfare and conquest. A hieroglyph of an Athelbrath king lording a spear over his enemies stood at least 12 stories tall.

Gavin's mouth hung open at the size and lavishness of the citadel. Veins of gold marbled the coarse stone exterior, hinting at the construction methods that allowed such a structure to exist. The tower went on seemingly forever, disappearing in the clouds above them.

"How did they build this thing?" Gavin asked, voice little more than a whisper. "What's it made out of that lets it be so tall?"

"You can't park here!" a woman shouted to their left. Two Athelbrath females, with their oversized arms, pale skin and dark hair, pointed toward the lopsided vehicle. They wore what looked like business attire; simple solid-colored dresses of blue and red.

Zaire jumped from the ramp and pointed toward a staircase to their right. "We need to go this way!"

"You better move that ship now!" one of the Athelbrath women shouted. "Or I'll call security!"

Gavin figured security would expand to military quickly once their identities were discovered. He bolted after Zaire, Isla by his side. Glancing back, Gavin saw Brek throw Phrensha'al over his shoulder and take off after them.

"Put me down now!" the Perennial screamed. "This is an indignity that shall never be forgiven by the Elder Race!"

"Can't have you running off before we get inside, now can I?" Brek said with a smile. Burgess ran next to him, trying to keep up.

Hurling themselves down the stairs, Gavin looked out on what appeared to be the roof of a factory of some type. Large smokestacks jutted from the building, billowing grayish-orange steam. The stench of rotting meat wafted from the industrial complex.

"We will cut through the factory on the lower level and make our way to the elevators on the far end as planned," Zaire said, looking back toward Gavin and Isla. "That will be our safest route!"

The stairs led to a metal catwalk ending at an oversized steel door. Without preamble, Zaire lowered her rifle and fired, blowing the barrier open with a puff of smoke. Thick stink rolled from the open door like a wall of death. Gavin covered his nose to keep from gagging on the smell.

"Why does it stink so bad?" he asked as they entered the putrid space.

"I do not know," Zaire answered, feet clanging against the metal walkway. "It is a textile plant manufacturing uniforms for citadel servants. It never smelled like this on my prior inspection visits."

"They are no longer weaving fabric, mother," Isla said as they reached an elevated platform looking down on the open factory below. "Look!"

Mists rose from bubbling troughs full of green liquid. Workers in yellow hazmat suits hooked hoses to the large channels, feeding the liquid toward strange glass chambers large enough to fit a man inside. Conveyer arms ran along the ceiling, picking up the strange caskets and taking them off to other areas of the manufacturing floor. It was three or four times the size of any warehouse Gavin had ever seen, with employees toiling in their protective gear from one end to the other. The roar of machines and the grinding of gears filled the warehouse with a droning of industry every bit as unappealing as the smell.

"This is an abomination," Zaire breathed, eye twitching in rage.

"What is this place?" Gavin whispered.

Isla slammed her fist against the railing and spat. "They are processing Cádavrite, but on a scale I have never before witnessed."

Gavin turned toward Isla, leaning his rifle across his shoulder. "Wait, they're reanimating people who just died and turning them into slaves?"

Brek ran up behind them, lowering Phrensha'al to the corrugated metal walkway.

"We have a problem," he snarled. "The Nythensus ran away. I could not stop him. He is likely alerting officials to our location as we speak. I believe military guards will not be far behind." He sniffed the air, a distasteful smirk contorting his already lopsided face. "It smells like death in here."

"Why have you brought me to this unholy place?" Phrensha'al whined.

"Look there!" Zaire said, pointing below to a procession of workers opening individual tubes. Green slime poured onto the floor in great gobs, dripping off what looked like naked people; humans and Athelbrath.

"What are they doing?" Gavin asked.

"It takes a day or two for the body to heal from a mortal wound inside the Renascence Chambers," Zaire informed. "Those specimens are being reintroduced to the environment for the first time after the process."

Several sickly pale men and women, all nude and stumbling, stepped out of the tubes and into the arms of their healers. What their mortal wounds may have been Gavin could only guess. His experience so far had taught him that even the most innocent or powerful person, once they became a Cádavrite, would be considered less than human and turned into a slave. Their skin grayed, retinas bleached, they would never be able to hide their discredited status. Escape from social expulsion would be impossible. Worse, they had been taught their entire lives to believe in such nonsense and thus would even consider themselves worthless and undeserving of even the most basic humanity. It made Gavin sick to think about.

Rolatok, former servant and now member of Gavin's Silverback Guard, acted as the perfect example of this flawed system. Even after months of reconditioning, he still saw himself as lower than an insect.

A group of over a dozen humans and aliens exited their rebirth compartments groggily. A worker in yellow hosed them off with the tenderness of a firehose and herded them toward a door on the far side of the factory. Gavin noticed several of the human men sporting tattoos on their arms; symbols he didn't recognize.

"Mother, do you see that?" Isla asked.

"I do, Isla'a," Zaire answered.

Gavin leaned farther over the railing, unsure of what they referenced. "See what?"

"The markings on their arms," Isla said. "Some of these men are inmates from a small prison colony."

"What does that mean?" Gavin questioned.

Zaire grabbed the railing with her left hand and squeezed with all her strength. "Someone is mass-producing Cádavrites. This many Renaissance Chambers and so much rejuvenation liquid means either someone is creating slaves against their will..."

"Or they are making an army," Isla concluded.

A terrified shout overpowered the buzzing of machinery. Seven lumbering Phylónethese military personnel entered the factory floor from the far side of the building, dragging an Athelbrath man kicking and screaming. Several workers met the uniformed soldiers with a friendly wave and pointed them toward an empty tube.

"We should stop this," Brek said, anger vibrating his voice.

"Stop what?" Gavin asked. "What are they going to do?"

As if answering Gavin's question, one of the brutish soldiers stepped forward and pulled a pistol from his belt. The Athelbrath cried out in words Gavin couldn't quite understand. The Phylónethese pulled the trigger, hitting the alien in the chest.

"No!" Gavin shouted, voice echoing through the space. The soldiers looked up, eyeing the group standing on the catwalk three stories overhead. "Shit. I probably shouldn't have done that."

"We need to run now!" Brek yelled, picking up Phrensha'al again and tossing him over his shoulder.

The Perennial slammed his fists against Brek's arms. "Be careful, you lumbering barbarian!"

Zaire took off toward a set of stairs on the far side of the factory. Gavin followed, holding Isla's hand as they descended the steps. Shouts from below followed them, but Gavin couldn't bring himself to look back.

The stairs led to another catwalk lower down that ran across some of the vats of green liquid. Breathing heavily from running, Gavin couldn't keep the rotten stench from filling his lungs.

"Up ahead," Zaire said as they charged toward the end of the catwalk. "Down below is the hallway that leads to the elevator. We must reach it."

"I don't see any stairs!" Gavin shouted.

Reaching the end of the walkway, Zaire locked her rifle to a hook on her belt and jumped onto the railing. In one motion she leaped out ten feet and grabbed hold of a conveyer arm as it hoisted a Renaissance Chamber from its housing below. She swung back and forth through wafting steam, dropping onto a ten-foot-tall tube filled with what looked like blue bath salts.

"Nothing stops her, does it?" Gavin said as Zaire landed gracefully in a puddle of water on the factory floor. Workers staggered away from her, shouting to a second group of guards eating lunch at a table less than 500 feet away.

"Mother!" Isla cried, pointing to the Phylónethese soldiers as they stood from their meal and locked eyes with Gavin.

"So much for this being a textile plant and there not being any guards," Gavin said.

"Go back!" Zaire shouted, eyes darting from the approaching soldiers to her daughter. "Find another way into the citadel! Take Phrensha'al! I will lead them away!" She pulled the rifle from her belt and fired orange blasts toward the ground in front of the guards. The sentries scattered in response to her assault, energy discharges blowing holes in the cement floor. One of the bulbous gray aliens ripped a pistol from a holster on his hip and returned fire.

"Zaire!" Gavin yelled.

"Run, now!"

An alarm began blaring. Red lights flashed from reflectors over the exits on the ground floor. It would only be a matter of time before they had no option for escape.

Isla grabbed Gavin's shirt and pulled him back the way they came. Brek led the charge, large feet thudding against the steel walkway and shaking the bolts with each thundering step. Phrensha'al bounced on his shoulder, face scowling back at Gavin like a man about to burst with indignation.

"Akteloth!" Brek spat, coming to a hasty stop.

Gavin poked his head around the large alien to see a group of advancing Phylónethese guards, each as big as Brek, stepping through a cloud of stinky fog directly in front of them on the gangplank.

"Drop your weapons!" the lead soldier commanded in a gruff voice. He leveled an absurdly large, three-barreled cannon at the trespassers, leaving no question as to his intent.

"Not likely!" Brek brought his bulky rifle up and fired. The bullet hit the guard's cannon in the lower left barrel, knocking him back into his comrades. The other sentries returned fire as best they could from behind their faltering commanding officer, blasts of orange and red energy flashing through the air around Gavin.

"Stop this violence!" Phrensha'al cried. His legs and arms flailed around like a toddler screaming for candy.

"Our position is untenable!" Isla said, pulling Gavin back to the far side of the factory.

"What's the plan then?" he asked as they ran.

Brek cried out in his guttural voice. Gavin turned to see him fall over, spilling Phrensha'al onto the metal catwalk. The Phylónethese had been shot, but how badly Gavin couldn't tell.

"We have to go back and help Brek," Gavin yelled.

Isla stopped and looked toward their wounded comrade. She opened her mouth to speak when a laser blast rang out from somewhere below on the factory floor, exploding the walkway next to them. Metal groaned and shifted, catwalk lurching to the right. Gavin grabbed a hold of Isla to keep them from falling over and dropped his rifle in the process. It spiraled in the air before splashing in one of the bubbling green cauldrons.

Below them stood three Phylónethese soldiers, each pointing a rifle at Gavin and Isla.

"Don't let the thieves escape!" one of the guards shouted.

"We didn't steal anything!" Gavin yelled back.

His claim did nothing to hinder the soldier's resolve. They opened fire, hitting the railing and footway under Gavin's boots. Isla pulled the trigger on her weapon in response, scattering the guards, but not before the elevated steel perch began to completely collapse.

"We need to jump," she advised, snapping the rifle to her belt.

The catwalk dropped several inches and shifted to the right as preamble to a full breakdown. Bolts twisted, sheering in half as supports overhead tore from the ceiling with the snapping of taut cables. Gavin glanced at the soldiers standing 200 feet away over an injured Brek. Phrensha'al tried to crawl to freedom like a pathetic slug before the towering brutes. Their section of walkway seemed secure at least.

Isla leaped onto the faltering railing and grabbed at a thick cable hanging overhead. Gavin did the same, grasping the line tightly as the catwalk fell out from beneath them and overturned a vat of emerald ooze with a splattering clang.

"Climb to that water drum over there!" Isla said, legs kicking beneath her toward a rusted cask.

"Alright, lets---"

The cable snapped, swinging the duo over the foul liquid. Careening through the air, Gavin saw an opening.

"Let go now!" he said.

Releasing the wire, both Gavin and Isla curved through a pillar of pink vapor and landed on the concrete just beyond the vats. They hit hard, muscles bruising against unforgiving cement. Several workers in their hazmat suits scurried out of their way like confused rats. Gavin slid to a stop, left arm scraping beneath him.

Isla shot to her feet, reaching for the rifle on her belt but finding only a broken clasp.

Through slightly blurred vision Gavin spotted her weapon ten feet away. "It's there," he pointed.

Shouting intensified as a group of 13 soldiers rounded the corner. Instead of being exclusively Phylónethese, this brigade consisted of humans and Athelbrath as well; two of them obviously Cádavrite by their pastel complexions. Isla pulled her gun from the floor and opened fire, hitting two of the uniformed guards and pushing the rest back.

"We need to find a choke-point," Isla said as she helped Gavin pull himself from the cement. "Then we must find my mother and verify she is alright."

Splashing through puddles of water mixed with chunky oils, Gavin and Isla turned past a series of rebirth chambers and slammed headlong into another group of soldiers, all armed and ready to fire.

Gavin pulled Isla behind a group of metal and glass cylinders, narrowly avoiding a cavalcade of laser fire.

"Back this way," Gavin said, squeezing the pair between two casks of smelly lubricant and into another aisle identical to all the others. Workers held their hands in the air while Gavin and Isla ran past, as if the duo would stop and steal their wallets.

An Athelbrath soldier holding a shock baton jumped in front of them from next to a row of large glass tubes.

"Drop your---"

Isla shot him in the knee, cutting off his order. The Athelbrath screamed in pain and dropped his riot stick.

Before Gavin could congratulate her on a precision shot, a second guard, this one brandishing a thermal rifle, sprung into their path, and fired without a word, hitting Isla dead center in the chest.

She fell forward onto her knees and toppled face-first toward the concrete. Her weapon skidded away and clattered next to a revival conduit.

"Isla!" Gavin screamed, turning her over so he could see the damage.

Eyes wide in shock, Isla coughed, blood dripping from the corners of her mouth. The hole in her sternum, two inches in diameter, sizzled like an overcooked steak. Gavin could see his hand against her back through the cauterized wound.

She tried to speak, mouth opening and closing, but no words penetrated the blood filling her throat.

"Isla!" Gavin cried, tears clouding his vision.

Her body tensed, fingers clawing at Gavin's shoulder. Eye's bulging like a terrified animal, Isla's lids fluttered and then she went limp as a rag.

Sobbing, Gavin held her close, hearing commands to surrender and lie on the floor coming from a hundred miles away. Only the sound of the shrieking alarm penetrated his faculties.

She was gone.

Isla was gone.

One moment her body bounded though space with all the vitality of a woman in her prime, and the next she was nothing more than a corpse waiting to rot in Gavin's arms. Fury competed with sorrow, coursing through his body like electricity during a thunderstorm.

Coming into sharp focus, his mind processed every detail of the moment, from the weight of her body to the number of soldiers encircling him.

Twenty-four.

Only 24 soldiers.

Piece of cake.

Gavin lowered Isla to the ground and raised his hands over his head in surrender. He breathed slowly, suddenly knowing exactly how many hairs grew on Isla's head, and the number of alternative exits that they could have used to escape the soldiers. Thousands of potential choices could have avoided all of this if Gavin had been more aware. If he had paid more attention.

Never again.

As one of the guards stepped forward to grab him, Gavin reached over and picked up Isla's rifle.

Still on his knees, Gavin fired, hitting the Athelbrath soldier in the face. The other guards jumped in surprise and tightened their fingers on their triggers, but they weren't fast enough.

No one could have been fast enough.

Twenty-three more shots rang out, each carefully angled and chosen to take out first, those quickest on the draw, and second, anyone else with a weapon. In front of him, behind him, it didn't matter. Changes in air currents telegraphed their movements and thus he knew where to fire without even looking. He could have killed them all with his eyes closed.

Each soldier fell, thumping against the cement like sacks of potatoes.

Gavin hadn't even stood up.

Ringed in bodies, Gavin finally pulled himself to his feet, rifle in-hand. Two hazmat-wearing workers whimpered against one of the rebirth pods, hands shaking in front of them as if pleading with Gavin not to shoot.

"Put her inside, now," Gavin said, motioning toward Isla's body with his rifle. The words had left his lips before his brain had fully evaluated the statement. "Now. Do it."

One of the hazmat covered workers, an Athelbrath by the size of their arms, nodded and stepped over to Isla. The second followed, trembling in panic. Together they lifted her corpse and placed her in the closest open chamber.

Gavin tasted the salt from his tears, hearing more shouting as the factory filled with military units.

"Save her, or I'll kill you both," he said.

"Please don't hurt us," a woman's voice cracked from beneath her full-body suit as the pair shoved Isla's cadaver haphazardly into the pod.

"Save her and I won't."

The Athelbrath woman pressed a button on the side of the unit, closing the doors with a hiss.

Isla's eyes remained open through the glass, mouth slack and lifeless. Thoughts of Cádavrites and social stigmas electrified Gavin's thoughts. If he brought her back, would she be happy or angry? Would she be condemned to a life of judgmental looks and scoffing overlords?

It didn't matter. He couldn't let her die.

In that instant he realized his true selfishness.

Even so, it wouldn't stop him.

"Start the process now," he ordered, gun still pointing at the workers. They pulled a hose from an adjacent hull and hooked it to the base of Isla's. The chamber hummed, electricity flowung to flickering internal lights. Liquid gurgled from somewhere behind the unit, filling vials along the sides in green slime.

A shift in the air flow told Gavin troops approached from the west. How did he know east from west and north from south from inside the building? He didn't care. He just knew.

"Is it started?" he asked.

The woman nodded, shaking uncontrollably.

"How long until she's okay?"

"I don't know," she sniveled.

"How long!"

Cowering, the Athelbrath woman continued. "I don't know…The process only works in half of the cases, depending on the injury and time between death and reawakening insertion. Please, don't hurt me! I have children!"

"Please!" the second worker chorused.

Gavin blew out a breath and threw his rifle to the ground with a metallic rattle. Turning, he watched 12 guards converge on his position, primed for a fight. Tired and lost, Gavin raised his hands above his head and fell to his knees. The alarm continued sounding, red lights flashing from above. No other sounds of battle echoed through the factory.

Maybe they had already killed Zaire too, and Brek. Maybe they would kill him then and there.

Who cares? He thought to himself as a soldier threw him to the floor and stomped on his neck.

CHAPTER 7

PINNACLES OF POWER

Two days in darkness. They had thrown Gavin into a windowless cell; door slammed behind him. That was 48 hours ago. At only six-feet by six-feet square, the prison didn't even allow him to lay down fully. Most of the time he crouched on the dusty ground, contemplating the universe and his place therein while smelling stagnant water and mold.

No visitors, no food, no light.

Strangely it hadn't bothered him. It felt deserved.

Gavin's thoughts lingered on Isla. Had she been resuscitated? Was she a Cádavrite that resented him, or had she simply never woken up? And if she had, would her hatred destroy their relationship?

If their places had been reversed, would she have been weak like he had and chosen to bring him back, or would she have been strong and allowed death to claim its prize?

He had no other choice; letting her die without trying something, anything, would have been a defeat too heavy to bear. Who in their right mind would have allowed someone they love to perish when they could save them? Still, he understood the cultural enormity of what he had done. Anyone on Earth would have made the same choice he had. Here on Cartoshí? Probably not.

For hours on end, he replayed the moments leading up to Isla's death, seeing dozens of alternate solutions, from rushing the Phylónethese on the upper catwalk to using Phrensha'al as a living shield to give them enough time to obliterate the enemy forces. A ghoulish alternative, but an effective one. Every detail of every plan coalesced in his mind with astonishing accuracy.

His parched tongue stuck to the roof of his mouth. Luckily, the lack of food and water had meant he had no need for a bathroom. The cell already stank of sweat and grief; no need to add poop to the mix.

Hinges squeaked as his door slowly opened. A shaft of light burned his eyes.

"Mr. Baller?" a female voice asked.

Gavin blinked, trying to focus on a dark shape haloed by blinding fluorescents. Pupils dilating, he finally made out a hand reaching toward him.

"I'm sorry that it took me this long to get you out of your cell." The woman spoke in perfect English, a hint of midwestern twang to her accent. "There are many levels of bureaucracy to navigate in matters like this, no matter how powerful the authority issuing the order."

"What do you want?" Gavin croaked, surprised by the gravely timbre of his own voice.

The woman smiled. Now that his eyes had fully adjusted, Gavin could see her long brown hair and cream-colored skin. He hadn't seen a Caucasian outside Seth, Ashton, and Raymond Halford since setting off from Earth the year before. He didn't think any white people existed in the Commonwealth, since all the humans had descended from one African tribe. Her sleeveless dress, black except for a pink stripe running from her left shoulder to right hip, hugged her body like a clingy boyfriend. She was beautiful, certainly. Was she also an evil minion of some shadowy Hierarchy? Who could guess?

"Mr. Baller, I'm here to get you cleaned up," she said, voice soothing and kind. "You've been summoned by the High Regency in the citadel above. It's a great honor."

Gavin pushed himself from the dirty floor. His legs ached as full circulation returned. "Where are my friends? Is Isla okay?"

"I'm not authorized to give you that information, I'm sorry," she said, reaching to take Gavin's arm. He swatted it away, stretching his back and neck. Two armored Athelbrath guards walked up beside the woman in response to Gavin's swiping. Their irritated stance telegraphed they wouldn't hesitate to spray him with paralytic ooze if he stepped out of line.

"I know you've been treated badly since your arrival in the Commonwealth," she continued, "and I'm sure your opinion of the Hierarchy and Plenipotentiary is probably worse. I bet you don't care for anyone who associates with them either, but trust me, all that's over now."

"Trust you? I'll pass."

"I understand." Sadness pulled at her eyes, real sadness, unless her acting ability rivaled Gavin's. "If you don't trust me, trust Lady Zaire. She's waiting for you upstairs."

"Zaire?" Gavin asked, hope rekindling in his chest. "She...she's okay?"

"She is. There are others waiting as well. I am to lead you to the bathing spas and then take you to the Regency Chamber. Will you follow me at least that far?"

The thought of a bath sounded better than sitting in a dank cell, whether she spoke the truth or not. Maybe there would be food, too. He'd suffered past the worst of the hunger pangs on the first day, but he wouldn't turn down something to eat, that's for sure.

"Fine, let's go."

"Very good, Mr. Baller."

The Athelbrath guards turned and began walking down the prison hallway with its beige walls and steel doorways. Gavin followed slowly, boots scraping against the cement flooring.

"I'm Aubrey, by the way," the woman said as she walked next to Gavin. "I'm from Iowa."

"How did you get here, Aubrey from Iowa?"

"A spaceship. You?"

"How long have you been out here?"

"Awhile."

Gavin nodded his head. "I can see you're not much for details."

"And I can smell you need a shower." Aubrey smiled and stopped next to a mirrored elevator door that looked like it had been plucked directly from some high-rise in New York. "Let's get you cleaned up and then maybe I'll give you some details."

The door opened and the two stepped inside, leaving the Athelbrath behind. The elevator interior, while similar to what existed on Earth, featured no floor buttons, only smooth walls covered in wood veneer. The doors closed and the lift shot upward, pushing Gavin's empty stomach into his butt.

"I've taken the liberty of ordering some food for you as well," Aubrey said, eyes forward. "Bathe as long as you like, eat whatever you want, but I'll be back in about an hour to escort you to the pinnacle. Hopefully you'll be recovered and in better spirits."

The elevator slowed, doors opening on a tiled room with a lovely veranda. Silky curtains drifted delicately in a pleasant breeze while afternoon sunlight framed a series of pools and tiny cataracts.

The sound of babbling water sent chills up Gavin's spine before he'd even noticed the fragrance of cedarwood and eucalyptus.

He stepped onto the smooth stone flooring, wishing he didn't have his boots on so he could feel the cool ground against his bare feet. Wind blew through his hair, massaging his tight scalp.

The entire spa looked out on the bustling city from several miles overhead. Gavin walked over to the glass railing and took it all in. His heartbeat quickened as a sense of vertigo tickled his inner ear. Heights had never bothered him, but even so, he grasped the railing tighter than needed. From that altitude, he could barely make out individual buildings on the ground far below. The ocean kissed the horizon and he remembered skimming across the water a few days before with this very tower in the distance.

"How high are we?" he asked.

"High," Aubrey answered. "We're at a point where the air starts to get thin. Don't worry, our climate processors keep everyone breathing just fine."

A platter of apples and bananas sat in a bowl on a table to his left: real Earth apples and bananas. He stared at them like they would disappear in a mirage.

Aubrey laughed quietly. "Those are actual Washington apples there, and the bananas are from Mexico City. Over on the counter is a medium rare steak from good old-fashioned Nebraska beef. Just don't eat too much and make yourself sick. There'll be food upstairs, as well."

Gavin rubbed his forehead. "I'm really confused…"

"Clean up and eat," Aubrey stated flatly. "You're by yourself here, and no one will be bothering you. I'll be back to get you in an hour." She turned toward the elevator and exited the spa.

Once alone, Gavin dove for the apples, sinking his teeth into the juicy red fruit. Looking back at the immaculate spa, Gavin saw a plate on a far counter covered in steak and a baked potato.

For the next hour, Gavin soaked in soothing pools and ate until his stomach groaned at him to stop. It was bliss. Unlike his cell, where his solitude had been oppressive, here in the bathing ponds, Gavin's seclusion brought freedom and relaxation.

Next to one of the pools lay a straight razor, hand mirror, and a can of Barbasol shaving cream. A vague question came to Gavin's mind of how the American-produced brand had arrived on an alien planet, but he quickly brushed it aside as he took the canister. Spraying the foam into his palm, Gavin breathed in the masculine smell of fougère and sandalwood. He smeared it liberally across his face and shaved, enjoying the razor's cold edge against his skin.

Fragrant towels waited for him upon stepping out of the pools. A fresh pair of tan slacks and light blue collared shirt lay across a nearby chair. Putting them on, Gavin smelled fabric softener and a hint of geranium. If there had been a bed within reach, he would have slept comfortably for a week.

Then he thought of Isla, eyes wide open behind the glass of a Renaissance Chamber. A week wouldn't be long enough. Perhaps he would sleep forever.

"Well, you clean up pretty nice," Aubrey said as she stepped off the elevator.

Gavin pushed Isla from his mind to better focus on the potential dangers that lay ahead.

"I didn't win *People Magazine's Sexist Bachelor 2018* for nothing," he said, putting on his polished 'Gavin Baller' swagger.

Aubrey looked him up and down, lips pulling into her cheeks as if she liked what she saw.

"How about we head upstairs?" she asked.

They stepped back into the elevator, leaving the spa behind, and rocketing toward the stratosphere. While gravity in the lift seemed fixed except for a tingle that almost imperceptibly lifted Gavin's hair, he knew they had to be traveling at speeds that would turn standard Earth elevators to cinders. Whatever relaxation he had retained quickly dissipated as worries about what awaited upstairs filled his frontal lobe. If Aubrey were being honest about Zaire, the Matriarch waited for him and had smoothed everything over while he'd sat bored in prison.

"You seem much looser than you did when I came to your cell," Aubrey observed in a conversational tone.

"Well, trading a jail for a warm hot tub will do that for you. Who am I meeting upstairs? It would be nice to prepare."

"Unfortunately, there isn't much time left for that," Aubrey said as the elevator slowed. "We're here."

"Seriously? That quick?"

The doors slid open on a long throne room at least 400 feet in length and 100 feet from floor to ceiling. Yellowish-brown pillars lined the walls along with designs and hieroglyphs like something from an Egyptian temple. Twelve Phylónethese soldiers stood at attention along the walls next to the rectangular columns, stoically staring into space like guards in front of Buckingham Palace. Granite tiles lined the floor, a purple carpet leading from the entrance all the way to a magnificent golden throne sitting at the top of a series of nine steps. The kingly chair sat unoccupied, sunlight streaming through massive windows behind it as the sun lowered in the sky.

A crowd of people Gavin recognized stood below the throne steps, chatting, and smiling next to a table laden with colorful fruits, meats, and steaming breads.

Aubrey nodded toward the group at the end of the hall. "I have a feeling some of these people are going to be very happy to see you."

"Gavin!" The shout echoed through the gallery, reaching his ears like a favorite song from his high school days.

Seth ran down the carpet toward his friend, arms outstretched in greeting.

"Seth!" Gavin grinned as he scooped the man up in a crushing bearhug. "What are you doing here? We thought you were going to be executed!"

"Everything's been worked out, man. We're all here."

Ashton and Bomb rushed toward the actor; pale, scarred Rolatok and the entire Silverback Guard proceeding behind. Brek limped along with the rest of the elite squad, arm heavily bandaged, face bruised.

"What...? I don't understand," Gavin floundered, lost for words.

"We're alright, mate," Ashton said, swatting Gavin on the shoulder.

Bomb came up beside Seth, wrapping her hand around his bicep. "I kept Seth safe for you, as I promised, Gavin Baller."

Tears welled in his eyes. "You did, Bomb. Dammit, you sure did." Gavin could hardly contain his excitement, emotion threatening to burst from his chest. "Is Isla okay? How did you all get here?"

"That would be because of me."

The voice, deep and familiar, spoke flawless California English. Gavin had heard that voice his entire life; dozens of movies capturing that exact tone and spewing it across screens from India to Delaware.

It was Gavin's voice.

A man approached, dark blue uniform hugging his muscular frame while an ornamental red and orange scarf hung from both shoulders down past his knees. Hair short, skin a light brown, the man's lips curled in a playful smile.

"Allow me to introduce myself," he said, extending his hand for Gavin to shake. "Gavin Baller, I am Abraxas-Mon."

Gavin stood dumbfounded, mouth hanging open. Other than a scar over the man's left eye, the two could have been twins so similar even their mother would be unable to tell the difference.

Abraxas-Mon; the man that had stood like a shadow over his entire life since Zaire first mentioned his name in the kitchen of a *PHAT Burger* off L.A.'s Skid row.

"Holy shit," Gavin finally gasped as he shook his doppelganger's hand.

"Right?" Seth said with a smile. "It's totally weird, isn't it?"

"I have wanted to meet you for a very long time, Gavin," Abraxas-Mon stated warmly. "I worried I would never get a chance, but it seems fate has brought us together despite all the odds."

"But we thought…I mean, you were supposed…" Gavin stammered.

"Are you alright?" Abraxas-Mon asked, placing his hand on Gavin's shoulder. "I've been working for the past two days to get you out of your cell. Do you need more time? I have doctors on stand-by. I'm sorry it took me so long to cut through the bureaucracy to secure your release."

Gavin smiled and shook his head, pushing his astonishment and euphoria aside. "No, no. I'm okay, this is just weird."

"I truly understand," Abraxas-Mon said, giving Seth a side glance. "Seth has been telling me so much about you and it's strangely comforting, knowing I would have made so many of the same choices you did if I'd been in your position. I would have selected many of the same friends, as well."

"This can't be real," Gavin said, hands running through the long hair on the side of his head. "I thought Aubrey was tricking me and that as soon as I stepped off the elevator, a firing squad would shoot me."

Abraxas-Mon laughed; a sound that sent uncomfortable chills up Gavin's spine like an echo originating from nothing. "Sorry about that. Aubrey isn't one to give superfluous information. I'm just glad I got to Cartoshí in time. Matriarch Brendant was planning on everyone's executions, thinking you guys had attacked Asha'asethol. That didn't seem right to me so I stepped in as soon as I could." His eyes moved to Gavin's female chaperon. "Aubrey, thank you for bringing Gavin here. You may take the rest of the afternoon for whatever personal duties require your attention."

"Thank you, sir," Aubrey said, stepping back into the elevator and giving Gavin a wink as the doors closed.

Gavin turned back to Abraxas-Mon, absolutely flabbergasted by their similarities.

"I seriously can't believe this," he said. "We thought you were dead. We seriously figured you'd been killed by whatever attacked the Perennials since no one had spoken with you directly in so long. Zaire was all worried about it."

"She told me," the warlord informed. "I am very disturbed by what she described in the factory at the base of this very tower. This would not be the first time someone tried to create a Cádavrite army, but to blatantly place it next to the Citadel betrays an ego bigger than the Gadabout. With Zaire's help, we will learn what we can and shut it down." He nodded his head toward the back half of the throne room. "She's actually right over there."

Looking over Abraxas-Mon's shoulder, Gavin noticed Zaire and Ogpog talking to someone in a shadowed crook across the hall.

"Zaire!" he shouted. "We did it! We found Abraxas-Mon!"

Zaire turned, a sad smile on her face. It was then Gavin noticed to whom she spoke.

Isla, dressed in a beautiful light-yellow gown, stood with her parents in a far corner. Hair pulled back into a regal bun, her eyes blazed pale blue like the waters of the Pacific. If the bleached irises hadn't been enough, her ashen skin confirmed her Cádavrite status. Instead of deep brown, Isla's flesh appeared tinged in gray, making her, if anything, more exotic than Gavin could imagine.

How anyone would ever think this woman less than spectacular and queenly, he would never understand.

The two paramours locked eyes for the briefest of moments

until Isla dropped her gaze and exited the room through a door on her right. Gavin stepped past Abraxas-Mon, reaching for the woman he loved, catching only empty air despite his best efforts.

"Give her time," Abraxas-Mon said like a kind older brother. "She's been through more than you understand."

Seth put his hand on Gavin's neck and squeezed lightly. "She'll be okay, I think. Look at me. Isla is ten times stronger than I am. I survived a year in solitary. She'll survive this."

Gavin nodded, though unconvinced.

"Come," Abraxas-Mon called to the group. "Let us continue our discussion and try to feel the joy of this wonderful reunion. There will be plenty of time for rumors of war and sadness tomorrow."

Gavin followed his friends as if in a funeral procession. Rolatok and Detrius came over to greet him, as did the wounded Brek. Voices spoke in gentle tones trying to lift his spirits, but nothing could nudge him toward happiness. Ashton gushed about how scared he had been until Abraxas-Mon had arrived to save everyone.

After a few minutes, Zaire approached and gave Gavin a hug. "I understand why you did it," she whispered in his ear. Her scent comforted him as she spoke, like grandma telling a young boy everything would be alright. "And I do not fault you for your actions."

"I'm sorry," Gavin whimpered. "I couldn't let her go. I wasn't strong enough."

"I know," she soothed. "We will discuss all of this later. She is not ready to be around anyone yet, and the only reason she came up here to begin with was to make sure you were alright. Trust in that."

Gavin nodded, feeling his spirits lift slightly. He remembered his conversation with Zaire back in the Gardens of Light when she admitted the hypocrisy of how Cádavrites were treated, but despite her understanding, she still saw them as abominations. Gavin prayed, embracing the woman who had become his most trusted mentor, that she would never consider her own daughter anathema.

"I'm sorry," Gavin repeated, hugging her close, unable to let go. "I'm so sorry."

"Shhhh." Zaire hushed. "You have been in a cell for several days and I know all of this must feel unbelievable, but we are going to need you at your best starting now. All of us are alive and well, but soon, millions of others won't be. The war continues, and whatever unknown is crouching in the darkness seems ready to strike. We must prepare."

"That is a strange sight to see," Abraxas-Mon said while taking a sip from a wine glass. "My Matriarch embracing me while I stand on the other side of the room!"

Everyone laughed. Even Gavin.

Zaire pulled from their hug and squeezed Gavin's arm. She looked over to Abraxas-Mon and nodded, as if giving him permission to continue speaking.

"I'm glad we can celebrate, if even for a moment," Abraxas-Mon continued. "From what I understand, the coming days will bring foul portent and tales of suffering and disaster like the Commonwealth has never known. I have interviewed our Asha'andasa emissary Phrensha'al, who Lady Zaire so bravely saved from the apparent decimation of the Elder Planet. He had many insights to share on both the past and future.

"Tomorrow we will form a council and discuss our options and the threats that loom. But for now, let us rejoice in this reunification and bask in a fleeting moment of frivolity. I am seeing my beloved Zaire, my kind Mala'apand, after several years of estrangement, and I am meeting my counterpart for the first time. For me, this is a day that I will never forget."

Seth nudged Gavin's ribs. "He gives a better speech than when you accepted your Oscar."

"Shut up," Gavin said with a shove.

Abraxas-Mon raised his glass above his head as if about to propose a toast. "It's appropriate that we are meeting in this ancient throne room. It was here that the last dictator of the Commonwealth, the Athelbrath Orthal-Oblin, reigned as king and ruler over the entire galaxy. Since then, we have enjoyed a more democratic system that has led to peace and prosperity. Without our Perennial fathers guiding us, it is possible none of the intelligent species currently living in the Commonwealth would have survived this long. It is a gift, as is this celebration."

"Now let's stop talking and continue eating!" Brek shouted, slapping Rolatok on the shoulder and practically knocking the slender man over.

"I agree fully, Commander," Abraxas-Mon grinned.

Stomach still full from his recent gorging in the spa area, Gavin wandered next to one of the pillars and watched everyone mingle. Abraxas-Mon, seemingly the best host in the universe, elicited laughter with each sentence. Even Brek, who rarely chuckled, and Rolatok, who felt himself unworthy of happiness, giggled and snorted like high school girls hanging around with the quarterback.

Seth held hands with Bomb, which didn't seem out of place but still made Gavin feel like he'd missed something; Ashton flirted with Zontol, one of Gavin's Silverback Guard; Zaire and Ogpog seemed to be avoiding Gavin as much as possible. Parties had rarely brought Gavin joy, but never before had he felt so alone in a room filled with people he actually cared about.

"You okay?" Seth asked, leaning against the pillar.

"Oh yeah," Gavin answered. "I just found out everybody is alive and safe, that Isla didn't die after being shot in the chest, and that my galactic warlord counterpart is every bit as awesome as I could have hoped."

"Then why do you look like somebody just ran over your

dog?"

"Because I feel like somebody just ran over my dog."

"Isla's going to be alright," Seth said, putting his arm around Gavin's shoulder. "This whole Cádavrite thing is a big deal. I haven't talked to her, but I can tell she's pretty depressed. Ogpog sure seems pissed about it."

"I couldn't let her die, man."

"I know. I would have made the same choice. For us, it's a no-brainer, but here in the Commonwealth, there are cultural things we just don't get."

Gavin watched as Bomb stood across the room in front of Ogpog, back ridged like a soldier giving a report.

"What's the deal with you and Bomb?" he asked. "When did that turn into a full-fledged thing?"

"We're taking things really slow." Seth smiled as Bomb bowed slightly to Zaire and Ogpog as they passed by the food tables. "She's something else. You'd think after everything she'd been through in the Gadabout zoo that she'd be a wreck, but honestly, she's the most impressive woman I've ever met. She inspires me. Plus, my ex-wife would hate everything about her, which is a huge plus."

"What do you think of the other me?" Gavin asked, eyeing Abraxas-Mon with needless suspicion.

"Our ship landed the morning before you guys arrived. We weren't sure what was going to happen to us. There were rumors we were going to be executed and stuff, but Abraxas-Mon showed up and ordered us released. Since then, he's been close by, getting to know everyone and asking questions about you."

"So, you like him?"

"I do," Seth admitted. "But not more than you. Think of him like a brother you never had. He's awesome, just like you … only different."

Gavin smiled, eternally grateful for Seth's friendship. He understood now what had been missing from his life all those years on Hollywood backlots.

"Thanks," he said. "Really. I'm glad everybody is safe. We spent so much time worrying about rescuing you guys, it's almost a let-down to know it was all for nothing."

"Well, according to Zaire, we all have plenty of stuff to still worry about since no one knows who attacked the Perennial planet." Seth looked longingly at the roasted meat ten feet away on a side table. "You care if I eat real quick?"

"Go," Gavin urged, pushing his best friend toward the beef. "I'll be fine by myself for a few minutes."

Seth grinned and rushed over to the platter.

Gavin stepped away from the column and up the steps toward the opulent throne. Whoever had sat here in times gone by had obviously been a powerful individual. Gavin rubbed his hand along the golden armrest and ostentatious ornaments reaching from the bolster toward the ceiling.

"Interested in sitting down?" Abraxas-Mon asked. "It's been 400 years since anyone has sat in that seat. I'm surprised the guards didn't tackle you before you got within ten feet of the thing."

"So, this is just a decoration now?" Gavin asked.

"More a reminder," Abraxas-Mon said, stepping onto the stairs. "It emphasizes where we've been and where we're going. For centuries, the men and women who sat in that chair ravaged the galaxy."

"I thought the Perennials brought everyone together in peace and prosperity," Gavin said. "That's what Zaire always told me."

Abraxas-Mon nodded. "They did, but there have been times when their power has waned, allowing for ambitious beings to wrest control from them. Orthal-Oblin the Athelbrath took power for almost 70 Earth years and decimated an entire intelligent species: the

Gronlins. They went extinct, unfortunately. Of course, there are those who argue that without Oblin's reign, there could have been no lasting peace; it was his atrocities that forced the people to reassert their rights and help the Asha'andasa regain dominion. I leave such theories to the historians."

"Where is Phrensha'al, anyway?" Gavin asked, looking through the crowd to see if he'd missed the uptight Perennial.

"Phrensha'al did not wish to join us. Once I told him rebuilding the Othpethoth Temple would be a priority, he began using my Speculates to show how all of the damage needed to be repaired and gave many opinions about how best to accomplish his goals."

Gavin smiled. "He certainly has a lot of opinions."

"He's been through a lot," Abraxas-Mon said. "Whoever attacked Asha'asethol has kept their invasion a secret for five years. Such a thing has never happened before in the entire history of the Commonwealth. I'm disappointed Phrensha'al couldn't give us more details about the threat. Right now, the Hierarchy and the Rebirth Militia are still amassing troops to fight each other while a much more dangerous menace looms. Their selfishness will be their downfall."

Gavin tapped his finger against the gold throne. "Well, now that you're on our side, maybe we can get them to pay attention to what's really important."

"You give them, and me, too much credit."

"This is really weird, talking to you." Gavin laughed, leaning against the throne.

Abraxas-Mon smiled, showing off those perfect teeth. "I know."

"I have so many questions," Gavin continued. "Like, how do you speak English so perfectly? You had shaving cream in the spa, and cow meat, and apples; holy crap, apples! Do you know how much I love apples?"

"I do," Abraxas-Mon said. "I like apples, so obviously so would you."

"How did you get it all here? I thought visiting Earth was illegal and all that stuff."

"Gavin, I think it's time you and I had a private conversation. There is a lot you need to know. Some of it you might not be prepared for, but you'll need to know regardless."

"I'm ready," Gavin replied with a nod of his head. "I'm tired of asking questions and feeling like I'm always behind the Eightball."

"Very well," Abraxas-Mon said, turning toward the chattering group. "Everyone! If I could, I request a moment alone with Gavin. I think it would be best if he and I had a little time to get to know each other. This is a very strange moment for the both of us. There is another banquet room to our right, through those doors. The servants will carry the food over there, so don't worry about taking anything with you. I apologize for the inconvenience and thank you in advance."

Everyone nodded and began shuffling toward the doors. Seth waved to Gavin as he exited the room. Athelbrath and Nythensus waiters muddled in and rushed platters and plates to the adjacent dining hall. Clanging silverware and fine china frittered quietly as servants bused them out, followed by the rest of the group.

Zaire looked at Gavin and Abraxas-Mon like a caring mother before exiting and leaving the two men alone, apart from the silent Phylónethese guards along the walls.

The sound of the doors closing echoed boldly through the throne room like the slamming of a tomb.

"You have no idea how long I've wanted to have this meeting with you, Gavin," Abraxas-Mon said, stepping close to the throne. "No idea at all. My entire adult life, I've been almost obsessed with it."

"Why?" Gavin asked.

"A lot of reasons." Abraxas-Mon ran his finger along one of the golden branches extending from the back of the chair. "It isn't often you come face to face with yourself and see only perfection."

Turning slowly, the warlord sat down on the throne, velvety cushion squishing beneath his perfectly formed glutes. He settled back comfortably like a father in his favorite recliner.

"Why are you sitting on the throne?" Gavin questioned, sweat suddenly accumulating in his armpits.

"Because it's mine," Abraxas-Mon stated without equivocation. "Gavin, there is so much you need to know, and it's time your education began."

CHAPTER 8

A SHADOW EMPIRE IN THE SUN

"Why are you sitting on the throne?" Gavin repeated the question, afraid of the answer.

"Most people don't know that Orthal-Oblin the Athelbrath was a genetically perfect being," Abraxas-Mon said, rubbing his hands along the royal chair's armrest like a tender lover. "Just like you and me. He reigned for decades and decades, never facing any real challenges. I mean, who could challenge him anyway? It wasn't until after he died that anyone even stood up to dispute anything."

Pinching his eyebrows together, Gavin scratched his forehead. "What does that have to do with you sitting on his throne? This is a democracy. You said so yourself."

"Democracy is a lie," Abraxas-Mon answered. "Democracy doesn't exist. People give up their rights, so they don't have to do anything. As long as there's money in their pockets, no one will fight back. You know where I learned that? Earth."

"You've never been to Earth," Gavin countered, mentally pleading with his counterpart to get off the throne so it wouldn't mean what he knew it meant.

"You're right, I haven't, unfortunately. But I've studied our history and cultures; everything I could get my hands on. Years ago, one of my operatives brought me a copy of your entire Internet. That was immensely helpful."

"Why don't we go to another room and finish this conversation," Gavin said, motioning toward the elevator.

Abraxas-Mon smiled. "Does me sitting on this throne make you uncomfortable?"

"Yes!" Gavin shouted.

"Like I said: it's mine. It was only waiting for me to sit down."

Gavin's head shook back and forth. "No, you're playing me. This is a joke. It's something I would have done to James Franco after the Golden Globes or something like that."

"And what would you have done to that man if it had been socially acceptable to kill him?"

"I wouldn't have…I would never have…"

The grin on Abraxas-Mon's face stretched wider. "But you've thought about it. I know for sure you have. Personally, I would have brought the man to me, feigning friendship, then set him up to be taken down by other enemies before finally being brought to me so I could cleave his skull with my own hand. Or perhaps I would have allowed him to think of me as his protector before swooping in and destroying this James Franco along with all his kin; burn his house before anyone is the wiser."

Gavin took a step to a lower stair, image of a burning home superimposed over a destroyed planet and cratered temple. Realizing for the first time how everything made perfect sense, Gavin put the pieces together in his mind. If Abraxas-Mon claimed that throne, then so much of the past few months suddenly came into focus.

"You attacked the Perennials. It was you. Admit it."

"Gladly," Abraxas-Mon said, hands wide in concession.

"What? Are you trying to take over the galaxy, or something?"

"Gavin, I already took over the galaxy." The warlord stated it in such a pleasant way, it disturbed Gavin, like a comedian describing a murder halfway through their routine. "I've ruled the Commonwealth since the day I destroyed Asha'asethol and basically wiped out the Perennials five years ago. Very few people know I'm running things, but that's why it works so well. Unlike you, I don't need the attention."

Looking to the silent guards standing next to the pillars, Gavin waved his arms over his head. "Hey guys! Hey you, Phylónethese! I'm talking to you, assholes! This guy just admitted to destroying the Perennials. Arrest him or something!"

"All these men have been by my side for decades, Gavin," Abraxas-Mon said with a swipe of his hand. "Many of them took part in the attack on Asha'asethol and dipped their hands in ancient blood. They are my comrades. I have nothing to fear from them."

"Other people are going to find out now," Gavin said as he stepped from the stairs and pointed toward the adjacent ballroom. "Zaire and everyone will fight back once I tell them."

"No, they won't," Abraxas-Mon said with a smirk.

"You think they won't choose to stand against you?"

Abraxas-Mon picked at a piece of fluff clinging to the fabric of the chair. "'Choose.' That's such a loaded word. People think they choose all the time, but in truth they don't. Every action is a predetermination of environment, biology, and circumstance. It's all data. If you know how to read it, then you begin to understand that there is no choice. Free will, like democracy, doesn't exist."

"Yeah, I remember this lesson from high school philosophy," Gavin said. "It's called Determinism. You don't believe in free will. It's not a new concept."

"You're right, it's not. But you and I are the perfect example of the truth of such a viewpoint."

"How so?" Gavin asked. "You and I are the same person, and yet completely different. My choices were different than yours and so I'm different. Your argument doesn't hold weight."

Abraxas-Mon leaned back in the throne, crossing his right leg over his left. "And yet, if Zaire had taken you into space as a baby instead of me, we would be having this exact conversation but from opposite sides. Not exactly a resounding endorsement of free will."

Gavin opened his mouth to retort but found no rebuttal springing to mind.

"You see, Gavin?" Abraxas-Mon continued. "Entire intelligent species taken together are no different than your immune system; acting in foreseeable patterns based off stimuli. We respond in predictable ways depending on the actions of other cells. For twenty years, I've known this truth and been able to anticipate betrayals, attacks, wars, death, all of it."

"So, you're a psychic now? Is that what you're telling me?"

Abraxas-Mon laughed, guffaw bouncing off the walls. "Psychics don't exist either, though I'm sure you know that already."

"This is nuts," Gavin said, turning as if to invite others to share in his conclusion. "This is a test or something, isn't it? You're just trying to see if I'm worthy of the great Abraxas-Mon. Admit it. Everybody is watching right now like this is a hidden camera show and they're going to come out and say, 'We really got you, Gavin.'"

Abraxas-Mon shook his head, a sad frown forming on his lips. "You're going to have to admit the truth to yourself at some point, Gavin. This is who we are. You became the greatest actor on

Earth. Where would you have gone from there? Have you ever thought about it? The Perennials believed you would naturally rise to a position of political power, and perhaps you still would have. I'm sure you felt constrained by your lifestyle before Halford arrived to retrieve you. I know I would have."

Forehead compressing, Gavin didn't want to think about the truth behind Abraxas-Mon's words. He remembered walking through his 34th birthday party at D.J. Cascade's house thinking about how he felt wasted in his current circumstances. Would those thoughts have led him down a potentially dark path?

"I can tell by your face that I'm right," Abraxas-Mon stated. "Don't be afraid of those feelings. I'm sure Zaire spouted the Perennial belief that fear is an infection and all of that crap just like she did to me as a child. Embrace fear. Fear is a wonderful thing that takes beings from the mud and turns them into kings. Once I bring the Earth into the Commonwealth, everyone will see what a culture dominated by fear can accomplish. Humans will become the new Perennials, the new ruling class. Did you know that there is a disproportionate number of humans in the Hierarchy? That's not a fluke."

"And you'll rule over all of them, right?"

"Exactly. I believe there's an Earth-saying about how sheep need a shepherd? Intelligent beings, no matter how smart, are nothing more than sheep, and we are the ultimate shepherds."

"We?" Gavin asked. "We're not the same person!"

"Yes, we are," Abraxas-Mon countered. "We are in every way. Tell me, while you were in that cell over the last few days, did you replay everything in your mind about what had happened with Isla? Formulating alternate scenarios down to the minutest of details? Did you picture yourself turning on the Phylónethese guards on the walkway behind you and going through them first? Better yet, did you think about using that sniveling Phrensha'al as a shield and sacrificing him so you and Isla could make it past? I know you did; I would have."

Gavin bit his cheek, uncomfortable with the accuracy of Abraxas-Mon's insights.

"You see?" the warlord said. "The only reason I left you in that cell was so you would have time to ponder all of the strategies you could have used to save Isla. I bet you came up with some impressive plots for your own personal revenge movies while crammed in that hellhole. Now you understand you can do it on the fly, not just after the fact. I'm sure your brain is feeding you all kinds of data right now on how to respond to me; how to escape this room; how to get to your friends over in the other chamber to tell them the amazing Abraxas-Mon is evil. I'm not evil though; I'm just trying to progress, like all living beings."

"Just tell me why you're doing this!" Gavin yelled, sweat dripping down the small of his back.

"Because of you," Abraxas-Mon answered.

"What do you mean?"

"Orthal-Oblin faced no real challenges his entire reign," Abraxas-Mon said, eyes looking toward the ceiling as if remembering a beloved fairytale. "He could anticipate everything and so rebellions were squashed before they could even start. Imagine what that would be like, never being able to progress; being stuck in kindergarten, as it were. I know what that's like. No one can stand toe-to-toe with me. No one. Except for you."

"I'm just an actor," Gavin countered. "What are you talking about?"

Abraxas-Mon stood, towering over Gavin from the step above. "Don't feign stupidity! You're not stupid!" he screamed. "I know for a fact that since leaving Earth you've slowly become aware of your brain's processing ability. I saw the security footage from when Isla got shot in the Renascence Plant; I saw what you did to those men."

"I didn't…I was…" Gavin faltered. "I never wanted to kill anyone. I can still see their faces: *all* their faces. Sometimes I have nightmares about it. I've only killed when absolutely necessary!"

Smoothing out the scarf draping over his shoulders, Abraxas-Mon breathed deeply. "You don't need to make excuses. I know what you can do, and you know what you can do. Don't you see? This is why I brought you out here."

Gavin walked down the steps and stood on the purple carpet, putting distance between himself and his delusional foil. "Zaire brought me out here because Raymond Halford wanted to use me to help the Rebirth Militia."

"And who ordered all of that?" Abraxas-Mon asked, walking down the steps to join Gavin.

"It wasn't you," Gavin said.

"It was."

"No, it wasn't!"

"Gavin, there are no secrets now. No secrets between you and me. I run everything; the Militia, the Hierarchy, the fleets, all of it. Everyone had become so used to receiving orders from some faceless Perennial that no one even noticed as I slipped in and took over. I started the Militia specifically to undermine the Athelbrath and put the Hierarchy on a course to alienate the people, so eventually I could come out of the shadows and they would beg me to take over. The Athelbrath are dying off anyway and won't survive another century or two. No big loss."

"So, you don't believe in the whole, 'life is sacred' thing, I take it."

Abraxas-Mon shrugged. "Insects live and insects die. As long as they pollinate the flowers, I don't tend to fret one way or another. Just know that, yes, you're here because of me."

Gavin didn't know whether to believe the man or not. "So, you sent both Halford *and* Zaire to go get me? Why not just one or the other? It would have been a lot simpler."

"Maybe," Abraxas-Mon admitted, moving slowly from the final step and onto the carpet. "But I couldn't make it too easy for you. There had to be opposition so you could be afraid and learn about yourself. It's only in times of trial and antagonism that we truly discover our strengths and overcome our weaknesses. That had to happen for you before you were ready to face me. I'll admit though that I didn't send Zaire specifically. She joined at the last moment and almost threw the entire plan off course. Even so, I knew you needed to have time to prepare; to process. I also knew that no matter what, you would survive and eventually make your way to me."

"You couldn't have known that," Gavin countered.

"*I* would have survived, so I knew *you* would as well. It all goes back to us not really having any choices. You will respond in a certain way, and I know that because I would respond in a certain way."

"Those were my choices, not yours!"

"And yet they led you here, like I knew they would. It's all cause and effect; our choices are determined by the causes and thus aren't really choices. They're determined by what came before. Nothing is arbitrary; it's all statistics."

"And yet you *chose* to take me from Earth," Gavin refuted.

"Based on my instinctive need for competition. If my unconscious has already determined my course before my conscious mind can even process the information, what good is my conscious choice? In truth, there's only one choice: to live or to die. If one thing can be said for free will, it is that I chose to live, and thus others must die."

Abraxas-Mon cracked his knuckles before continuing. "But that's all secondary philosophy. This moment right now is real. Everything has led up to today. Through all this running around and fighting, I needed to see if you could actually pose a threat to me, and the wonderful answer is that you *can*! You are me and I am you. Which means for the first time in my life, I have someone who can act as a real challenge; someone who won't roll over and die without a fight." He closed his eyes, a look of pleasure spreading across his face like a believer at a Baptist revival. "Finally! Finally, I have a challenge! Finally, I have a worthy adversary!"

Gavin slowly stepped away from the animated military leader. "Dude, you're fucked up."

"I want you to be a threat," Abraxas-Mon breathed, following Gavin step for step. "I truly do. I need you to be. You can't be anything less than me at my greatest moment. The only way that will happen is if you have something to fight for."

"Right now, I'm willing to fight to get out of this room," Gavin said, still backing away.

Abraxas-Mon advanced. "You need to be a threat, and that means I need to take everything from you. Your entire life needs to be burned down so you can come at me from the ashes. Don't you see? That's the only way."

"What more can you take from me?" Gavin asked, standing firm for the first time. "You've already pulled me from my planet and thrown me out into space. It's not like you can destroy my house again."

"I like that your mind doesn't immediately jump to the more pernicious aspects of what I'm talking about," Abraxas-Mon said, still moving closer to Gavin. "It will. Eventually you'll be as artful in your violence as I am."

"Maybe I just don't want to believe the great Abraxas-Mon is capable of murdering innocent people."

"I am," the warlord said. "And so are you. Give it time."

"You wouldn't hurt any of my friends," Gavin assured. "If you're anything like me, you wouldn't hurt them."

With a grin that could light up a Hollywood sound stage,

Abraxas-Mon continued. "I don't have to hurt them. No, no, no, no, no. I will do something so much worse. I'll make them love me. They will love me like they never loved you. Love is so much more powerful than hate. Seth will stand by *my* side in our battle; your Silverback Guard will fight *you* to the death. Zaire will lead my armies…and Isla will warm my bed as my wife."

With a primitive scream, Gavin leaped toward his genetic twin, bringing his fist against the man's face with the rage of a wounded wolf. He punched again and again, but Abraxas-Mon didn't fight back. Blood dripped from his nose and mouth as Gavin pummeled him, but the smile never left his lips.

Abraxas-Mon stumbled back, falling onto the steps. Gavin paused, looking over his shoulder at the still-motionless Phylónethese soldiers.

"Aren't they going to come and help you?" Gavin asked, standing over the man with shaking fists. "They're not going to rescue their king?"

"My guards would help if needed," Abraxas-Mon said, wiping blood from his chin. "But they're not needed right now."

"I'm going to beat you to death!" Gavin cried.

Abraxas-Mon sat back on the steps and spat blood onto the carpet. "No, you're not. My gore has done more damage to that ancient rug than you've done to me. And I want to thank you. No one has dared stand up to me in many years. I'm already so happy with how things are going."

"You son of a bitch," Gavin growled, raising his fist again.

"Here's what's going to happen, Gavin," Abraxas-Mon said, taking a deep breath. "I'm going to order my guards to kill you. And they will; without hesitation. The thing is, you're going to escape out that door and back down the elevator. I know how I would do it, but I'm going to let you figure that out. From there, the only stop the elevator is programmed to make will be on the upper landing bay where a single ship is waiting for you. I know you've learned how to pilot a vessel and you can take it wherever you want."

"You think I'll just run away?" Gavin asked, stepping closer to the sitting man.

"I know you will, because if you don't, my guards will kill you. I'm not going to hold back in anyway. I'd be disappointed if you died at this point, I really would. I'd be inconsolable. But I'm not going to hold back. You get the ship and run, or you die. And if you died, I'd have no reason to keep everyone else alive, so there's that too."

Gavin looked down at his blood-smeared knuckles. His brain sifted everything Abraxas-Mon had said. Staying now would mean swift defeat and the deaths of all his friends. Running would at least give him a chance. Footsteps behind him drew his attention to the soldiers. They all slowly walked forward, spears at the ready.

"You better make your choice quick, Gavin," Abraxas-Mon said.

"What're you going to tell Seth and Isla about why I left? They'll know something is up. They'll know you're a liar."

Abraxas-Mon came to his feet, seeming bigger and broader than he ever had before. His face registered no anger, only extreme enjoyment. "I don't know what I'll tell them to be honest. I really like improvisation; the words tend to come out more authentically, I've found. And about them not believing me? I wouldn't worry too much about that. You see, it turns out I'm a pretty great actor."

Before he could lunge at the man again, a spear flew by Gavin's head and forced him to retreat. Twelve Phylónethese soldiers rushed forward, snarling like rabid animals. Their asymmetrical faces meant each looked completely unique from the others, but even so, they merged into a roiling gray mass. Gavin saw an opening between two of the guards and dove to the floor, rolling past them while three more converged.

"Go ahead and kill him," Abraxas-Mon shouted. "Don't worry, Gavin, I know you'll find a way out. I would, and you and I are the same person, after all!"

A spearhead slammed into the stone floor, spitting tiny chunks of masonry into the air as Gavin jumped to his feet. The gigantic alien soldiers moved to cut off the exit and hedge Gavin in place. No weapons in-hand, Gavin chose instead to spit in the eye of the closest Phylónethese. When the brute stumbled back in surprise, Gavin grabbed his spear and smashed it into his nose.

One of the soldiers thrust his weapon, but Gavin pivoted, allowing the spear tip to plunge into the belly of the alien he'd just spit on. Strafing to the left, Gavin moved around the impaled soldier and slid like a baseball player between the legs of another, smacking the Phylónethese in the crotch with his fist as he went. With no one standing between him and the door, Gavin ran at full speed, knowing he could outpace the unwieldly aliens.

"That's not how I would have done it," Abraxas-Mon shouted over the sound of the grunting soldiers in their pursuit. "But you still have some things to learn, after all."

"Would you shut the hell up?!" Gavin cried as the elevator door opened 50 feet away.

"Take your time before you come back to fight; please," Abraxas-Mon continued, voice echoing from farther away with each stride Gavin took. "I don't want you to rush anything! Ours will be a meeting that will be spoken of for millennium."

Jumping between the open elevator doors, Gavin turned back to see the charging Phylónethese guards closing in. Behind them, Abraxas-Mon stood, a contented smile on his bloodied face.

"I'm going to come back here and kill you!" Gavin yelled as the elevator began to close.

"I sincerely hope you do!" Abraxas-Mon replied.

The doors closed just as the soldiers drew within reach. Their bodies slammed against the barrier, sending a shudder through the elevator before it shot toward the ground with the aid of unseen gravity apparatuses.

Gavin's mind raced, wondering how things had fallen apart so quickly. Everything he'd believed about the Commonwealth; hell, everything Zaire had believed, turned out to be completely false. What they had assumed to be a bright beacon of galactic peace and hope had in truth been broken since before the Athelbrath ship appeared over Gavin's pool in the Hollywood Hills. The entire Commonwealth system had crumbled to dust years before Raymond Halford even set out to procure a clone.

Gavin licked his lips and tasted sweat; nerves ready to fray along with his understanding of the universe.

Breaks hissed as the elevator slowed so quickly Gavin almost fell over. The doors opened on a landing bay the size of a warehouse, full of crates and what looked like engine parts and pieces of machinery. A single silver spaceship, shaped like a metallic wasp about the size of a moving truck, floated amongst the storage items. Light from the setting sun shined through the open access gates and reflected off the vessel's chrome surface. Storm clouds gathered over the ocean in the distance, slowly cutting off the sunset in favor of darkness and lightning.

Where would he take the ship? Gavin had no idea where to go. Could he fly the thing back up and just crash into the throne room without hurting any of his friends? Could he even find the throne room along the 30-mile-high tower?

Screaming in frustrated impotence, Gavin ran toward the ship. He tripped on a discarded aluminum tube and tumbled forward, catching himself on a steel drum stained in some type of dried oil. He looked down on the flat lid, catching a warped reflection of himself between the spots of grime on the cover.

He barely recognized the face looking back. Was it the face of Gavin Baller, or merely the image of Abraxas-Mon's clone?

"I hate you!" he screamed at his dingy reflection. Pushing the barrel over, Gavin grunted in defeat. The metal drum slammed against the ground loudly, oil seeping from a loose seam along the rim. Veins rippled along Gavin's neck and forearms as his muscles tensed.

For over a year, Gavin had envisioned meeting Abraxas-Mon, fearing he'd feel inadequate and laughably insignificant before the great leader. Once while daydreaming during one of his language sessions with Zaire, Gavin had fantasized about hanging out with his genetic duplicate and finding in him the perfect cohort; someone who understood his every emotion, joke, and insight. That's what Gavin had wanted. For a moment in that throne room, he thought he might have found a brother.

Now all his expectations turned to cinders in a week-old campfire.

Instead of a comrade, he'd gained an enemy; one so methodical and talented he'd overthrown the entire Commonwealth system without anyone even noticing; a man driven insane by his own success to the point he would accept death if it meant finally finding a superior being. Unfortunately, Gavin knew he was not superior to Abraxas-Mon. He may have the mind, but he definitely didn't have the experience.

Their final battle would not be one of a hero's victory, but instead the burning of both houses, at best. And how many would die in the service of their egos? Numbers compiled in Gavin's brain, too large for less-than-genetically-perfect-men to fathom.

And what of Seth and Isla? Could Abraxas-Mon really make them fall in love with him?

Of that, Gavin had no doubt.

How many men and women had Gavin charmed during his life and then used to get what he wanted? One time, he'd met a 75-year-old U.S. Senator who disagreed with Gavin's stance on gender politics and climate change. Within ten minutes, the actor had the man practically eating out of his hand and wanting to hang out like old friends. If Abraxas-Mon was half as skilled as his clone, Seth and Isla would fall prey unless given ample evidence of his duplicity.

At that moment, the only evidence that existed was Gavin himself. And he had no choice but to run away like a coward.

Deep breaths filled his lungs as he slowed his racing thoughts.

Think, he said to himself. *Don't rush. Just breathe.*

A breeze tickled his arms, blowing at a steady three miles per hour; 42 individual barrels of green liquid marked 'flammable' sat in a nearby corner; a swarm of insects billowed over a dumpster on the far side of the hangar, 372 individual bugs taking their turns diving into the trash for a snack. Everything came into focus.

Good options still existed. He could put the ship on autopilot and send it off, then sneak back into the Citadel and find his friends, doing the opposite of what Abraxas-Mon wanted.

That could work.

Charging up the ramp, Gavin darted into the small ship and made his way down the main hall. Every surface on the liner seemed perfectly smooth, as if Gavin had just stepped into the Cadillac of spacecrafts. Unlike the organic vessels he had grown accustomed to in the Commonwealth, this one seemed far more manufactured and less welcoming.

The door to the main bridge folded back, revealing a command deck with a single pilot's chair. Gavin ran over and sat down, waiting as the tendrils slithered up from the floor and wrapped around his hands.

"Alright ship, I need autopilot settings."

A buzzing sound, like when someone gets a wrong answer on Jeopardy, echoed through the bridge.

"Gavin," a voice said, resonating from the very walls. "This is Abraxas-Mon speaking, though I'm sure you already know that since we have the same voice. Anyway, this is a recorded message just so you know how serious I am about all of this."

"Holy shit, would you just shut up for once?!" Gavin yelled.

Abraxas-Mon's recording continued. "Just to reiterate what I'm sure we touched on during our introductory conversation: free will doesn't exist. I know you want to put the ship on autopilot and then sneak back in so you can get help from your friends. I'd have thought about it too. But that's not going to happen. I took the opportunity to disable the autopilot before you were ever taken out of your cell."

"Son of a bitch!" Gavin screamed, thrashing against the control vines.

"Anyway, I'm sure our conversation upstairs was enlightening for you and I wish you all the luck in the universe. Take your time before you face me so we can have a lot of fun, okay? I'm looking forward to it. I'm also looking forward to meeting you, since this is, after all, a recording that I'm making about twelve hours before you'll be released from your prison cell. Free will's an illusion. Fly safe."

Gavin wailed in exasperation. All the veins in his body seemed to push against his skin and claw to escape. How could he beat a man who knew what he would do in any given circumstance? What options existed at this point?

Back during his Hollywood days on Earth this would have been the point where Gavin would have thrown in the towel and said, 'Yep, this is too hard. Time to run away.'

Not this time.

Doubts had to be tossed aside.

If Abraxas-Mon could figure out how Gavin would act in a given situation, then Gavin could do the same for the would-be emperor. Whether or not that knowledge would be enough didn't matter; it was all Gavin had to use at the moment.

For the first time since speeding away from his burning

mansion so long ago, Gavin felt truly alone. No Seth. No Zaire. No Isla.

He needed new friends; influential, ambitious, slithery friends. Fortunately, he knew where to find some, in an unfortunate place.

"Alright, Raymond Halford," he said to himself. "I hope you're still hiding out on that shit-hole, because I'm about to need your help."

CHAPTER 9

WELCOME BACK TO THE GADABOUT

"No, I understand I'm not on the right course to land in one of your stupid bays. That's why I'm going to need you to do that tractor-beam-thing you guys do when you're capturing a ship. Is that too much to ask?" Gavin spat; hands wrapped in gray vines growing from the floor at his feet. The Gadabout expanded in the front window and he didn't care to debate proper landing procedures.

"Look, pal," a man's voice echoed across the pale blue walls of the small bridge, as if coming through a dirty speaker half a mile away. "You can do what you want, but I'm just warning you that if you try to land in a brand-new jump-ship like the one you're in, you're going to draw the attention of some bad people. You're lucky I'm the first guy to answer your beacon, because other radio operators wouldn't waste time trying to save your life."

The enormous Gadabout city state floated on an ocean of stars with its haphazard array of ramshackle structures. The last time Gavin visited this collection of slums and derelict buildings, he had spent most of his time hiding in the zoo with Dan and Ashton. While he hoped to avoid repeating that experience, he needed to get onboard the space station as soon as possible to find Raymond Halford.

Gavin's hands squeezed the tentacles snaking between his fingers. "You think I'd have spent the last four days trying to track down your crappy Gadabout if I didn't know you were full of a bunch of stinky dickheads? Just reel me in so I can talk to Fralt Randok. Or if you know Raymond Halford, that would be great too."

"I'm not friends with Fralt Randok," the man said, exasperation evident in his digitized voice. "And I'm not a snare operator. I can't just pull you inside. Plus, you're moving way too fast."

"I'm not friends with Randok either! One of my colleagues shot him in the knee, for crap-sake. I just need to talk to him and work out a deal so he can help me find Raymond Halford. You don't know Raymond, do you?"

"I don't know where Fralt Randok is, and I don't know this Ray woman either."

"Then what the hell good are you?!" Gavin asked, kicking at the base of the chair beneath him. "And Raymond is a guy's name!"

Static answered his query.

"Well screw you then, buddy," Gavin said, tugging on the vines and moving the ship closer to the Gadabout. Lights ran along what looked like an open docking area not far from his current position. Mists of air blew into space from the berth, a natural wall of pressurized atmosphere holding back the cold vacuum. "I'll just land this thing myself."

The space-faring slum drew closer in the window. Gavin visually confirmed that he was indeed approaching a hanger similar to what he had seen on the Silver Hammer, but he was also moving much too fast, as the man on the radio had warned.

"Alright Buxbaum," Gavin whispered through clenched teeth. "You need to slow us down, buddy, or we're going to have a very unpleasant landing."

The ship remained silent, not even warming Gavin's hands or flashing veins of color along the walls. The Gadabout landing bay grew larger and larger through the window.

"Alright, you want to crash, Buxbaum? That what you want? Because I don't want to crash." Gavin continued pulling against the vines, but the ship's momentum carried it forward with only slight evidence of slowing. Parked vessels came into view inside the dock, along with colorful tents that made the entire area look like a swap meet or bazaar. Individual people looked up and pointed at the hastily approaching craft.

"Buxbaum!" Gavin shouted. "You're supposed to stop us, so we don't crash!"

The ship began vibrating as it traded vacant outer space for pungent atmosphere. They entered the docking area with speed to spare. Gavin swerved to try and dampen their velocity, but only managed to throw them to the left and scrape against a transport vessel parked next to what looked like an alien diner of some type. Pulling as hard as he could, Gavin managed to miss slamming into the far wall and careened instead across the hanger toward a grouping of smaller ships.

Aliens and humans scurried out of the way as the vessel's nose pointed toward the concrete. Buxbaum's underbelly skipped across the cement, tearing through the marketplace, snagging tents and bending poles as it went. Gavin rocked in his seat like a passenger on a rusted roller coaster, and eventually came to a stop in a shower of sparks.

Releasing a pent-up breath, he looked out at a collection of colorful tarps pinned against the front window and completely obscuring his view.

"Thanks for the help there, Buxbaum," Gavin said as he pulled his hands out of their slimy confines. "I'm just glad I didn't name you after Mordecai. Now *that* was a ship that knew how to stop!"

Gavin stood up, noticing the vessel listed to the left about five degrees. He wanted to make a comment about the incompetence of the landing but had to admit he couldn't blame everything on the spacecraft. Biting his tongue, Gavin made his way to the side door.

Shouts met his ears, along with the smell of smoke and week-old cabbage. The ramp lowered to the wet cement below, scrapping the ground due to the ship's uneven angle. A group of Athelbrath and Dubaku men ran up, pointing angrily toward the line of tents that Gavin had destroyed during his little wreck.

"Nobody got hurt, did they?" he asked, hands wide to show he held no weapons.

The same couldn't be said for the greeting party. Several of the men pulled out knives, while one of the Athelbrath brandished a rifle over his head with an angry cry.

"Crap," Gavin said, leaping from the ramp and darting behind the ship as the group charged. "It was just a couple of tents!"

Splashing through a puddle that smelled surprisingly like urine, Gavin darted toward one of the adjacent rust-heaps that passed for spaceships on the Gadabout. An elderly Nythensus woman stepped out from behind one of the broken tents carrying a platter of squid legs. Gavin twisted to avoid running into the diminutive grandmother, but instead tripped on a section of tangled fabric and fell to the floor.

"Knife the Aktelothing scab!" one of the men shouted as they rushed around the ship.

Gavin clambered to his feet, almost pushing over a Dubaku woman holding a toddler. Apologizing to the mother, he took off again toward the cluster of parked spacecrafts. People began to crowd the area, pointing at the crashed vessel and the man running for his life.

A pillar of steam rose from a metal grate on the ground, billowing with the fragrance of wet towels and cat hair. Gavin jumped through the mist and right into a group of men sitting at a table playing what looked like a game of dominoes, except with finger bones. Knocking over the table, Gavin spilled their money and skeleton pieces onto the floor.

"Sorry about that," he muttered, turning to run. Before he made it two steps, Gavin charged into the stone-hard chest of an abnormally large Phylónethese. He looked up into a lopsided, three-eyed face with mucus dripping steadily from one of two noses. "I said I was sorry," Gavin said, stepping away from the brute.

The double nosed Phylónethese roared, spit slapping against Gavin's cheeks.

"You're pissed, I get it," Gavin said, striding back.

With a grip that would make a gorilla jealous, the Phylónethese grabbed Gavin's arm and tossed him into a food cart ten feet away. Hot oil seared Gavin's forearm as the buggy tipped over and spilled half-cooked fish heads onto the concrete. A Cádavrite chef shouted for the men to leave his business alone. Gavin flipped onto his back, hearing metal spoons and knives skid across the ground while the Phylónethese stomped in his direction.

Gavin lay there and closed his eyes, picturing the scene. There had been three humans and four Athelbrath playing their game around the table; another 12 men had chased him from the crash site. Add the Phylónethese to that number and you had the makings of a very bad day. Gavin could disarm the Athelbrath carrying the rifle and use that in a surprise offensive, but if he killed anyone, it would likely make matters far worse. He needed to make a statement that would force everyone to back off until he could get his bearings.

A large serving spoon tipped back and forth on the concrete to his right. Gavin smiled, knowing what to do.

Grabbing the spoon, Gavin jumped to his feet and faced the towering Phylónethese with the ladle as his only weapon.

"What's this pup doing?" one of the Athelbrath laughed, pointing at Gavin. "He's gonna spoon Ugnol to death!"

The Phylónethese snorted in disgust, glancing from the silverware to Gavin. More men arrived on the scene, finally catching up with their quarry.

"Choke him with his own intestines, Ugnol!" a Dubaku man with face tattoos goaded. "He broke my tent when he crashed over there. Rip him in two!"

"I don't want any trouble," Gavin warned, swishing the spoon through the air like a sword. "But trust me, I know how to handle myself."

Ugnol the Phylónethese grunted and lunged for Gavin.

Flipping the spoon in his hand so the tapered end pointed up, Gavin shoved the piece of cutlery up the aliens second nose. Eyes wide, the Phylónethese stumbled back, clawing at his face and snorting painfully. He bellowed and stamped his feet, trying desperately to dislodge the spoon with his oversized fingers. The onlookers stepped back, unsure how to respond to the surprisingly effective assault.

Gavin reached down and picked up a pair of salad tongs from the toppled food cart. Tossing them end over end, he smiled. "Who's next?"

Several of the men backed away, hands in front of them. Ugnol continued pinching at the spoon, unable to grasp the silverware lodged in his nostril. He whimpered like a puppy while everyone else stood wide-eyed.

"Come here," Gavin said, swatting the Phylónethese's elbow. "Let me get it out for you. You're whining like a baby. It's just a spoon."

An angry look wrinkled Ugnol's face, but he bent over

nonetheless to allow Gavin a chance to pull out the silverware.

"Hold still," Gavin said, clamping the round end of the spoon between his forefinger and thumb and yanking quickly.

Ugnol bawled loudly, thick gobs of phlegm now drooling from both his noses.

"Like I said," Gavin shouted, handing the spoon to Ugnol, and patting the alien on the shoulder. "I'm not here to make trouble, but I can make trouble if you want."

The men nodded in nervous unison. One of them, an Athelbrath with a long scar running down his face, raised his hand like a student in Catholic school. "We don't want no trouble," he sniveled.

"That's good," Gavin continued. "Now, if any of you can point me to Fralt Randok, I would appreciate it."

A murmur swelled through the crowd at the mention of Fralt's name.

"Nobody talks to Fralt Randok no more," the scarred Athelbrath said. "Not in months now."

"He'll want to talk to me," Gavin assured. "Any of you ever heard of a guy by the name of Raymond Halford, by chance? Pale guy, gray hair, kind of an asshole?"

Heads shook as confused faces met Gavin's gaze.

Ugnol lumbered over, wiping snot from his face. "I've worked for Randok before," he said, glaring down at Gavin. "I can take you to him. I don't know the other guy you mentioned, but Randok, I know."

"Thanks," Gavin nodded. "And sorry about the spoon thing."

"It was a good move," the Phylónethese grumbled. "My face hurts now, but it was a good move. Good strategy. I'll take you where you need to go. Aratob! Frold! Let's get this guy to the Veredok."

"Let me grab a knife, at least," the scarred Athelbrath said.

"Be quick, Aratob," Ugnol admonished.

"I'm ready to go," Frold the Dubaku said, scratching his bald head.

Ugnol nudged Gavin. "Come on. It'll take us a full cycle at least to walk. We could take a transport, but we'd draw a lot of attention. You don't want to make too big a deal about anything around the Veredok."

"I will defer to you, Honorable Ugnol," Gavin said.

The Phylónethese shrugged. "We don't care about pretty titles here, pale Dubaku."

"My name's Gavin."

"Whatever," Ugnol said, turning toward one of the tunnels on the other side of the landing bay.

Gavin bowed to the crowd, clacking the tongs together and making several women jump in fear. "When I get back, I expect my ship to be right over there and in one piece. You get me?"

More nods. Gavin smiled and tossed the salad tongs to a nearby Dubaku boy, who caught them and grinned like he'd just been gifted Excalibur.

Gavin followed his globular guide into the bowels of the Gadabout. Frold and Aratob scampered alongside, getting more nervous the longer they walked. The group passed through several large city areas similar to what Gavin had seen on his initial visit to the space station. Each reflected different architectural styles and cultural trappings, but they all had the same rundown and overcrowded feel to them. Water dripped from cracked pipes high overhead, giving the streets and walkways an eternal dampness that added to the gloom. Smells ranged from offensive to downright pleasant as they passed food vendors frying meat and fish over open flames. Gavin's mouth watered. He'd only eaten the fruits and vegetables grown by Buxbaum since leaving Cartoshí four days before, and the thought of biting into a greasy slab of beef-like protein excited him.

His desire for food was tempered by the fact that he was about to walk into probably the most dangerous place in the galaxy. Especially for him. The last time he had seen Fralt Randok, the clan leader had been kneeling in a puddle clutching his missing knee. Zaire had shot it off without regret.

Not a great first meeting. Still, as a clan leader, Fralt had power and ambition; both of which Gavin could manipulate. And hopefully he would know how to find Raymond Halford.

The thought of potential peril and death didn't worry Gavin as much as it used to. Maybe being in a war, killing soldiers by the dozens, running around between planets, being chased by monsters, and finally learning you're the clone of the biggest bastard in the galaxy had a way of tempering one's fear. Whatever the cause, Gavin appreciated the evolution. He looked at his current mission as one of diplomacy, not violence; but if violence became necessary, it wouldn't bother him.

Eventually that violence would lead him back to Abraxas-Mon, and he'd beat the wannabe king over the head with it.

"How do you know Randok?" Ugnol asked after they'd walked for over an hour.

"He and I met about six months ago…sorry, about a half annular-cycle. Anyway, he wanted to steal my ship and kill me. You know how it is."

"So, you're not friends with the clan leader?" Aratob asked.

"We are not friends," Gavin answered.

Frold the Dubaku ran up, seemingly interested in the conversation. "Then why go see him?"

"He's a guy who seems willing to make a deal, and I have one he's going to want to make."

Ugnol grumbled, pushing a pedestrian out of the way as they

entered a crowded marketplace. "Fralt has lost some of his standing among the clans since an incident involving the Dubaku Matriarch."

"Really?" Gavin asked, suddenly very curious.

"Yeah," Aratob added. "He got shot and let her escape with some zoo animals."

"They were people," Gavin amended, remembering running through the streets being chased by a giant spider and a hoard of pissed off Gadabout residents.

"Since then," Ugnol continued, "Fralt has been trying to reassert his power. He's been more brazen, and more dangerous. A lot of us Phylónethese have stopped working for him because of his overwrought aggression."

"Well, just take me to him and we'll see if he and I can help each other out."

A woman walking past Gavin on the right caught his eye. For an instant he thought it was Isla, only to be disappointed when he took a second glance. The woman grabbed the hand of a young child, a girl about three years old, and skipped off singing a lullaby and laughing.

Isla. Four days ago, he'd locked eyes with the woman he loved, and she'd run away in shame. Her status as a Cádavrite didn't bother Gavin in the slightest, yet he knew it was likely tearing her apart.

Was Abraxas-Mon there to help her through it? Was Abraxas-Mon even now sitting with his arm around her as she cried? What lies had he spun about why Gavin had left? Questions burned in his chest, the desire for vengeance almost overwhelming him. Hopefully, she would see through his mask and maybe kick him in the balls for good measure. The thought made Gavin smile.

Ugnol slowed his pace, squinting at Gavin as they walked past a series of tents filled with aliens and humans trying to sell everything from fabrics to small stones carved to look like Easter Island heads. The baubles again reminded Gavin of how similar

Perennials looked to the ancient Earth monuments.

"You look very familiar," Ugnol said with a sneer, voice raising in volume to compete with the bazaar's clamor. "Have we met before today?"

"I'm pretty sure I would have remembered an eight-foot tall Phylónethese guy with two noses," Gavin said as a glowing cloud made up of several hundred bright yellow Luminaries wafted in their path and swirled around him. He swished his hands about, trying to dispel the swarm. "Shoo, guys! Go away."

"Speculates don't normally like strangers," Ugnol commented, eyebrow lifting over two of his eyes.

Gavin continued waving away the Luminaires, but they eddied and merged into a single mass. "I'm just a nice guy, is all. They're like puppies; they can smell it on me."

The Speculates formed into the face of a woman…Isla's face. Frowning in impotent anger, Gavin stomped through the billowing lights and continued the way they'd been walking.

Ugnol came back beside him, pushing a scarf-waving vendor roughly aside. "I realize where I've seen your face."

"If you say I look like Abraxas-Mon, I'm going to shove a spoon back up your nose."

"I will merely say there is a resemblance," Ugnol said with a nod. "My cousin fought for him many years ago. We would follow his exploits and adventures with the warlord's army until he died honorably in battle on Granthus."

"Abraxas-Mon and I are nothing alike," Gavin said, eyes focused on the teeming marketplace in front of them. "Trust me when I say that. And he isn't as great as you think, either."

"Most men aren't," Ugnol agreed.

After another twenty minutes, the crew left the market and descended a long flight of stairs into a dark and even more seedy section of the Gadabout. Where most of the ceilings throughout the station rose at least two hundred feet overhead, here they dropped to less than 25. Rodents that looked like a cross between a rat and a beetle chewed on garbage before hissing and running away as they approached.

Men, faces marked with glowing tattoos of orange or purple, began following them the farther they advanced through the sector. Aratob and Frold huddled close together like terrified lemmings. Athelbrath and Nythensus women waved from the steps of derelict apartments, offering pleasures Gavin assumed would end with infections and burning urination.

Ugnol stopped in front of a building with curved walls like a flattened cylinder covered in graffiti Gavin couldn't read. Eight human men stood in front, wearing similar colored clothing and jackets, like intergalactic gang members. Several large turquoise lizards, easily as big as dogs, sat leashed next to one of the men. The animals growled menacingly as Gavin approached.

"What do you want at the Veredok?" the man with the lizards asked roughly. The gentleman, easily seven feet tall with long dreadlocks falling past his shoulders, stood from his seat and tugged on the leashes to lead his reptiles toward the newcomers. Gavin looked up at the towering human, noticing several purple teeth in the gangster's mouth. "What do you want?" he repeated.

"I need to see Fralt Randok," Gavin answered, catching a whiff of the lout's cologne; a rich scent of body odor and lemon, which didn't smell as bad as Gavin had imagined it would.

"Threx, he just needs to talk to Randok," Ugnol said, stepping next to the tall man. "He's proven himself an adept warrior in single combat. I bring him here in peace."

"You left this crew," Threx said, unimpressed by the Phylónethese's size. The lizards hissed and scratched at the metal grates beneath their paws. "You want to come back now, Ugnol? That what you want?"

"Look," Gavin replied, hoping to keep things from turning

into an incident. "Fralt will want to see me, I guarantee---"

"Who in the name of Aktelothing Renki'itomet are you scabs talking to up here?" a voice shouted. Gavin looked over to see Cass Randok, the first man he ever met on the Gadabout, stroll up with a sour look on his face. Familiar green tattoos glowed under his left eye, exactly as Gavin remembered, down to a four-inch long black beard. Scars on his shaved head evinced his violent life, while his left arm ended in a stump covered in an unpolished and stained golden mace. He brought up the spiked club to scratch his chin before he continued. "The party starts in like…"

Cass blinked, staring at Gavin while his cheek twitched in delayed recognition.

"Cass," Gavin said with a nod of his head. "It's good to see you again. I'm looking for your dad. Any chance he's here?"

"Galta'arok…" Cass cursed under his breath, emerald tattoos turning red as blood.

Gavin looked up at Ugnol. "See, I told you they'd recognize me."

With a rage-induced scream, Cass charged through his underlings toward Gavin, swinging the golden mace over his head. "I'll kill you!" he cried.

Ugnol stepped in front of Gavin and blocked the incensed man before he got within three feet. The lizards went wild, tugging against their leashes and forcing Threx to pull them back toward the building entrance.

"I lost my hand because of you!" Cass screeched trying to push past the Phylónethese barring his way. Aratob and Frold ran across the street nervously to stand next to a group of prostitutes while the Clan leader's son thrashed and wailed. "You took my hand, you puss-bag whore!"

Gavin withdrew a few feet, trying not to smile at the tantrum-throwing man. "Technically it was the giant spider thing who's name

I can't pronounce that chopped off your hand. And honestly, I wasn't even there for that!"

"I'll kill you!"

"What is going on?!" The deep voice, resonate and forceful, pulled Cass from his frothing. A broad-shouldered man limped over, leaning on a cane. Despite his impairment, the older gentleman exuded menace in every line of his face. Short cropped gray hair came down over an aged forehead painted in intricate green tattoos, while a single purple tooth stood out against yellow mates.

"Father," Cass gasped, gesticulating toward Gavin.

Stepping forward and pushing Cass out of the way like a rabid fan at a movie premiere, Gavin grinned at Fralt Randok with all his charm.

"Just the man I wanted to see," he said gregariously. "Fralt Randok, it's been too long."

A sneer pulled at the older man's lips. "Gavin Baller; the man who, if stories be believed, single-handedly beat the Militia on Kr'thotok. The man who escaped me along with that Galta'arok of a Matriarch who shot me in the knee."

"I'm glad you remember me," Gavin said.

Fralt hobbled up, smacking one of the agitated lizards with his cane. "I wish I'd known you were the clone of Abraxas-Mon back when I had you cornered in the south square. That would have changed everything."

"I doubt it," Gavin said.

"You must have known I would kill you if I ever saw you again," Fralt replied, running his tongue over his teeth and patting a sword strapped to his right thigh.

"I did," Gavin answered. "But that must make you wonder why I'd risk so much to come see you."

"It does."

"I'm looking for Raymond Halford. You're a powerful man

here on the Gadabout and a friend of mine found some documents with your signature that alluded to the fact that Halford was here and you were involved somehow. Beyond that, Abraxas-Mon has taken over the Commonwealth and I need your help to stop him. There will be a lot of money and prestige involved if you do."

Cass spat on the ground. "Let me kill him, Father!"

"Shut up, boy!" Fralt bellowed. He turned back toward Gavin, a half-smile on his lips. "You think I'd go against someone like Abraxas-Mon? You had a stroke or something? No one steps in front of Abraxas-Mon and lives to tell about it. Everybody talks about how wealth and prosperity flow wherever he walks, right? Not before his enemies are crushed beneath his heel. I won't be one of those enemies."

Gavin nodded. "There's more. You'll at least want to hear it. You know where Raymond Halford is or not?"

"Possibly," Fralt grinned. "With the proper incentive."

"I just landed in a brand-new ship directly from the Citadel on Cartoshí," Gavin said. "Other than a few scratches that need to be buffed out, it's in perfect condition, and it's yours."

Fralt scoffed. "It was mine the second it landed. I control everything in this sector. What else you got?"

"A plan," Gavin answered. "Something that will make you richer and more powerful than you could ever imagine."

"Imagination is something I have plenty of." Fralt stepped back, leaning on his cane. "I've heard offers like this before, from men who lacked the means to provide them. What makes you different, Gavin Baller of Idumea?"

Gavin took a deep breath. "Because I'm Abraxas-Mon's clone. What he can do, I can do. You want wealth and honor to flow here on the Gadabout? You step in line behind me."

Fralt grinned like a Cheshire cat, spittle hanging from his yellow teeth. "I like this one," he said, turning to his gathered posse.

"Maybe we can talk a bit before I kill you."

"No, father!" Cass protested, pushing next to Fralt. "I want to beat him to death now! He took my hand!"

"Back off, junior," Gavin said. "The adults are talking."

Cass seethed, veins throbbing along his scared forehead. "I challenge!" he yelled, pushing the men standing next to him away as if forming a rudimentary boxing ring. "I issue an Honor Challenge right now, in the name of Renki'itomet the Golden God!"

"What does that mean?" Gavin asked Fralt with an annoyed smirk.

"The boy wants to fight you," Fralt answered.

"Once I beat your kid, you still good to talk?"

"If you beat Cass, I'll take you to Raymond Halford right now," Fralt said with a smile.

Gavin rotated his shoulders and stretched his neck. "Done."

The group stepped away, forming a circle around the two combatants like fighters on an elementary school playground. Cass twisted the mace on his wrist in preparation for righteous retribution. The gilded weapon screwed off its base like a lid from a peanut jar. Cass let go of the spiked club and allowed it to dangle from a twelve-inch-long chain concealed in a housing where his left hand had once perched.

"Are there any rules to this Honor Fight, or whatever?" Gavin asked the crowd.

"Not really," Ugnol said with a shrug.

"Do I get a weapon or something to---"

Cass rushed Gavin, swinging the spiked mace with full force. Caught off-guard, Gavin barely avoided the strike as it plunged past his skull. He spun, moving to the other side of the ring.

The crowd cheered, spitting, and laughing in barbaric joy.

"What, no foreplay?" Gavin asked, heart beating faster. "You just get right to it, don't you? You must be super popular with the ladies."

Screaming like a rabid canine, Cass darted forward, mace arching with skilled precision. Again, Gavin dodged the blow, gaging his opponent's strategy. Cass led with his right foot and would swing the mace less than a second later. The man showed expertise with his weapon, but rage clouded his focus. Gavin had options.

Stepping aside after a third blow, Gavin drew close to the ring of men currently overjoyed at the potential for bodily injury. They pushed him back toward Cass with jeers and taunts. Quickly, Gavin reached over and pulled Fralt Randok's cane out of his hands.

"Hey!" Fralt yelled. "I need that!"

"You'll get it back in a second, don't worry," Gavin guaranteed, testing the staff's heft and balance.

Cass spun the mace back and forth in front of him to keep whatever attack Gavin had planned at bay.

Studying the speed and angle of the mace, Gavin planted his right foot and lobbed the cane like an Olympic javelin. Timed perfectly, the staff passed between Cass's slinging club and thumped the man right between the eyes.

Cass stumbled back in surprise, losing control of his weapon, and slamming the spiked mace into his own right knee. A sickening crack followed, along with a stream of blood left behind by the two-inch barbs. Crumbling to the ground, Cass screamed in pain and clawed at his eviscerated leg.

"Ouch," Gavin said through clamped teeth, neck tightening at the sight.

Ugnol nudged one of the gang members standing next to Fralt. "You should see what he can do with a spoon."

Screams echoed through the humid air and down dark corridors. Gavin turned to Fralt, who's mouth hung open in a mixture of surprise and amusement.

"You good to take me to Halford now?" he asked, leaning down to pick up the man's staff.

"You've earned it," Fralt said.

"I hope I didn't damage your cane," Gavin said, handing the stick back to its owner. Cass continued to whimper pitifully.

"Ah, it's little worse for wear," Fralt replied, running his finger up the smooth ebony surface. He waved his hand toward several of his underlings. "Pick Cass up off the street and take him to the meds. From the looks of it, he'll be needing a cane for a while, too."

Fralt marched toward the main entrance and motioned for Gavin to follow. As he took his first step, an oversized hand grabbed Gavin's shoulder.

"I'll be waiting here when you get back," Ugnol said.

"You don't have to do that, Ugnol. You brought me here, and I appreciate it. You can go back home."

Ugnol craned his head as if in thought. "I'll be waiting here when you get back," he repeated firmly.

Gavin understood. "Alright. Keep an eye on things. If this meeting with Fralt goes south, we'll probably need to fight our way out."

"I like a good fight," Ugnol said.

Smacking the Phylónethese on the arm, Gavin turned to follow Fralt through the double-doored entrance to the Veredok. "I know a Commander Brek who will want to meet you," he said over his shoulder.

Fralt led Gavin down a set of stairs toward the sounds of techno music. Colored lights flashed along the walls like a 1970's disco parlor, complete with blinking tiles on the floor at the base of the staircase. Walking into what looked like an alien dance club, Gavin smelled smoke and alcohol. Women and men, some

Athelbrath, others human and Nythensus, danced and gyrated inside gravity wells not unlike what Gavin had seen produced by singularity bombs. Music thumped in his ear as he bumped into hooting patrons and avoided eye contact with scantily clad, or in some cases fully naked, dancers.

Several of the performers sported the pale eyes and grayish skin of Cádavrite. Gavin wondered if they were being forced to exploit themselves, or if things worked differently on the Gadabout.

"Let's head back to my private booth," Fralt said, nodding across the room to a series of purple drapes running along a wall.

"This is weird," Gavin admitted, shouting over the throbbing beat.

"What is that?" Fralt asked.

"I wouldn't have expected an alien strip club to feel so familiar."

Fralt laughed. "I can get you a private performance if you'd like."

"I'm good."

Two muscular bouncers nodded to Fralt as they approached and parted the curtain for their benefactor. Gavin slipped through, noticing less smoke and a more pleasant fragrance on the air. Even the music changed, switching from a harsh pounding of discordant melodies to a softer and more recognizable tune. A woman's voice sang in English of home and new love after a painful relationship.

"Is that Linda Ronstadt?" Gavin asked, looking to the overhead speakers.

"It is," a voice said from the shadows of a nearby corner. "I'm surprised you know the song. Your generation rarely appreciates truly talented artists that are more than twenty years old."

Gavin gave a side glance to Fralt. "So, when you said you knew where he was, you meant, 'he's downstairs.'"

Raymond Halford sat forward on the couch, light peeking from between the curtains and hitting his face. He held a wine glass and wore a collared shirt and pair of slacks, though without his usual thousand-dollar tie. A bottle of half-empty turquoise liquid sat on the table in front of him.

"Gavin," he said with a tip of his glass.

"Raymond," Gavin replied.

"What brings you to this hellhole?"

"The end of the universe."

Raymond took a sip of his liquor. "That sounds dramatic."

"You know me; I won't get out of bed in the morning unless there's a 50-million-dollar contract and an Oscar involved."

"I'm going to assume things have gone badly, otherwise you wouldn't be coming to me at all, am I right?"

Gavin scratched his cheek. "You could say that."

"So, you need my help?"

"Yep."

Raymond smiled and grabbed the bottle of light blue liquor, refilling his glass. "Shit. If you're that desperate, I'm probably going to need a few more drinks before we talk."

CHAPTER 10

THE ENEMY OF MY ENEMY IS STILL A JERK

"I don't believe you." Raymond leaned back on his couch and glanced nervously over at Fralt Randok.

"It's true, whether you want to believe it or not," Gavin replied.

The lounge sat empty except for the three men. Music still blared from the strip club on the other side of the curtains, but lights had been turned on inside the salon, transforming what normally would have been a seedy sex chamber into something closer to a bar in a bad part of town. Other than the purple accents and gaudy cushions everywhere, Gavin accepted their surroundings as probably the most professional setting the Gadabout had to offer.

"You're saying Asha'asethol has been completely razed?" Fralt asked.

Gavin leaned forward and tapped his finger on the glass coffee table between where the men sat. "I was there. I was chased by an Axelroth. I walked up the steps of the temple in the capital city. I don't know how many Perennials survived."

"Abraxas-Mon wouldn't do that," Raymond protested with a shake of his head. "I've met Abraxas-Mon. He's a ruthless tactician, but you're talking about slaughtering the entire planet; millions of Perennials and dignitaries from other species and planets. You can't just do that and have nobody notice."

"He's been controlling things for years," Gavin reiterated. "He was sending out messages that made it look like people were coming and going on the Perennial planet, but in truth, nobody was. He probably did the same for months before to make sure anybody that would actually be missed would avoid the assault. It's what I would have done. And look how easily I fooled you back on Earth when I stole your ship. I barely even knew what an alien was, and I was terrified half the time. How much easier would it have been for Abraxas-Mon to trick everybody?"

Raymond frowned. "And you would know the mind of Abraxas-Mon, that's for sure. What a scary thought."

"I still don't understand…" Fralt said, green tattoos turning slightly yellow. "Asha'asethol is gone? Just like that? All the cities and people, gone for years now?"

"Yeah," Gavin answered.

"Like I said," Raymond continued, "I don't believe you. A couple times now you've pulled the wool over my eyes; you stole my ship back on Earth, you convinced me you had joined the Militia and then punched me in the face and took one of my best military units with you. What's the difference today?"

Gavin stood, stretching his back. "Why would I come to you now with some story like this? Why? What good is it going to do me? Both the Hierarchy and the Militia want me dead; I don't exactly have a great relationship with anyone on the Gadabout; and the only Perennial I've ever met thinks I'm disrespectful to their stupid traditions."

"They would think that," Fralt agreed. "That's definitely their way."

Gavin took a seat on the couch's backrest, feet plopping up on the cushions. "Look, I need people willing to fight. I need powerful people who will listen. That's all I want from you, Raymond. After that, you can go back to drinking and whoring, or whatever you're doing here on the Gadabout."

"That's just the thing, Gavin," Raymond said, eyes looking down at the floor. "You think I'd be here if I had anywhere else to go? No offense, Fralt."

"The Gadabout is a required taste," the clan leader admitted.

"When I stole that ship after the battle on Kr'thotok, I reported immediately to the Plenipotentiary High Tribunal who had originally sent me to goad leaders like General K'litok into open warfare. They told me my failures had put their plans in jeopardy and that I would be arrested upon my rendezvousing with the fleet. I've burned through all my contacts. Nobody will have anything to do with me. I've been blacklisted for all intents and purposes. I got them exactly what they wanted: war. And they tossed me out like a damn rotten banana. The Militia thinks I'm a traitor and the Hierarchy won't have anything to do with me. I don't know what you thought I could deliver but trust me when I say my influence has waned in the past few months."

"Damn it," Gavin said. "You, everybody, has been manipulated by Abraxas-Mon. He issued your orders; he wanted the war; he's running both the Militia *and* the Hierarchy. Don't you get it? Everybody has been played. We're fighting ourselves while he sits back and drinks a beer. The Commonwealth is on the verge of collapse."

"That doesn't change the fact that I don't have anyone in a position of power that will answer my calls," Raymond retorted.

"Alright." Gavin bit his lip, furiously pondering through alternative strategies. He hated to think he came to the Gadabout for nothing. "Give me a minute to switch things around in my brain."

Fralt laughed. "He wants to fight Abraxas-Mon and he only needs a minute to strategize. This is going to be a swift defeat."

"Shut up and let me think," Gavin said. "We don't have a lot of time. If I can surprise Abraxas-Mon and come at him quick, we'll be in a better position."

"Whatever you say, clone," Fralt replied.

Gavin smacked his hand against the glass table. "Look, Abraxas-Mon has certain expectations. He's been waiting his entire life for this. If I can make him disappointed and then surprise him, catch him off-guard, things will go well for us. I know what happens when I have expectations that aren't met, and I can tell you — I don't respond well. Neither will he."

"So, you just want to take out Abraxas-Mon, not launch a full-scale war," Raymond surmised.

"Exactly. He made this whole thing very personal. People that are important to me may or may not be by his side during any potential battle. I don't want them getting hurt. Misdirection and a good strategy are our best bets at this point. We need people willing to fight long enough for me to get close to him. If we can make that happen, his whole shadow cabinet thing will come crashing down. We might even be able to stop the fighting between the Militia and the Hierarchy."

"Unlikely," Raymond said, shaking his head. "Both those organizations are boiling over. That war will happen one way or another. And you realize there must be people in the Hierarchy that are a part of all of this, right? Abraxas-Mon obviously has a team in place that won't be easy to ferret out."

"At least we can save what's left of the Commonwealth if we act quickly," Gavin said.

Fralt took a long drink from a wine glass filled with sparkly pink liquid. "And what does that mean to me; to anyone on the Gadabout? The Commonwealth shuns us, and we hate them in-kind. If they fall, what will it matter to us?"

Gavin looked straight at the man. "When the dog dies, the fleas die."

"What's a dog?" Fralt asked.

"When a nation burns the scavengers burn," Raymond rephrased.

"Now that makes sense," Fralt said, pointing at Gavin. "Why didn't you just say it that way?"

Rolling his eyes, Gavin continued. "Whatever, just know that if war breaks out then only one man wins: Abraxas-Mon."

"Again, I hate to repeat myself," Fralt said, "But why do I care? I'm a survivor, as is everybody else on this station. The Commonwealth can rot, and we'll be just fine."

"What if you could be better than fine?" Gavin asked. "What if you could be on top for once? I was going to make you an offer for helping me, but now if Raymond can't get what we need, I'll turn to you with something much bigger, and you'll probably want it."

Fralt's eyes narrowed. "What do you mean?"

"Yeah, what *do* you mean?" Raymond questioned.

"I'm going to defeat Abraxas-Mon with or without your help. I won't let my friends become his pawns. If Abraxas-Mon knows every choice I could make, then I know every choice he could make. That puts us about even. But if you help me, Fralt, you and the Gadabout, once this is over — you can have the Citadel on Cartoshí, and the authority that goes with it."

Fralt's eyes widened slightly, like a gambler trying to hide a straight flush.

"That's not yours to give," Raymond warned.

"It will be if this works." Gavin scooted off the backrest and slid down onto the cushions once more. "The Citadel will be yours, along with the power base on Cartoshí."

"You sure you're not trading Hitler for Stalin, there Gavin?" Raymond asked. "Again, no offense, Fralt."

"I don't know who those people are," Fralt admitted. "Though if they are dangerous men, then I take no offense."

"We'll jump off that bridge when we come to it," Gavin said.

"I want the surrounding city too," Fralt leveraged. "Not just the Citadel. My crew gets first pick of everything and then the rest of the clans can have what's left."

"You bring them all in line and it's a deal," Gavin agreed. He turned to Raymond. "Whatever contacts you have left, we need to find anyone who has access to the Cádavrite Guild. Zaire has mentioned the organization to me before. I know Cádavrite don't have representation, but there has to be leaders of some type."

"We have many Cádavrite onboard the Gadabout," Fralt added. "They flee oppression and seek a new life here. We don't treat them as thralls like in the Commonwealth."

Gavin pointed to the curtains and the unharmonious ballad thundering on the other side. "So, the Cádavrite dancers I saw out there aren't your indentured servants then?"

"They're whatever they can be," Fralt said flippantly with a wave of his hand. "Whatever they are, at least they make their own choices."

"What do you want with the Cádavrite Guild?" Raymond asked.

"Before we were captured, we made our way through basically a Cádavrite factory next door to the Cartoshí Citadel. They were killing people and then turning them into Deadites to make what we assume is an army."

Fralt spat on the table, saliva spraying the crystal surface. He pointed his cane at Gavin, face tattoos flaring orange and then red.

"Are you being honest with me, boy?"

Gavin blinked, surprised by the sudden antagonism from the clan leader. "Yeah, I'm telling the truth. We saw guards executing people by shooting them in the chest and then putting them in those Renaissance Chambers."

Seething, Fralt clawed at the couch's armrest and smacked the tip of his staff against the floor. "That's been done before, about 40 annual cycles ago. A thousand Dubaku were captured and forced to become Cádavrite to serve in an army on Panta'aloth. It was a dishonorable outrage. Many of the Dubaku who now live here on the Gadabout emigrated because of that degradation. My father's brother was one of the victims. If Abraxas-Mon is once again forcing beings to become Deadite soldiers, he is worthy of evisceration."

"Okay, now we've got some common ground," Gavin said, trying not to smile. "What I want to do is get that army to revolt at the right moment."

"You've met Cádavrite, Gavin," Raymond said, picking up his glass of wine from the table and examining it to make sure none of Fralt's spit had smeared the sides. "Kids are taught from the time they can first walk how terrible it is to get resuscitated and turned into a monster. It's their version of the Boogeyman. Most of those people are going to want to die and feel like they're worthless now. They're not going to revolt."

"Some of them will." Gavin wagged his finger to emphasize his words. "I have to believe someone can come back from this; that they're not completely emotionally destroyed by it. I have to. Some of them will be pretty pissed off and all they need is an excuse to fight. If we can get some of them to join, I'm sure others will follow. That will give us the opening we need. First, though, the Gadabout needs to change course toward Cartoshí."

"That will require the approval of all the clan leaders," Fralt said, tattoos still a pale shade of crimson. "Normally the station floats freely along the gravity rivers and only alters direction for specific raids."

Gavin sat forward, tiring of the discussion. "Let's get approval then. The faster we can get things moving, the better off we're all going to be."

Fralt stood, leaning on his cane. "I can call an emergency summit. The soonest all the clan leaders could congregate would be tomorrow midday."

"That's perfect," Gavin said, standing up next to the man with an excited bounce.

"But know this, Gavin Baller," Fralt spoke, an edge to his voice. "The tribes are not likely to follow you. They take great pride in being pirates and having no leader. They aren't afraid of being attacked here in the safety of their station-fortress. They understand payment, just as I. Don't assume a single Dubaku or Athelbrath at that gathering will listen, let alone join you. They may plot your death for merely presuming to speak with them."

"It's a chance I'm willing to take," Gavin said.

Fralt nodded and glanced down at Raymond Halford. "Very well. It looks as if we are about to have an interesting meeting."

When Fralt said 'meeting,' Gavin assumed the clan leaders would gather in some sort of conference room, or at least the alien equivalent of a seedy Italian restaurant. No such luck. This collection of brigands apparently always met in the central Gadabout square, surrounded by hundreds of onlookers, guards, and curious passersby. Gavin stood in the center along with Fralt, Raymond, and Ugnol, like a group of petty thieves about to be tried before a mismatched and sweaty array of tribunal judges.

The clan lords, eight men and three women, some human, others Athelbrath and Phylónethese, stood in a circular plaza ringed by tall buildings reaching toward a ceiling 40 stories above. The skyscrapers seemed much better kept than the rest of the Gadabout, but even so, the best the station had to offer still reminded Gavin of some of the worst sections of LA.

Hushed conversation filled the square as people pointed and elbowed for better positions to view the proceedings. Each of the clan leaders looked like they'd stepped out of one of Gavin's movies; a pirate with a disfigured face; a reject from *Beyond Thunderdome*; a Phylónethese with Athelbrath and human skulls attacked to his shoulders. Two of the women, small and hunched over with age, seemed frail and weak, until Gavin locked eyes with one petting a red-striped racoon and felt a cold chill run up his spine. No one at this gathering had ascended to their position by being anything less than terrifying and ruthless.

"I hate the Central Square," Ugnol said, leaning close to Gavin. "It always smells of a chemical flower fragrant, and the temperature is kept too cold."

Gavin shivered slightly in the pale blue artificial sunlight. Where most of the Gadabout seemed climate-controlled to be as uncomfortably hot as possible, here wisps of vapor blew from Gavin's mouth like a cold spring morning.

"It could smell a lot worse," he said, rubbing his hands together and placing them inside the pockets of a black Tom Ford three-button coat that had likely cost Raymond Halford upwards of $7,000 back on Earth. "This is actually the most comfortable I've been since arriving here. I'm glad I took Raymond's advice and borrowed a jacket."

"Don't get used to the comfort," Ugnol warned. "Everyone here would kill you because of nothing more than the shadow you cast, or the fine coat you lent from the Idumean."

Cracked concrete, sporting small triangular patches of yellow grass, clicked under Fralt Randok's cane as he paced in front of the line of eleven scowling delegates and their respective entourages.

"Clan leaders," Fralt began, raising his arms above his head like a ringmaster at the circus. "I have called this gathering at the behest of one who brings distressing news."

"Cease with the oratory, Fralt!" an Athelbrath leader with rings piercing up and down both sides of his face said with a salivatory shout. "My spies have already told me you have the general from the Battle of Kr'thotok here with you; the one who looks like Abraxas-Mon."

One of the old ladies stepped forward, pushing the Athelbrath slightly with her walking staff. "He's a clone!" she crowed. "And there's a price on his head!"

Raymond shot Gavin a side glance. "Did you know about that?" he whispered.

"I was not aware," Gavin replied.

"I, too, received word from the Matriarch Brendant's official Thought-Mech as we were walking into the square," another clan leader said; this one a Dubaku woman wearing official-looking robes and a hairdo that stood at least a foot taller than she did. "The Hierarchy has issued a formal decree that the capture and imprisonment of this man will be met with titles and land on Cartoshí and the green fields of Panta'aloth."

Eyes went wide, followed by a murmur from the crowd.

"I hate Abraxas-Mon," Gavin groaned.

The pirate-looking clan lord stomped forward, pulling a long knife from his belt. "The Prea'alok Clan makes first claim on this clone!"

"The Randok Clan made first contact," Fralt protested, holding his cane like a weapon. "It will be the Randok Clan that reaps the rewards!"

More voices joined in, all claiming the right to throw Gavin at the feet of the Hierarchy Matriarch. Things would descend into chaos before Gavin even had a chance to state his case.

Weighing his options, Gavin quickly scanned the crowd. To his right stood a Dubaku bodyguard protecting one of the elderly clan matrons. A pair of large purple revolvers hung from the man's belt.

Gently pulling his hands from the warm confines of his coat, Gavin darted forward and pulled both weapons from the guard's holsters before the soldier realized what had happened. Gavin stepped boldly in front of the clan leaders, pistols held in the air, and fired twice. Earsplitting gunshots refracted off the glass and steel structures; bullets hitting pipes far above with whimpering clangs. Everyone jumped at the surprise assault.

Instantly, dozens of rifles, pistols, and paralytic-shooting hands swung in Gavin's direction. Angry eyes twitched, ready to unleash hell on the disrespectful actor.

Gavin swung around, guns pointing in all directions as his eyes fed his brain every spec of data he required.

"Now that I have everyone's attention," Gavin shouted, still spinning in a circle, revolvers at the ready. "I can see there are currently 117 guns pointed at me, along with 31 Athelbrath hands ready to lob some sticky crap my way. But I can also see that only 12 of you have steady enough aim to hit a moving target.

"Now, I have two guns, each with 7 shots left, which means I could kill the 12 most skilled marksmen easily with two bullets to spare, while stealing any number of other rifles and continuing to mow all of you down. I have the skill of Abraxas-Mon and the patience of a Phylónethese who just got stabbed in the back. If any of you ever wondered what would happen if you faced the great warlord in battle, I am more than happy to show you now. Or, if you'd prefer, we could talk before I have to kill all of you. How does that sound?"

Not a single weapon dropped, though confused faces now permeated the crowd.

"I don't feel like dying today, Gavin," Raymond said, hands up in surrender. "I have a date with a very loose Athelbrath dancer later tonight."

"Shut up, Raymond," Gavin ordered. "I am Gavin Baller, and

yes, I'm Abraxas-Mon's clone. That is true. Which means anything Abraxas-Mon can do, I can do. Any story you've heard about how deadly that guy can be is true and I can give you a demonstration if you'd like." He cocked the revolvers to accent his meaning.

The standoff continued silently for another minute, Gavin never flinching or pulling his fingers from the triggers.

Finally, the elderly matron petting the red racoon-like creature stepped forward and looked Gavin in the eye. Her lopsided gray afro bounced as she spoke. "I, Pleash Athro'ok, matriarch of the Athro'ok Clan, concede the floor to the Hierarchy fugitive known as Gavin Baller. I for one would like to hear what this young Gro'otolok has to say!"

Gavin looked over his shoulder toward Raymond. "What's a 'Gro'otolok?'"

"It's a sexual term," he answered with a half-smile. "You really don't want to know more than that. Let's just say she likes you and leave it there."

"Gross," Gavin said.

"I, Agboss Underlurch of the Underlurch Clan, second Pleash Athro'ok's motion," shouted a wrinkled Phylónethese clan leader holding an axe over his head. Silence fell except for the dripping of water from punctured plumbing somewhere above.

Fralt stepped back, waving his hand toward Gavin. "The plaza belongs to you, clone."

"Thank you," Gavin said, lowering his weapons. "Alright, I'm just going to give you guys the bullet points. Abraxas-Mon has destroyed the Perennials, taken over the Hierarchy *and* the Rebirth Militia, and has been secretly running everything for five annular cycles. He brought me here so I could pose a threat to him and, I guess, give his life meaning. He plans to rule like the Athelbrath guy, what was his name…Orthal-Oblin, and take control of everything. I would assume that includes the Gadabout. He's forcing Dubaku and Athelbrath men and women to become Cádavrite and building a Deadite army; I know some of you here have personal experience with things like that. Your way of life is about to end. The Commonwealth is about to end."

The red racoon growled, but other than that no one spoke.

Gavin continued. "I have a plan, but it's going to require everyone's help. The Gadabout itself will need to set a course for Cartoshí so I can get in front of Abraxas-Mon and end all of this."

"What's in it for us?" one of the onlookers shouted from somewhere in the crowd. Heads nodded, followed by whispers of agreement.

"I don't suppose you guys will help just because it's the right thing to do, will you?" Gavin asked, fully aware of the rhetorical nature of his question.

Fralt chuckled, eliciting laughter from several of the gathered clan lords.

"Look," Gavin said, tossing his revolvers to Ugnol. "I've stolen speeches from movies and used quotes from smarter men to get people to join me in a fight. I'm not going to do that. If you guys don't help, Abraxas-Mon will kill all of you within a single cycle once he steps out of the shadows and takes control. I don't like the Gadabout or really anybody on it, so I know he doesn't care for it either. Abraxas-Mon will cleanse this station, I can guarantee it. If that's not enough, I already promised Fralt Randok that the citizens of the Gadabout could claim the Citadel on Cartoshí once the battle is over."

An excited buzz rumbled through the crowd, whispers of 'citadel' and 'golden tower' making their way from one end to the other.

"If we agree to join you," the pierced Athelbrath said looking back toward the mob. "We will only be exposing ourselves to death by standing before Abraxas-Mon. The authority that comes with the Citadel will do us no good as corpses."

"First of all, from what I understand, the Gadabout is the most heavily armored vessel in the galaxy," Gavin shouted before the thought of dying in battle could invade the minds of the nervous flock. "You guys are constantly welding new armor to the exterior. This place can survive a lot, and for good reason since everybody pretty much hates you."

Fralt snorted and nodded his head as if conceding the point.

"Secondly, I have a plan."

"And what plan is that, my Gro'otolok?" Pleash asked in her scratchy old voice, a curl of smoky breath slithering from her mouth on the cold air.

"Ew," Gavin said. "Alright, first I need someone to send a report, if you ass-hats haven't sent one already, saying that I'm here on the Gadabout."

"You want us to tell the Hierarchy you're here?" Ugbol the Phylónethese questioned.

Gavin bobbed his head. "Yes. I want several reports to go out that I crashed here, which is true, and that I'm in an infirmary injured and under arrest, but that the clan leaders won't turn me over unless the Matriarch comes herself to give the deed for the lands and stuff she promised."

"And then what?" a voice shouted from somewhere behind Gavin.

"And then we kidnap her and use her access codes to undermine Abraxas-Mon. Brendant has to be working with him, I have no doubt. We get her, we can make things difficult for him. After that, we get what we can and adapt as necessary. If everything goes the way I think it will, we'll avoid any actual fighting in favor of a Cádavrite rebellion and a head-to-head between me and Abraxas-Mon. At the very least, you'll have a very high-profile prisoner to ransom. Sound good?"

Everyone collectively looked at the clan leaders, waiting for someone to protest or offer challenge.

"I like this sexy Gro'otolok," Pleash said with a grin that revealed several missing teeth.

"Please stop, ma'am," Gavin interrupted.

Pleash continued. "...But how do we know you won't run away like an Aktelothing coward once the battle begins?"

Again, the crowd showed their agreement with nods and curled lips.

Gavin craned his head back and closed his eyes in exhaustion. "Alright, which one of you is the best fighter here?"

Ugnol chortled loudly and took a step away from Gavin.

"I am!" a Dubaku guard said with a raised hand. The man pushed several other attendants out of the way and marched forward. His muscular arms, heavy armor, and scarred face backed up his claim of superiority. He had at least six inches of height on Gavin as well. "Are you issuing a challenge? I am Fanthis of the Edrom Clan, and if so, I accept." the man said with an angry grimace.

"If I beat this guy, will everybody follow the plan and join me?" Gavin asked.

A cheer roared from the mass of people thronging the square like Madison Square Garden during the NBA Playoffs.

Gavin clapped his hands. "Alright. Anybody got a spoon?"

CHAPTER 11

SNATCH AND GRAB

"That Fanthis guy isn't going to be able to walk right for a month," Raymond said as he and Gavin ambled between the parked ships in the main Gadabout landing bay. Their boots splashed through shallow puddles; remnants from the cleaning crew that had power washed the concrete the night before in preparation for Brendant's arrival.

"That was three days ago," Gavin dismissed. "You'd think I handicapped the guy."

Raymond shook his head. "The warriors in Edrom Clan are still mad you shoved that spoon up his---"

"Gavin!" Ugnol shouted, cutting Raymond off. The brawny Phylónethese tromped up on the stained concrete, pointing toward the enormous departure doors a half mile away. "The Matriarch will be landing within a hundredth-cycle. The harnesses are in place."

"Thanks for the update, Ugnol," Gavin said, stopping to look at the stars twinkling through the atmosphere barrier holding back the cold of space. "Get the clan leaders ready."

"Yes sir," Ugnol said before setting off toward the primary bay entrance.

Raymond leaned against a rusted ship, instantly grimacing and dusting particles of oxidized metal from his gray suit jacket.

"Why do you always wear a suit?" Gavin asked, looking around the deserted landing area. The usual tents and marketplace structures had been cleared and removed over the past three days, opening a broad zone for Brendant's ship to land. Only Gavin, Raymond, and a selection of Gadabout leaders would be attending the Matriarch's advent.

"My dad always told me to dress for the job you want, not the job you have," Raymond answered.

"You're a secret Hierarchy operative for a galactic commonwealth," Gavin said. "I don't think a suit really matches that job description."

"Like I said, I'm dressing for the job I want," Raymond winked. "At least I don't look like I just crawled out of a Marilyn Manson concert."

Gavin looked down at his black shirt and dark gray pants. "It's all Fralt had that would fit me, other than all the jackets he has chains and spikes attached to. This was the most unpretentious thing I could find. I got tired of wearing the clothes Abraxas-Mon had laid out for me. Yesterday I burned them."

"What did you do with my Tom Ford coat?" Raymond asked, suddenly very worried. "It was a gift from the Prince of Saudi Arabia."

"It's in my room; chill out," Gavin said. "And someday you're going to have to tell me your life story, because I have a feeling it would probably make an unbelievable movie."

Raymond chuckled. "It would. But I'd demand a more attractive actor play me than you."

"Good luck with that one."

The two men continued walking, passing a large 747-sized transport unit. They approached Fralt as he talked to four other Gadabout leaders.

"We got the communiqué," Fralt said, waving to Gavin. "Brendant is on her way. If you look closely, you can see her flagship, the Aklethrobí, out there among the stars."

Squinting into the black of space, Gavin couldn't make out any ships against the points of light in the vacuum.

"We ready?" he asked.

"They'll never know what hit them," Fralt grinned, purple tooth sparkling like a diamond. "Hold your hands behind your back so it looks like you're restrained. No one has weapons of any kind, as ordered by the Matriarch, so your plan better work, otherwise we're all dead."

"It'll work," Gavin nodded, placing his hands behind him like a prisoner.

A shape moved against the black nothingness in front of them, drawing Gavin's eye. A ship came into view, rocketing toward the Gadabout landing platform. The closer it drew, the bigger it became, exterior lights shimmering on a chrome surface. Unlike other Hierarchy ships Gavin had seen, this one featured wings like an Earth airplane, extending from a cylindrical mass ending in a point at the front tip. Gavin gasped at its size, suddenly less than convinced in the success of their rudimentary plan.

"It that thing going to fit in here?" Gavin asked.

"Oh yeah," Raymond answered. "With room to spare. Trust me."

Wind blew with gale force as the vessel penetrated the atmosphere. Gavin covered his eyes to keep dirt and grime from hitting them. Engines thundered throughout the bay, pounding everyone's eardrums as the yacht approached.

A series of 12 finger-like claws lowered from the bottom of the ship, digging into the concrete, and leaving behind thick gouges. Stopping less than 100 feet in front of them, the ship tilted toward the ground. With a squeal, the ramp extended on the front end, light shining from deep inside the craft.

"Here we go," Fralt said.

Fourteen Dubaku soldiers, seven male and seven female, descended the ramp wearing blue uniforms and yellow cloaks, each armed with a silver, tree-limb rifle. Helmets covered their heads and faces like executioners. They formed two lines in front of the gathered leaders, bringing their weapons to the ready in case anyone on the Gadabout decided to attack.

Gavin had never seen guards like these before. They weren't Praetorians like Ogpog and Zaire used. Each held perfectly still, rifles trained on the group. Whatever they were, these men and women knew how to kill, Gavin had no doubt.

Following closely behind the soldiers, Brendant stepped out regally. Periwinkle robes wafted around her body like curtains in a breeze. A stern face, beautiful and majestic, glowered as she approached. She looked the same as Gavin remembered from the view screen on the Silver Hammer's bridge, except now, instead of a yellow streak running up her tall hair, pale purple accents weaved to the tip of her bun, matching her garb. She held a crystal in her hand tightly, like a woman clutching her purse in a particularly bad neighborhood.

"Matriarch Brendant," Fralt said with an exaggerated bow. "Welcome to the Gadabout."

"Fralt Randok," Brendant forced, as if the words made her ill. "Raymond Halford."

"Brendant," Raymond said.

"I heard you scurried to hide in some hole after your failures," Brendant declared with contempt. "It would be difficult to find one slovenlier than the Gadabout."

Raymond smiled. "One man's failure is another man's victory."

"Spoken like a true vagrant." Brendant turned to Fralt. "I see you have my prisoner."

"Do you have my payment?" Fralt asked.

"Before we get to exchanges and stuff," Gavin interrupted, stepping forward with his hands still behind his back. "Are you and Abraxas-Mon, like, together, maybe? I'm just thinking that I find you extremely attractive, so naturally, he would too."

Brendant blinked slowly as if trying to keep herself from slashing Gavin's throat. "I am sure the clone has spoken many interesting lies since crashing here."

"You guys *are* sleeping together," Gavin smiled. "That's good to know. Abraxas-Mon and I really do have similar tastes."

"Here is your payment," Brendant said, handing her crystal over to Fralt. "Lands and titles to the Veradelach Valleys on Cartoshí, as well as the Sovereign Lake on Panta'aloth."

"Pleasure doing business with you, Matriarch" Fralt said, taking the gemstone and flipping it into his palm.

"One more question before you take me away, oh sweet Matriarch," Gavin said. "Can you breathe in space?"

Brendant motioned with her hand for one of the guards to collect Gavin. "No," she answered flatly.

"Then you better hold your breath," Gavin said.

The lights ringing the landing bay entrance flickered and died, releasing the gravitational hold on the atmosphere. A roar like a thousand locomotives cascaded through the hanger as the vacuum of space pulled on the air with overwhelming ferocity. Hurricane winds buffeted Gavin's back as he leaped toward a shocked Brendant and grabbed her arm. Using his momentum, he spun the Matriarch toward Ugnol's waiting grasp.

Several of the blue-uniformed guards fell backward in the

tempest. They stumbled and clutched for purchase as cosmic infinity threatened to suck them out of the Gadabout. Two of the female soldiers ran up the ramp toward safety inside the ship.

"Grab the tether!" Raymond shouted, wrapping his arm in a leather strap attached to a nearby scaffold. He tossed a belt to Gavin, holding close to Fralt and the other leaders as they gripped their harnesses.

"Give me a second!" Gavin cried, allowing the wind to pick him up and throw him against one of the soldiers. Kicking the man to the ground, Gavin stole his weapon and fired on the two closest guards. A third shot back, energy blasts never coming within a foot of Gavin. He leveled his weapon to fire on the soldier when a brass barrel took flight in the tempest and hit the woman in the helmet. She tumbled into the air and spun toward the open port doors. The other caped warriors did their best to scatter while several held fast to seams in the concrete to keep from blowing away.

Gravity tore at every surface, picking up wooden crates or tools and sending them on an unending journey through the cold universe. Within a few seconds heavier material, like people, would be unable to withstand the force.

The air grew thin. Turning, Gavin glimpsed Ugnol struggling with Brendant as the alien attempted to pull the Matriarch to one of the cargo crates and lock her inside. The woman obviously had more strength and tenacity than Gavin had given her credit.

As he took a step toward his Phylónethese friend to lend a hand Gavin's feet scraped along the floor. The nothingness of space slowly pulled him toward the open bay door.

He turned and reached for Raymond but realized he'd been dragged too far away to grab hold of his tether. Several energy blasts blew by him, fired by one of the soldiers. Taking aim, Gavin shot the man in the chest and sent him careening toward the stars.

The soles of Gavin's boots slowly peeled off the blemished concrete. Arms waving like a swimmer in a riptide, he tried to fight a force infinitely stronger that he could ever hope to be.

Just as Gavin lifted into the air, the lights along the exit reignited and gravity once again separated the dock from outer space. The rumble of wind ceased, leaving behind an eerie silence. Gavin landed heavily, bringing his rifle up in case any remaining guards decided to put up a fight.

"Send in the squads!" Fralt screamed behind him.

A battle cry replaced the quiet, followed by the scraping of metal against metal. Sections of the floor slid open, revealing Gadabout warriors and several makeshift cannons that had been hiding beneath their feet. They charged up ladders and jumped to the ready, brandishing rifles, pistols and swords like a band of buccaneers about to raid a merchant skiff.

More Hierarchy soldiers ran down the ramp to reclaim their Matriarch, but before they could respond, guns blazed and hewed them down like dried grass under a lawnmower. Shells exploded against the side of the pristine yacht, rocking the silver vessel back and forth. A group of Athelbrath shot green paralytic from their hands as another squadron of troops charged out of the ship. Unfortunately, the ooze had no effect against the soldiers' blue armor, allowing the intruders the opportunity to return fire and kill a line of Gadabout fighters.

"Blow up the ramp!" Gavin commanded as he ran back toward the clan leaders. Fralt and the others sheltered behind a series of metal crates, avoiding the battle in their unarmed state. Looking around quickly, Gavin saw no sign of Ugnol or Brendant, until he noticed a pair of enormous gray feet poking out from behind the landing gear of a nearby ship like a passed out drunk on Hollywood Blvd. Had the Matriarch somehow overpowered the Phylónethese fighter?

Gavin's head turned left, then right. "Where's Brendant?!"

A fist flew past his periphery too fast for him to react, walloping Gavin's face with brutal precision.

"Disgusting clone!" Brendant spat, swinging both her hands and slamming them against Gavin's ears.

He stumbled back, hearing gunfire and shouting echo from far away, as if he'd been knocked to the other side of the Gadabout. An intense ringing impaired Gavin's senses, pain moving from his inner ear to his sinuses. Before he could blink, another strike impacted his nose, sending blood gushing forth.

Brendant's blurry shape advanced. Gavin focused as best he could and blocked her next attack with his right forearm. She swung again and he blocked with his left.

The air swirled around her, giving Gavin an idea of where her next barrage would originate, but she moved with such speed and fluidity that he barely had a chance to defend himself before her next kick or jab forced him back. Even with his brain feeding him data, his body couldn't react quickly enough to give him an advantage.

"They're retreating!" Fralt yelled somewhere to Gavin's left. "Some of her guards are even joining us in the fight!"

Brendant's soldiers were defecting? Had Gavin heard right? Another punch from the Matriarch knocked the thought clean out his cerebellum.

Concrete buckled with a sickening crunch as the Hierarchy ship pulled up from the ground. The claws retracted, dropping hunks of broken cement indiscriminately on advancing Gadabout combatants and Hierarchy soldiers alike. Gravity fluctuated somewhat as the engines cycled to life and pushed the craft toward the exit.

Brendant seemed unfazed by her cadre's retreat. Her battering of Gavin continued unabated until he tripped on a thick cable and stumbled backward. Using his falter to her advantage, Brendant lunged, kicking Gavin in the stomach and following up with a brutal elbow to the thigh. The hit moved through the muscle to the bone and sent Gavin tumbling to his knees.

She raised her fist for another blow, when one of the female, blue-armored guards ran to her side.

"Matriarch!" she shouted through the voice modulator on her helmet.

Brendant turned quickly to her subordinate with a look of impassioned rage. Suddenly Gavin noticed something in the woman's gauntleted hand: a glob of green paralytic from one of the Athelbrath. Without another word, the woman threw the goop in Brendant's face, sending the Matriarch faltering. Brendant cursed while trying to wipe the ooze from her cheek, but before she could remove the sticky snot, she fell to the floor unconscious.

A jubilant cheer rose from the motley army as humans, Athelbrath, Nythensus, and Phylónethese fighters celebrated their victory. Gavin glanced around quickly to see dead soldiers lying next to bleeding Gadabout ruffians. The skirmish hadn't been pretty, but luckily, they'd won.

Gavin tried to stand but found his left leg completely numb. A second female soldier ran next to the woman who had incapacitated Brendant and handed her a dirty rag. The armored guard cleaned what remained of the paralytic from her metallic glove.

"Shoot them!" Fralt yelled as he advanced on the two soldiers.

"Wait!" Gavin protested, still trying to stand. "She saved me."

"We can't risk their betrayal of the Matriarch being a possible ruse," Fralt reasoned. "Shoot them now!"

"She saved me!" Gavin reiterated.

"And I saw them attacking some of the other Hierarchy guards," an Athelbrath affirmed.

"Let them speak!" another soldier shouted.

Raymond ran over and grabbed Gavin by the shoulder, helping him off the ground. Standing shakily, Gavin looked at the two women with a grateful nod. It became clear to him who wore at least one of the helmets.

"You know," he said between tired breaths. "You could have done that sooner. Or at least called in advance so I wouldn't have tried to suck you into space."

The taller of the two soldiers reached up and pressed the release on the side of her helmet. Mist sprayed from the seams with a hiss. Zaire pulled the mask from her head, thick hair tumbling out in tiny ringlets.

"It is hard to send a message when you are avoiding detection on a Matriarchal vessel," she said with a hint of humor.

"Son of a bitch," Raymond gasped.

"Galta'arok..." Fralt stuttered. He lunged forward, cane swinging overhead. "The Matriarch that took my Aktelothing knee!"

Zaire pulled a pistol from her belt and held it to Fralt's forehead. "And I would be more than happy to take your head as well, Fralt Randok of the Randok Clan."

More guns raised, the sound of clicking hammers and fore stocks chorusing Gavin's breathing.

"Will everybody just calm down for a second," Gavin said, steadying himself on his wobbly left leg. He looked to the second masked woman, hoping Isla's face would smile at him from beneath the mask, but knowing by the height and build it had to be Bomb. "How did you guys get here?"

"Abraxas-Mon sent us," Zaire said, stepping toward Gavin. "He was very worried about you after you attacked him. He ordered me to find you and bring you back safe, but Brendant would not allow me to join the search. I fear she has taken control of the Hierarchy. Was she the reason you fled? Did you learn something about Brendant's plan?"

Bomb pulled off her helmet, blond ponytail swishing back and forth. "Why did you leave, Gavin Baller?"

Blood dripped from Gavin's nose. Wiping it away with the back of his hand, he blew out a frustrated breath. "I'm fairly sure Brendant's a part of all this, but she's not in charge. Abraxas-Mon is." Gavin looked over at Fralt, the clan leader's neck tight as a steel cable. "Can we go somewhere and talk this all out?"

"Yes," Zaire agreed. "The paralytic I threw at Brendant had already begun to break down in the air. She will not be unconscious for much longer."

"I'm in charge here!" Fralt seethed. He stepped closer to Zaire, eyes bulging. "I give the orders! I make the plans, not this woman who shot my knee off! I should have my men round up the lot of you and line you against the wall to be shot!"

"Fralt," Gavin said, shaking the man's shoulder. "We're so close to accomplishing our goals. Now's not the time for this."

"It will be soon enough," Fralt replied, teeth clenched like a rabid dog.

Gavin turned toward the clan soldiers. "Alright everybody, great job! Let's take a little bit to figure things out. Get a bite to eat and we'll report back in a little bit. And somebody check on Ugnol and make sure he's okay."

The crowd began to disperse, regaling each other with heroic tales of the fleeting scuffle. Ugnol sat up groggily, touching a swollen eye and bloodied nose. Several Nythensus women walked over and began dragging dead bodies toward one of the hidden pits under the landing bay floor. Gavin didn't want to know what happened to corpses aboard the Gadabout.

He hoped none of them ended up in any of his meals.

"What did you mean when you said Abraxas-Mon is in charge?" Zaire asked as she leaned forward and gave Gavin a hug.

"There's a lot we need to talk about," Gavin replied, smelling her familiar fragrance of lavender and honey.

"It's good to see you, Zaire," Raymond said. He stepped

between Gavin and the former Matriarch and extended his hand in greeting.

"And I never thought I would say this," Zaire said, looking down at the offered appendage. "But it is good to see you as well, old colleague, despite our recent differences." She shook his hand quickly and dropped it like a venomous snake.

"It's been a while since we've worked together," Raymond continued. "Luckily, I don't hold a grudge. Plus, in my defense, I was ordered to do all those things by the Plenipotentiary Council, so I was only doing my duty."

Zaire's eyebrows pinched together. "Even so, you are lucky I am not one to kill unarmed men."

"I will kill an unarmed man, if Zaire wants," Bomb said, stepping closer to Raymond.

Smiling, Raymond looked at Gavin. "I like the blonde. Is she available?"

Gavin clutched his left thigh as a dull ache began to bud like a rotten weed. "Let's go someplace with fewer dead bodies and maybe a chair to sit down."

"That cannot be true, Gavin," Zaire said as she took a bite from an overripe piece of Galbrath fruit.

Shouting intruded through the open window of Gavin's temporary apartment. Two people argued on the street below in a language Gavin didn't understand. The smell of roasted meat wafted in as well, reminding him he needed to go down and ask the vendor for a snack once the conversation ended.

Zaire glanced over as the yelling grew louder. "You must have misinterpreted his meaning," she continued.

Gavin sat back on the dingy couch, massaging his leg. Bomb sat across from him chewing on a piece of dried meat next to Zaire, while Raymond stood in the kitchen trying his best not to touch any of the surfaces for fear of staining his suit. Humidity dampened Gavin's armpits as much as his frustration.

"There was nothing to misinterpret," he said. "He's taken over and he wants me to come at him so he can stop being so bored, I guess."

"Abraxas-Mon asked me personally to come find you," Zaire admitted. "He pleaded with me to bring you back safe and said he understood your jealousy."

Smacking his hand against the cracked coffee table in front of him, Gavin grimaced. "Jealousy. That damn prick."

"It was Brendant who stood in our way at every turn," Zaire said. "She would not allow me to join her and threatened my arrest. If it had not been for Bomb sneaking us inside, I would not have arrived this morning to help you."

"Brendant is lying woman," Bomb said between bites of jerky. "She lies like the worst of men."

"Yeah, she's not the only one," Gavin agreed. He grabbed a bruised fruit from the bowl on the table and took a bite. While flavorful, the texture belied its rotting condition. He chewed, hoping the answer to his next question didn't derail his ability to keep fighting. "How's Isla?"

Zaire's gaze dropped. "When I left two roused-cycles ago, she was in better spirits. Abraxas-Mon has been very kind to her since her transition, doting on her and trying to make her smile. It has been a joy to see, despite my own difficulties with her condition."

"So, he's been flirting with her."

"Do not let your anger cloud your judgement."

"*My* judgement?" Gavin howled. "I'm the only one who knows what's actually going on here, Zaire!"

"Gavin," the former Matriarch began, "the Abraxas-Mon you are telling me about and the one I have known for the past 35 years are not the same person. Granted, I have not always agreed with his methods or how he would sidestep Commonwealth protocol in procuring his victories, but still, I know deep down he is a good man. His kindness toward Isla'a and Seth particularly defend this position."

"And what did he tell you after I left? How did he convince you that I was somehow at fault?"

"He said you had argued with him about Isla and that you were jealous. He said when you stormed out, he pleaded with you to stay but you grew even more angry and attacked him, and then you ran off. He came to see us immediately after and asked if Seth would go and talk to you. It was half a roused-cycle before we realized you had absconded with a ship. I knew something must be wrong, but I did not know exactly what. Once Brendant began impeding my efforts to find you, I hypothesized you had learned something about her and was forced to flee for your life."

Gavin rubbed his temples in an attempt to force away an oncoming headache. "So, he's charmed everyone just like he said he would."

"It is not that I do not believe you, Gavin, it is just that Abraxas-Mon has never shown this side of himself to me or anyone else. Even before I left two days ago, Seth and Ashton had been made his personal counselors; your Silverback Guard ordered to protect the Commonwealth as official Praetorians. His kindness has brought my daughter joy after her resuscitation."

Tears came to Gavin's eyes at the thought of Isla and Seth laughing with Abraxas-Mon at that very moment. "He's the bad guy," Gavin said, muscles tensing like a man about to step onto the gallows "He's the bad guy; you have to believe me."

"I believe," Bomb said flatly.

"You do?" Gavin asked, wiping at his tears.

"I can tell something not right with Abraxas-Mon" she continued. "He walk and move like hiding secrets. He be good at smiling, but under, I see darkness."

Zaire sat forward, looking closely at Bomb. "Why have you not mentioned this before, Bomb?"

"Because I think it men's way. Men lie and smile to get what they want. But with him, it much worse. Gavin speak true. Only Seth and Dan honest men who love me."

"Dan was an honest man," Zaire agreed.

"And Seth does love you, I'm sure," Gavin replied.

Zaire stood, walking over to the small window. "I do not wish for this to be true."

"Well, it is!" Gavin said, jumping to his feet.

"You do not understand," Zaire continued, eyes glazed like a daydreaming teenager in math class. "Everything has fallen apart. The Asha'andasa have been decimated; the Commonwealth is on the verge of open civil war; my daughter is a Cádavrite. Any one of these things would be enough to break me. Now you say Abraxas-Mon is to blame for it all? It is too much to bear. I have no more tears to shed."

Gavin walked over and embraced Zaire. He squeezed her close and wept for them both. The moment lingered, allowing each to mourn in their own way.

"Can I say something?" Raymond asked. "I don't want to interrupt your crying, or anything."

"I hate you, Halford," Gavin said, letting Zaire go.

"Duly noted. Forget for a second that we're going to arrive at Cartoshí the day after tomorrow and we'll find out for sure if Abraxas-Mon is really the devil incarnate; we have the Matriarch of the Dubaku people currently tied up downstairs with Fralt and Ugnol. Gavin, you said back at the hanger that you think she and Abraxas-Mon are sleeping together? We could just ask her."

"She will not falter," Zaire replied with a shake of her head. "We Matriarchs are well trained. She will not give us any information; she will not break.

"I could break her arm and make her talk," Bomb said with a crack of her knuckles.

"No," Zaire said. "I will speak to her, with Gavin. Just the three of us. Perhaps I will be able to glean something from the interaction."

Raymond nodded. "Alright, you guys go down and we'll wait up here."

Gavin opened the door but turned back before leaving. "Bomb: if Raymond here lies to you about anything, you have my permission to break *his* arm. Sound good?"

She smiled broadly. "It does, Gavin Baller."

Zaire and Gavin made their way down the crooked stairs to the graffitied main building lobby where Ugnol and Fralt sat brooding. Brendant, tied to a chair and gagged in the corner, simmered like a pot about to boil over. Glass doors on the far side of the parlor exited onto a busy street full of pedestrians and lumbering vehicles. Two Athelbrath men stood screaming at each other in front of a smoking, six-wheeled automobile, giving Gavin a visual of the argument he'd heard earlier. The muted sounds of the dispute and thoroughfare outside reminded him of Times Square on a Friday night.

"We need to talk to her alone," Gavin said with a nod to Ugnol. "How's your eye doing?"

"She caught me by surprise," the Phylónethese grumbled while wiping at his two noses like an irritated toddler. "It won't happen again. We just got word that the Matriarch's flagship has fled closer to Cartoshí where it looks like a few other ships are gathering. We'll have more details later this evening."

"Thanks, Ugnol," Gavin said. "Go ahead and leave us alone for a bit."

Fralt stood, kicking his chair back against the wall. "I'm not leaving, and I'm no taking orders from either of you. If I must, I'll bring the clan lords down here right now. You're not our boss, Gavin Baller, and I'm not your Galta'arok! I want my reckoning with the high and mighty Zaire for what she did to my leg."

"You should learn forgiveness, Fralt," Zaire said, feet firmly planted like a statue. "You will find it is very freeing."

"I'll show you forgiveness!" Fralt said, stepping forward in a rage.

Gavin sidled in front of the unbalanced man. "You only respond to violence, right?"

"It usually gets the point across, yeah."

Gavin grabbed Fralt's face and smashed the back of his head into the drywall behind the man. Chunks of pink chalk crumbled to the ground along with Fralt's limp body, which smacked the tile without resistance.

Kicking the clan lord to make sure of his insentient state, Gavin dusted his hands and turned to Ugnol. "Would you take him out please and put him somewhere he won't cause us any problems for the next few hours?"

"That I will," Ugnol said with a chuckle. He scooped up the unconscious man and walked through the cracked glass doors toward the street beyond.

Zaire picked Fralt's discarded chair off the floor and sat in front of Brendant. She pulled the gag from the Matriarch's mouth and stared into her eyes.

"If you are expecting a ransom, you will be waiting a very long time," Brendant said evenly. "I have strict orders in place never to pay for a captive no matter how high-ranking."

"Did Abraxas-Mon attack Asha'asethol?" Zaire asked as if the Matriarch hadn't spoken.

Brendant stared forward without responding.

"Are you working with Abraxas-Mon?"

Again, no reply.

"Have you betrayed the Commonwealth and plunged us into war?"

Clacking her tongue against the roof of her mouth, Brendant smiled. "I will not be answering any of your inquiries. You are a disgraced former Matriarch who was cast aside because of your inability to fathom our bright future."

"Bright future?" Zaire smirked. "You see the death of billions as a bright future?"

Gavin leaned against the wall, eyeing the fresh hole in the sheetrock. "When did you and Abraxas-Mon start working together? Was it always his plan to replace Zaire with you? You fell in love with him, of course; if I can make someone like Isla love me, you would be no problem for Abraxas-Mon."

Brendant shook her head. "You are grasping at air, clone."

"Really?" Gavin breathed. "You'll keep his secrets while he trades you in for a younger model? You're about to join the Ex-Girlfriend Club."

Pursing her lips, Brendant's eyes glanced at Gavin.

"What, you don't know?" Gavin continued. "He's currently putting the moves on my girlfriend just so he can get a rise out of me. Did he tell you how he wants us to face each other in battle and how the only way I'll be ready is if he takes everything from me? He's going to seduce the woman I love and marry her just to piss me off."

Brendant blinked, eyes looking left than right.

Without another question, Zaire balled her fist and punched Brendant with enough force to pitch the Matriarch back against the wall. Left hand, then right, each came down with crushing force and pulled away spattered in blood.

"Zaire!" Gavin shouted, wrenching his mentor away from her bound target. Struggling, Zaire eventually pushed away and paced to the far side of the lobby. Gavin reached over and pulled Brendant's chair back onto its four legs. "What are you doing?! She's tied up."

Brendant spit blood onto the floor, lip swelling like a Hollywood starlet with too much collagen.

"You are telling the truth," Zaire said finally, breathing raggedly while pressing her hands against a support pillar covered in spray paint and clan symbols.

"I know! You can *see* that she's tied up."

"About Abraxas-Mon," Zaire amended. "I could see it in her eyes when you mentioned Isla'a. It is all true. The man who was supposed to become a light for the entire galaxy has become nothing more than another tyrant."

"He is so much more than that," Brendant coughed.

Gavin kicked a metal can littering the floor and pointed at the restrained Matriarch. "Shut up, lady, or I'll let her at you again."

"Everything has crumbled." Zaire turned, tears running down her cheeks. "I have pledged my entire existence to lies and shadows."

Trying to think of what Zaire would say if their roles were reversed, Gavin felt an impression he couldn't deny. "At least now you know," he said softly. "It's better to know the lie than to keep living it. Remember back on Earth when you told me I was going to have to choose whether I saw myself as just a copy of Abraxas-Mon or as something more? Now it's your turn. Are you the sum of all of these lies, or are you something more than that? It's time for all of us to let go of our fear."

Zaire touched a tear rolling to her chin and rubbed the saline between her finger and thumb as if crushing the emotion it represented. She turned toward Brendant, still bleeding in the corner. "Brendant of the Ooglak family, I hereby strip you of your rank and title."

"You have no authority to do so!" Brendant countered.

"I have every right!" Zaire screamed.

Her rage sent cold tremors up Gavin's spine. He had seen Zaire angry; he had seen her disappointed, he had seen her annoyed many times, but he had never seen her enraged. Eyes bulging, fists clenched, Zaire looked ready to rip off Brendant's head and use it as a soccer ball.

Stomping forward, Zaire continued. "You have betrayed the Commonwealth! You have profited from war and placed your own power above others." Zaire's breathing slowly came back under control. "Your title as Matriarch is now revoked and being reclaimed by its rightful holder: myself."

"The Hierarchy will never ratify your claim," Brendant protested.

"There is no Hierarchy anymore," Zaire said. "The Hierarchy will be torn down and left to rot. Their power has corrupted them. I see that now. After all of this is done, it will be laid to waste."

"After what is done?" Gavin asked.

"After you kick Abraxas-Mon's ass," Zaire said with a nod.

Gavin grinned and kicked Brendant's chair leg. "Now *that's* what I wanted to hear! I knew you could swear given the right circumstances."

CHAPTER 12

CALLING ALL MERCENARIES

"To all beings loyal to the Commonwealth and the glory of the Asha'andasa, this message is for you!" Zaire's voice echoed through the speakers hanging along the buildings in the Gadabout square. She wore official matriarch robes, or as official as could be procured on the derelict space station and seemed once again the pinnacle of grace and wisdom. Several thousand Luminaries swirled around her like tiny cameras, sending her image to anyone within broadcast distance: including the capital planet Cartoshí, now less than six hours away.

Each of the eleven clan lords, including a very pissed-off Fralt Randok, stood by her side, ringed in soldiers, legionnaires, civilians, and even an Athelbrath man trying to sell t-shirts. Cold air bit at Gavin's bare hands as he blew a cloud of steam from between his lips. Bomb, wrapped in a hairy Grothloth pelt blanket, shivered in the perpetual wintery conditions in the square. Humidity and uncomfortable heat had never bothered her, but obviously her time in the climate-controlled Gadabout zoo had not prepared her for the wet cold.

Despite the frigid temperatures, Gavin beamed at Zaire, hoping the transmission would reach the ears of Isla, Seth, Ashton, and anyone else who needed to know the truth.

"I am Zaire, rightful Matriarch of the Dubaku, member of the Hierarchy, and delegate to the Asha'andasa." Her voice rose and fell in perfect intervals like a seasoned orator delivering a speech that would be studied for centuries by high school students. "I have reclaimed my station and title after discovering a conspiracy in the Hierarchy that has bred dissent and war. Abraxas-Mon has attacked the holy planet Asha'asethol and left it in ruins, including the holy temple of Othpethoth. He is currently leading both the Hierarchy and the Rebirth Militia in hopes of plunging the Commonwealth into civil war.

"For those of you in the sound of my voice, know that I speak the truth. If you have a difficult time accepting my words, I advise you to look closely at your leaders and their intent. I am confident you will discover the cracks in their narratives. Once you do, I admonish you to join us in standing against the oppressors who wish to rule over us. At this moment I am leading — along with Gavin Baller, the hero of the battle of Kr'thotok — a military force against Abraxas-Mon. The Gadabout clan leaders have thrown their support behind the endeavor as well. Join us now that we may end this shadow tyranny threatening to destroy our peace and enslave our children. I am Zaire, and I pray you will heed my call."

The Luminaries quickly dispersed, leaving Zaire alone before the gathered throng. A hesitant cheer rumpled through the square; nowhere near as resonant as Gavin would have hoped. Enthusiastic volunteers wouldn't likely be found on the Gadabout under the best of circumstances, let alone for a potential battle. At least the people hadn't revolted or petitioned the clan leaders to turn tail and run.

"Stirring speech, Matriarch," the old and wrinkled Pleash

said as she walked over to Zaire while petting her furry red racoon. "While I feel your cause is just, I must admit I don't believe many will join you in fighting Abraxas-Mon."

Zaire leaned over and stroked the strange animal in Pleash's arms. "It does not matter, Pleash Athro'ok of the Athro'ok Clan. The correct people will hear and understand what I had to say. And if our designs work, there will be no pitched battle at all, and hopefully as few casualties as we can manage."

"That's what we're shooting for," Gavin said.

"Hopefully, you survive to spend some private time with me, virile profligate," Pleash replied with a lick of her lips.

Gavin shuddered.

"Can we go to warm, please?" Bomb asked, teeth chattering as she nudged close to Gavin.

"Yeah," he replied, pointing toward a column of steam rising from a grate on the ground nearby. "Stand over there and you'll feel the heat from the interior exhausts. That will warm you up."

Bomb smiled with a nod and jogged over to the promise of warmth.

A cane clacked against the cold ground as Fralt approached, followed by seven strong and tattooed bodyguards. He passed Zaire with an angry side glance, stopping in front of Gavin, chest out like a peacock.

"Once all of this is said and done," Fralt began, "you're gonna pay what you owe me, Baller."

"You'll get the Citadel, as promised," Gavin assured. "Just make sure all of the ships have left the hangers as agreed."

"You're going to pay with more than the Citadel," Fralt threatened, massaging the back of his head.

"Look, Fralt, you want to end up in the infirmary next to your son, I'll take your other kneecap and make it happen," Gavin said, moving within inches of Fralt's face. "Right now, you're a cog.

Don't step out of line, otherwise I'll respond from angles you don't yet know exist. I'll have your own guards kill you and they won't even realize they're doing it. You get me?"

Fralt's eyes blazed with impotent fury. He turned and stomped away, bodyguards scowling at Gavin before following their leader.

"You have become very skilled at issuing threats, I see," Zaire said, standing next to Gavin.

"I was always good at threats," he agreed. "Being an actor helps with that. The difference now is that I find them to be less 'threats' and more 'promises.'"

Zaire nodded in understanding. "So much has changed since we first met. If you had told me such things would transpire that would shake my faith and turn you into a menacing warrior, I would not have believed."

"War will do that to people, I guess," Gavin said.

Kicking at a tuft of yellow grass growing between a crack in the sidewalk, Zaire blew out a nervous breath. "Are you confident in our plan? Perhaps we should wait and look at other options."

"No," Gavin disagreed. "We have to hit him now when he thinks I'm not experienced enough to stand against him. He's going to underestimate me."

"Perhaps you are not experienced enough and will be playing into his hands. Have you thought about that?"

"He wants a glorious war," Gavin said, blowing warm air between the palms of his hands. "He doesn't want to beat me; he wants us to stand face to face and kill each other. As sad as it sounds, I'm starting to understand him a little bit. He's going to be taken off-guard."

"A lot of innocents will potentially die if things do not go exactly as planned," Zaire cautioned. "There are many moving parts. If even one falls through, we will have much to answer for."

Gavin put his hand on Zaire's shoulder, giving *her* courage for once. "There is no perfect solution, Zaire. We need to know where our friends stand and take down Abraxas-Mon and the Hierarchy quickly and definitively. Our strategy is solid. Trust it."

"Gavin!" Ugnol shouted, pushing his way through the milling crowd. "Raymond Halford wishes to speak with you back at the Veredok. He has made contact with members of the Cádavrite Guild. I brought a Slaver Transport to take us there now."

"Would you like me to join you?" Zaire asked.

Shaking his head, Gavin waved to Ugnol to let him know he understood. "No, I'll be fine. The Veredok is only a ten-minute walk to the main elevator that can take us to the forward bridge. I'll meet you there in about an hour; sound good?"

"I will be there," Zaire confirmed.

Gavin followed Ugnol out of the square toward the main boulevard running through that section of the Gadabout. Wheeled vehicles blew smoke from pipes on their roofs like steampunk-inspired automobiles, while gravity-defying motorcycles zoomed past. A mech-unit, not unlike what Gavin had seen used by the Rebirth Militia, sat parked along the gutter next to the plaza. Four sets of spider-like legs reached from the asphalt toward an extended cab, about the size of a taxi, eight feet above the ground. A Nythensus driver nodded at Ugnol from the open-air cockpit.

"This is Frank," Ugnol said, stepping up on one of the legs and grabbing the transport door.

"Frank?" Gavin asked with a snicker.

Ugnol looked down at him and blinked. "Yeah, Frank. What's wrong with that?"

"Nothing at all. It's just nice to see some names transcend planetary boundaries."

Pushing off from the spider legs, Gavin climbed into the strange arachnid-taxi and sat next to Ugnol. The cab lurched forward, climbing over other vehicles as it entered the thoroughfare and set off at a surprisingly fast pace toward the Veredok. Gavin clutched handholds on either side of him as the space-carriage rocked back and forth, weaving through traffic while ducking below cables strung between buildings.

"Did Raymond say whether he was able to convince anyone to help?" Gavin asked as a bat-like creature dove through the air and almost landed on his head.

"All he told me was that you'd want to know what they said," Ugnol answered.

Gavin sat quietly after that, enjoying his trip through the Gadabout. Most of the areas he'd explored offered little in the way of memorable aspects, but here near the main plaza, at least things seemed more colorful and vibrant. Advertising banners hung from the ceiling high above, changing color and images like billboards on the Las Vegas Strip. Bubbles of gravity danced overhead filled with warriors sparring with swords or families laughing and playing.

Of all the places Gavin had visited so far during his journey through the stars, the Gadabout reflected humanity the most accurately. That fact didn't make him feel particularly good about his species, but still, the realization comforted him somewhat as he looked forward to the coming engagement with Abraxas-Mon.

After ten minutes, the taxi entered a long tunnel that smelled like a recently flushed toilet and emerged in the familiar rundown neighborhood controlled by Fralt Randok. The circular Veredok building came into view after another few minutes.

"Have Frank wait here so he can take us to the elevators on the far side of the neighborhood," Gavin said as the taxi lumbered to a stop in front of the same guards Gavin had dealt with less than a week earlier. This time, the men waved him by as Gavin climbed down from his ride and sauntered into the building toward Raymond's usual spot in the back room. Dancers called out Gavin's name and shook their butts in his direction. He kept his eyes locked on the purple curtains, feet never hesitating.

Pushing the drapes aside, he walked into the VIP area. Earth music played through the speakers much like when Gavin had first entered the room after fighting Cass Randok. Cat Steven's *Fathers and Sons* competed with the more raucous tune beating in from the club.

"Did you bring your entire collection of music with you into space?" Gavin asked as he saw Raymond standing at a table, looking at a collection of Luminaries shaped like the Statue of Liberty.

"I did," Raymond said, erasing the statue with a wave of his hand through the Speculates. "I took all my cassette tapes with me the first time I left in the mid 1980's. Every time I go back, I add to it."

"You got any Counting Crows in that collection? I would love to hear something from their *Films About Ghosts* album."

"Sorry. I was never much of a Counting Crows fan."

"Why were you looking at an image of the Statue of Liberty?" Gavin asked, pointing to the Luminaries as they swayed back and forth like slow dancing lightening bugs.

Raymond smiled through a look of sadness. "I've had a lot of time to think since arriving on the Gadabout, Gavin. For decades, I've kind of done my thing and gotten power and influence in payment. Losing all of that pretty much overnight has made me a bit nostalgic, that's all."

"What did your contacts at the Cádavrite Guild have to say?"

"They said that they knew about the army-building but didn't feel it was their place to make waves," Raymond said. He reached down to a nearby table and poured brown liquid from a corkscrew-shaped bottle into a shot glass. "You've met enough Cádavrite to know how they are. Fortunately, they did say that a lot of the soldiers are pretty disgruntled to say the least, and that if you really do plan to face Abraxas-Mon, they will send out a command code allowing soldiers and servants alike to disrupt things as they see fit. I doubt we'll have many that will do anything, but even a handful could cause a lot of problems for the opposition."

"That's good to hear," Gavin said. "Are there any near Abraxas-Mon?"

"It looks like the Big Guy is on his personal warship, Bolta'atrox; the Serrated Cleaver."

Gavin blew out a mocking breath. "I would have called it, 'Blood Dawn Death-by-Axe' but that's just me."

Raymond smirked. "Look, Gavin, I know it's going to look like we have a lot of ships and soldiers, but we don't. If Abraxas-Mon calls your bluff that's going to be it; we're all dead. You have doubts about any of this?"

"None at all," Gavin said. "Since I first took off after talking to Abraxas-Mon, everything has seemed so clear to me. There won't be a full-fledged battle. He's not going to see this coming."

"The classic Baller overconfidence."

"Which Abraxas-Mon shares," Gavin informed. "Now, are there any Cádavrite on his ship or not?"

"There are," Raymond confirmed. "All of which I sent messages asking for their help along with the timetable you gave me."

"Any word from Rolatok?" Gavin asked.

"I found his personal Thought-Mech code through the Cádavrite Guild and sent him your message for the Silverback Guard, as well as about relaying evacuation orders for the Capitol City, but I won't know whether he received the message or not until after everything is over. Why do you want the city to think they're going to be bombed if you're not planning on an attack?"

Gavin held his hand out, calling the Luminaries toward him. They churned on air vent drafts and formed an image of the Cartoshí Citadel and surrounding city.

"Because something like 12 million people live there in

Mantatol surrounding the tower, and whether things go according to plan or not, I want as few civilians as possible in the crossfire. Plus, it will add a level of disruption that will work to our advantage."

"I feel like you're not telling me everything."

"That's because I'm not."

Raymond's lips pulled up slightly. "Still don't trust me?"

"I know you have plans already in place for how you can survive this whole thing. You're every bit as self-interested as I used to be, so no, I don't trust you."

"And yet, you tell me to trust me," Raymond disputed.

Blowing the Luminaries like dandelion flush, Gavin focused his thoughts until the tiny glow bugs reformed into Isla and Seth's faces.

"You can trust the fact that I'm willing to put my own life on the line here and that I want as few others hurt or killed as possible, and that includes you."

"I'll accept that."

Fathers and Sons ended, giving way to a lonely acoustic guitar solo. A man's voice quickly followed, singing about packing his bags and standing outside doors.

"Is that John Denver's *Leaving on a Jet Plane*?" Gavin asked.

"You have a good ear," Raymond said. "I was surprised you caught that Linda Ronstadt was singing *Feels Like Home* when you first found me on the Gadabout."

Gavin listened closely to the lyrics, feeling a sense of loss he couldn't explain. "My dad loved this song. He'd listen to it after my mom died, but even before that, I always felt it was just such a sad song; like the guy leaving was never really going to come back."

"I don't think he ever did," Raymond agreed. "It's kind of ironic that John Denver ended up dying in a plane crash. Songs like this remind you of what you give up in life, and that coming back is never guaranteed."

"I'm intrigued by your taste in music," Gavin said as a wave of sadness overcame him. "If we both survive the next few hours, we should sit down and maybe go through some songs and talk."

Raymond smiled and looked down at the floor. "Gavin, we're about to challenge Abraxas-Mon with only a handful of Cádavrites who may or may not help us, and a few Gadabout clan leaders who are just waiting to stab us in the back. There aren't going to be any winners in all this. Best case scenario, you take down Abraxas-Mon and things get worse than they are now. You won't be seen as a hero by the people of the Commonwealth. They don't even understand what's really going on. Worst case scenario, neither of us survives the next few hours. You've got to be smart enough to see which of those eventualities is more likely. We're both dead men."

The song ended, leaving the two erstwhile adversaries standing in silence. The cold of space seemed closer than it ever had since Gavin left Earth.

"Maybe the guy in *Leaving on a Jet Plane* did come back," he said finally.

"Maybe," Raymond replied.

The main Gadabout command bridge looked to Gavin like a cross between an aircraft carrier he had toured once while preparing for a movie role, and an abandoned *Arby's*. Dust gathered on every surface, strange balls of hair rolling around with the slightest air current. Only one of the captain's chairs appeared to have been recently used, with handprints swirling around in the grit on the armrests. Every time Gavin took a step, his boots squelched along the floor as if syrup covered the ground. The old bird needed a cleaning crew decked out in hazmat suits.

Ugnol had told him that this primary control hub had been the original Gadabout ship; all the other sections of the station being added to it over the past two centuries like houses in a slum.

Glass windows looked out on Cartoshí, now close enough to touch. Zaire stood gazing at the planet; lips moving silently as if in prayer. The citadel poked through the atmosphere just over her right shoulder, framed by massive sections of the Gadabout's jagged hull. Through the clutter, Gavin made out a fleet of 1,268 spacecraft floating between him and the planet. An enormous ship even bigger than the Silver Hammer led the charge; Abraxas-Mon's command vessel, the unironically-named Serrated Cleaver.

"I brought the Speculates," Ugnol said, lumbering onto the bridge holding a metal box a foot square, gilded in gold tree limbs and blossoming flowers. "These were stolen from a Hierarchy yacht last Festival Season. Pleash Athro'ok has been using them for her personal communications and donated them to our cause."

"We better wash our hands after we use them," Gavin said.

Zaire wiped her finger along one of the computer consoles and grimaced. "Why could we not use another, more fully functional section of the Gadabout?"

"Because maybe you need to get your hands dirty, Matriarch," Fralt said as he pushed Brendant into the room. The Hierarchy official, hands tied behind her back, stepped forward gracefully despite the clan leader's harsh shoving.

"Thank you, Fralt," Gavin said. "Now you're sure this command deck will dislodge and take us out safely?"

Fralt spat on the floor and licked his purple tooth. "You nervous?"

"Just remember to have all the ships in position for my broadcast," Gavin said. "As long as we have Brendant, Abraxas-Mon won't fire on us. If he killed the Matriarchs together on the same ship, he'd lose too much support. He still needs the powerful families by his side to keep the common people in check. It's standard tyrant stuff."

"I'll remember that when I'm sitting in my citadel," Fralt

replied.

Gavin chuckled. "I have a feeling you're going to be fighting with a lot of other clan leaders for that honor."

"Don't worry," Fralt said. "I can handle myself. Just keep up your end of the bargain."

"I will."

Bomb came up behind the clan lord and nodded to Gavin. "Fighters are ready in hangar," she said. "I choose many good servants for second wave."

"Thanks Bomb. And Fralt; I feel like we're going to take Abraxas-Mon by surprise. Be happy."

Fralt nodded and stepped out, leaving Gavin, Zaire, Bomb, Ugnol and Brendant on the antique command bridge. The door folded shut behind him.

Bomb curled her lips in disgust. "He is walking-liar."

"Walking-liar?" Gavin asked.

"Seth say men who never stop lying are walking-liars." Bomb sat down in one of the seats behind Gavin and threw her leg over the armrest.

Gavin's lips pulled to the left. "That sounds about right."

"You realize Fralt, and the other clan heads will betray us at the first sign of our defeat?" Zaire asked. "Bomb is right to show concern."

"That's why we're not going to get defeated," Gavin grinned. "Plus, they're going to be picking up pieces instead of prizes after all this. Fralt Randok won't be the only pissed of clan lord. We can handle it. You know how to fly this thing?"

"I do," Zaire said, leaning over a control panel.

"Whatever you have planned, it will not work," Brendant said, staring forward toward the fleet now uncomfortably close. "Abraxas-Mon will see every move you make before it happens."

"That's what I'm counting on, sweetie," Gavin said. "Take us out, my Matriarch."

"That I will, Mr. Baller," Zaire answered.

A tremor rumbled through the room, dust dancing across every surface. Gavin planted his feet, feeling the vibrations in his molars. Metal rubbed on metal as the command module pulled away from the rest of the Gadabout and moved into open space toward the armada. Gravity lessened as they drew into the vacuum but remained powerful enough to keep anyone from floating off the sticky floor.

"Get us ready to broadcast," Gavin said to Ugnol. The Phylónethese bent over and picked up the gold-accented box and placed the container next to Gavin. He pressed the lid with his bulbous index finger, which opened like a flower and released several hundred Luminaries. Billowing and swirling around, the points of light encircled Gavin.

"I have attached the Speculates' signal to my Thought-Mech," Zaire said as she continued piloting their rickety ship toward the Serrated Cleaver.

Details became visible as they approached. Abraxas-Mon's command vessel looked intimidating in the extreme. Unlike the Silver Hammer or other Commonwealth spacecraft which tended to be oval or shaped like insects, the Cleaver took a more triangular shape, like a pyramid lying flat, covered in lighted windows and extended cannons. It tapered toward the back like a long spear tip, the front end coming to a much more flattened prow. The overall dark gray tint made the ship blend in with the starfield behind it and give the illusion of space itself shifting and moving as they drew closer.

"That's a big ship," Ugnol breathed.

"Keep it together," Gavin said. "We ready to broadcast?"

"We are," Zaire confirmed. "We should reach all the ships in the vicinity, as well as anyone else within range. As soon as---"

A high-pitched screech cut off Zaire's sentence and made

Gavin jump in surprise. The Luminaries spasmed like startled flies and danced around frantically in an agitated mass. Swiftly they swarmed away from Gavin and pulled together into a single shape.

"What's going on?" Gavin asked as the Speculates formed into a man's head. "What the hell's happening?!"

"You are being outmatched," Brendant said, smiling for the first time since Gavin had met her. He didn't find her grin to be appealing.

Before details could form on the man's visage, Gavin knew who he would see in the Luminaries' holographic depiction.

"Gavin, this needs to stop now," Abraxas-Mon said, voice booming through some hidden sound system. A five-foot tall face looked down on Gavin, worry and care expertly written across every line and tug of the cheeks. "I don't know why you've arrived here with a war armada, or what I did to offend you, but this has to stop."

"You don't have to pretend anymore, Abraxas-Mon," Gavin responded. "We already told everyone about your attack on the Perennials and how you've taken over. Feel free to drop the act."

Abraxas-Mon's head lowered, eyes looking at the ground. He shook his head. "Gavin, please, just come on board my ship and let's talk about this. There is no need for anyone to get hurt. I received word from the surface that you threatened to bomb the city of Mantatol? You've started a needless evacuation and panic, and for what? Did you really think you would get far enough to bomb the Citadel? That tower has stood for a thousand years and will stand for a thousand more. Just to let you know, there are going to be 12 million pissed off people when they find out you had them abandon the Citadel and their homes based off an empty threat. And I don't know how you brought Zaire into this madness along with the entire Gadabout, but even so, there will be no battle today. If you want to fire on me then go ahead, but I will not respond with violence unless you turn your weapons on Cartoshí itself."

"The Gadabout is ten times as big as your warship and built

to be an interstellar predator," Gavin informed, keeping his voice even. "It would take you a week to get through its defenses."

"Yes, the Gadabout is feared throughout the Commonwealth," Abraxas-Mon agreed. "But if you wanted to get people to join your cause against me you probably shouldn't have thrown your good name behind a collection of thieves and rapists."

"You're going to show your true colors one way or another," Gavin said, walking over to Brendant. "We have your girlfriend here with us and she's corroborated everything we've said about you."

The glowing head shifted, looking sadly at Brendant. "Matriarch, I am so sorry you were pulled into this. I will do whatever I can to make it up to you."

"It was not your fault, great Abraxas-Mon," Brendant said.

"Oh, for crying out loud!" Gavin yelled. "I don't want to fight, but the people need to see you for what you really are. Ugnol? Order the Gadabout ships into position."

"Yes sir," Ugnol said, touching the Thought-Mech bracelet on his wrist. Instantly a dozen Gadabout cruisers moved past their vessel on an intercept course with the Cleaver.

"I'm sorry, Gavin," Abraxas-Mon replied. "I didn't want to have to do this, but you leave me no choice."

Before the warlord had finished the sentence, the Gadabout ships turned and encircled the command pod like hunting dogs on a wounded game bird. Through the glass, Gavin watched 13 spacecraft of varying shapes and sizes move in for checkmate.

Gavin turned toward Ugnol. "What are they doing?"

"I don't know!"

"Gavin," Abraxas-Mon continued. "I was contacted three days ago by Fralt Randok and two of the other clan leaders on the Gadabout. Did you seriously promise to give them the Citadel on Cartoshí and the authority that came with it just to get them to fight me? You can't just give that stuff away. Now, I'll admit I had to make a deal with them in return for their promise to not fight today, but it was a small personal price to ensure lives weren't lost in your needless bravado."

"What about the Cádavrite army?!" Gavin shouted. "You're killing people and turning them into your own soldiers. The Gadabout hates that!"

The holographic head nodded. "Yes, rogue members of the Hierarchy were indeed making a Cádavrite army illegally and against all moral judgement, but as soon as I found out what was happening, I shut that plant down. You can ask Isla'a. She led our forces into the factory and destroyed everything. We are currently trying to find all the soldiers so they may be liberated."

Gavin glanced over at Zaire who watched the exchange intently. She nodded her head as if giving Gavin permission to continue.

"You've thought of everything, haven't you?" he asked. "You've pulled the wool over everyone's eyes."

"I have no desire to destroy you, Gavin," Abraxas-Mon warned. "But if you proceed to attack anyone in the Commonwealth, I will blow up that ship despite Matriarch Brendant's presence onboard."

"I will consider my death an honor," Brendant said with a nod.

"Surrender now, Gavin, otherwise you will get innocent people killed. If you won't listen to me, listen to him."

The Luminaries whirled as if Abraxas-Mon had stepped away, restructuring into the face of Seth Kemp. Gavin's neck tightened, knowing Seth likely believed every word spewing from Abraxas-Mon's mouth.

"Hey Gavin," Seth said, eyes sad despite the forced smile on his holographic face. "What are you doing, man?"

"Seth, you need to listen!" Gavin urged. He stepped closer to the Luminaries as if he could bridge the space between the two ships and touch his friend. "It's all a lie, okay? You have to believe me! He's the bad guy here, Seth. He's Lex Luthor!"

"Gavin, please, just give up and let's talk face to face, okay? This doesn't need to continue. Do it for me. Better yet, do it for Isla."

Looking down at his boots, Gavin nodded his head. With the Gadabout betrayal there would be no point in continuing. If he pushed things too far, Abraxas-Mon would reluctantly destroy their ship to save face in front of everyone.

Gavin had to admit that the warlord earned an Oscar statue for his performance today…and a Golden globe, and an Emmy. Hell, Gavin would give him a vote for a stupid *People's Choice Award*. No one suspected a thing; not Seth, not the people in the Commonwealth, not even Zaire originally. Would Isla be different? Would Isla see through the charade? Gavin hoped she would. He had to find out. Above all things he had to see Isla and learn for himself if Abraxas-Mon had truly won.

He looked back up into the hopeful eyes of his best friend's holographic image. "Fine," Gavin said finally. "We surrender."

CHAPTER 13

FIRE FROM HEAVEN

Handcuffed and heavily guarded, Gavin, Zaire, Bomb and Ugnol ambled down a long corridor toward the unknown. Each of the 14 soldiers surrounding the prisoners wore the same full-body blue uniforms, yellow capes, and helmets used by Brendant's guards. They walked in perfect unison, polished footwear thumping the glistening metal floor like goose-stepping Nazis through Nuremberg. Half of them were obviously human under their armor, while the other half were stocky Phylónethese; Abraxas-Mon's favored warriors.

Gavin's wrists chaffed against his tight restraints. Cold steel scraped his skin; heavy cuffs completely encasing his hands in front of him.

Nothing in Abraxas-Mon's ship felt organic. Gavin had come to expect certain comforting aspects of Commonwealth vessels that didn't seem to exist here. Where Mordecai and the Silver Hammer had felt grown and natural, exuding peace, comfort, and pleasant odors, this one seemed manufactured like any boat on Earth. Plastic smells filled the hall, while the air felt sanitary and lifeless.

The contrast made Gavin realize how much patience existed behind everything the Perennials had built. They never rushed or panicked, and their ships and cities demonstrated that fact. Even Phrensha'al in his uptight and Draconian rule following always allowed space to flow and never permitted time to hurry him from his tea or a pleasant conversation.

Waiting for a spaceship to grow and mature over centuries forced Commonwealth citizens to take a longer view of existence stretching far beyond their own lifespan. Gavin had felt it. Slowly his perspective had changed as well, and he appreciated the feeling of being a part of something that would live on for millennia.

Now walking through a factory-made vessel, he felt cold and empty, as if he sailed through space in a dead body whose spirit had long since fled to some fathomless heaven.

Here on the hysterically named 'Serrated Cleaver,' patience didn't exist. Gavin expected a producer to storm out of one of the rooms they passed and start barking about how they only had 20 minutes to film a scene because after that, the sun wouldn't be in the right spot and they'd have to scrap the day. Stress dripped from every surface. The air itself seemed fidgety as they marched toward the end of the hall and a towering door 15 feet tall.

Sliding open as if on hydraulics, the entrance led to a large command center with floor-to-ceiling windows looking out on the planet below. Soldiers and support staff manned computer consoles that looked every bit as manufactured as the rest of the ship. *Star Trek* sprang to Gavin's mind, if *Star Trek* had taken place on a warship with no appealing design elements whatsoever.

Abraxas-Mon stood on the far side of the room on an elevated platform next to thirty-foot tall windows. His smiling reflection looked back at Gavin while Isla and Seth stood by his side, concern evident on their faces. Brendant walked over and joined them, though she looked more amused than anything.

Gavin hadn't seen Isla or Seth in person since before his original conversation with Abraxas-Mon. Both of his loved ones seemed healthy and strong. Seth, dressed in an official dark blue uniform, exuded authoritative compassion, like a general who would save you instead of destroying you. Glancing from Gavin to Bomb, the lines on Seth's forehead deepening as he saw their shiny iron restraints.

Isla wore a pale cream uniform with a blue stripe down the right shoulder not unlike what she had been wearing the first time Gavin had ever seen her. The stripe had been red at that first meeting, and she had worn a full-face helmet, but the memories flooded his mind, nonetheless. Her black hair, pulled back into a bun on the top of her head, stood out against the grayish tint of her brown skin. Cádavrite eyes in all their alabaster glory, looked down on Gavin with a mixture of confusion and pity.

"I'm glad you chose to surrender," Abraxas-Mon said, turning toward his shackled guests. "I'm surprised you got the Gadabout involved. Normally, they won't do anything unless there's already money on the table. The promise of giving them the Citadel was shrewd, but undeliverable."

"Can we take off their cuffs?" Seth asked. "At least Bombs? She's not a threat."

Abraxas-Mon smiled and nodded, motioning for one of his guards to step forward. The soldier approached and placed a yellow crystal into a slot on the left side of Bomb's manacles. A hiss of air shot out from a latch on the bottom and the guard pulled the chrome shackles off the blonde woman's hands. She rubbed her wrists and looked longingly at Seth.

"Don't worry," Abraxas-Mon said to Seth, hand patting the man's shoulder firmly. "She won't be held accountable for Zaire's actions."

"Where are my Silverbacks?" Gavin asked, searching for his

loyal guards and seeing no sign of them on the spacious bridge.

"They are on-duty with the rest of the fleet," Isla answered, looking away from Gavin as if embarrassed.

"Are you okay, Isla?" Gavin asked.

"I am fine, Gavin," she replied, eyes meeting his once more.

"We never had a chance to talk after…" he began before Abraxas-Mon stepped between them.

"I don't understand why you've done any of this, Gavin," the warlord said with a shake of his head. "And Zaire; what could he have said that would bring you to the point of attacking a Commonwealth vessel and putting your family at risk? Ogpog has been beside himself since your broadcast. All of us have."

"Where is the Prelate?" Zaire asked.

"I have returned your husband to the Konti'ikont along with the remaining women you rescued from the Gadabout zoo," Abraxas-Mon said.

"They're safe, Zaire," Seth added.

"How could you have been so deceived, my kind Mala'apand?" the warlord asked.

"I stand by what I said," Zaire answered. "I love you Abraxas-Mon as any mother could love a child. But I fear you have strayed from your chosen path."

Abraxas-Mon stepped down from the command platform and approached them. "Hopefully with time, I can convince you that I'm not your enemy, and I never was. Please, remove their restraints. They are not a danger to me."

"You sure about that?" Gavin asked.

"Positive," Abraxas-Mon smiled.

The same guard that had taken off Bomb's cuffs stepped forward, followed by a second soldier holding an ornate club with four blunt blades on the head. They stood side-by-side ready for a surprise attack. The sentry slowly inserted the crystal into Zaire's restraints, followed by Ugnol's. The Phylónethese rotated his shoulders and growled, forcing the soldier with the club to raise his weapon in response.

Gavin grinned, waiting for his turn, when the guard looked at Abraxas-Mon expectantly.

"Are you sure I should release this prisoner, Exalted One?" the soldier asked, nodding toward Gavin as two Phylónethese soldiers inched closer in response to Ugnol's grumbling.

"I am sure, centurion," Abraxas-Mon answered.

Placing the crystal in its housing, the cuffs released, and Gavin's hands felt cool air again. He rubbed his fingers to help recirculate his blood flow.

A door on the far side of the bridge opened and Ashton ran in, breathing heavily. The blond man charged forward wearing a simple gray shirt with black sleeves and matching pants.

"Why didn't anyone tell me where you guys were going to be? I've been running from one end of this deck to the other trying to find everybody."

"Ashton, it's good to see you," Gavin said with a small wave.

"Gavin! Holy crap, what the hell are you doing, man?"

"Only what's right," Gavin answered.

Ashton turned to Abraxas-Mon; eyes suddenly wide. "They're not going to be executed, are they?"

"Of course not." Abraxas-Mon laughed good-naturedly. "I would never do such a thing, Ashton my friend."

"I think you *should* execute them," Brendant said, still standing on the platform with her superior smirk.

"We will discuss punishments at a later date, Matriarch Brendant," Abraxas-Mon replied.

"I'm so glad you're pals with everybody now," Gavin

murmured.

"Would you rather we be enemies?" Abraxas-Mon asked. "I must say, I am beside myself with confusion regarding you, Gavin. I want us to be brothers, but it seems you're determined to destroy any relationship we could possibly have. It's like your time as a celebrity or whatever you were on Earth has made you incapable of accepting me as your friend and equal."

"What happens now?" Gavin questioned, ignoring his counterpart's statement. "You've convinced everyone I'm crazy. What now?"

"I hope to bring you back to reality. I hope through time and the care of your friends you can rejoin us here. I worry that your time alone in the prison and your shame over what you did to Isla'a have somehow shattered your grasp on reality. You've been through so much in so short a span of time; it's natural to go through psychological breaks like this."

"Gavin," Seth said, moving slowly down the stairs toward his friend. "We have a room for you right across the hall from mine, just like when you lived with us after your mom died. We can get through this together."

Looking at Seth, emotions threatened to overcome Gavin's resolve. His best friend stood there with love and empathy in his eyes, wanting nothing more than to help, never knowing the man he served would destroy them all.

"I'm sorry Seth, I really am," Gavin said, tears coming to his eyes. "I know it's hard to believe, but I'm telling the truth."

Abraxas-Mon looked back at Seth, a pained expression contorting his face. "Give it time, Seth."

Gavin's muscles strained beneath his tight black shirt as he called on all his will to keep from jumping at his double and throttling the man. He needed patience now more than ever. He could see the dominoes falling into place, he just needed to set up a few more.

"Isla, I love you," he said, looking past Abraxas-Mon to the beautiful woman still standing on the raised command dais. "I've loved you from the first moment I saw you; from the first time you looked at me like I was a huge disappointment. I will never stop loving you, even though I'm stupid and thoughtless and I screw up all the time. I love you."

Abraxas-Mon waved his hand to the guards. "Please, take them all to the infirmary and make sure they're comfortable." He stepped in front of Zaire. "Matriarch, can I count on you not to escape and harm any innocents on this vessel?"

"Wait," Isla said, stepping down the stairs to the prisoners' level. "Abraxas-Mon, let me say goodbye, please." She reached over and ran her hand along the warlord's shoulder as she once had to Gavin. Fingers lingering, Gavin could see her affection for the man on muted display.

Abraxas-Mon had done his job well. Perhaps nothing Gavin could've done would have stopped any of this from happening.

He doubted himself for the first time since setting off for the Gadabout.

Isla reached up and touched Gavin's face. "You are going to get through this; you and my mother both. Just know that I forgive you for what you did to me in the Renaissance Plant. I understand your weakness, and I do not fault you for it."

She pulled him into a hug, patting Gavin's back like a treasured friend. No affection, certainly no love, radiated from her body during the embrace. Gavin's stomach dropped slightly. He had gotten the answer he had dreaded from the moment he saw her dead eyes behind the glass of the rebirth chamber. He may have saved her life, but he had doomed their relationship.

"Thank you for the moment," Isla said to Abraxas-Mon, stepping beside him.

Gavin wanted to die. His plans forgotten, hope crushed, he longed to slip into oblivion and see nothing but darkness ever after.

An almost imperceptible movement caught his eye and pulled him from his despair. Isla reached over with the speed of a trained warrior and yanked the club from the soldier's hand. Before anyone could register her action, she swung the weapon directly at Abraxas-Mon's face with enough force to shatter bone.

Reflexes honed on a thousand battlefields, the warlord reached up and caught the blow, halting the bludgeon a mere inch from his face. He closed his eyes and shook his head, holding firm despite Isla's struggling. A smile spread Abraxas-Mon's cheeks, eyebrows pointing downward.

The surrounding soldiers bolted to action, raising their rifles and swords without the need for an order.

"I didn't want this," Abraxas-Mon said through his white teeth. He swung the club to the right, forcing Isla to let go of the bat as she stumbled. The weapon clattered on the floor, discarded by the warlord. "I was this close!" he said, bringing up his finger and thumb together to illustrate the miniscule distance. "I thought I had all of them."

"What's…going on?" Seth stammered.

Abraxas-Mon turned and pointed to Seth. "I had most of them; that's something. But Isla…" he said, grabbing her by the arm and throwing her to the floor. "…just couldn't play along!"

"You son of a bitch!" Gavin yelled, rushing forward. Abraxas-Mon turned and brought up his boot, kicking Gavin in the stomach and sending him tumbling back toward Zaire and Bomb. Ugnol bellowed, ready to rip the smug military leader limb from limb, stopped only by a pistol shoved under his chin by one of the soldiers.

"Gavin!" Isla cried, trying to stand back up.

Brendant walked over and kicked Isla in the thigh, sending her crashing back down.

"I will kill you for that," Zaire said, standing tall and majestic despite the weapons pointing in her face.

"We shall see," Brandant retorted.

Seth ran down from the command platform and dove to Isla's side. "What the hell are you guys doing?!"

Ashton rushed over as well, placing his hand on her wounded leg.

"I hate to break this to you Seth, but Gavin was telling the truth the whole time," Abraxas-Mon said with a laugh. "I had you going, didn't I? When we talked that evening and I cried and you were all like, 'Don't worry, we'll get Gavin back if we work together,' I knew I had you. And Isla'a, let me tell you, your acting matched my own! You almost convinced me. Almost."

"Are you freaking serious?!" Seth yelled. "Gavin?"

"Sorry, buddy," Gavin groaned, still hunched over.

"Bomb?" Seth asked, as if looking for support after finding out Santa Claus never existed.

She shook her head, ponytail swishing like a whip. "He is walking-liar."

"And I'm apparently the biggest dumbass in the world," Seth said, still helping Isla to sit up.

"Don't feel so bad," Abraxas-Mon said, twirling like a madman. "Ashton fell for it too."

The New Zealand native raised his fist and flipped the warlord off with a look of disdain.

Gavin stood back up, rubbing his bruised stomach. "This is between you and me, Abraxas-Dickhead."

"Dickhead?" Abraxas-Mon said. "I hope you have better retorts than that up your sleeve." He strode close to Gavin; hands pressed together as if pleading for mercy. "And I pray...I *pray* you didn't just come here with the Gadabout and think you stood a chance. Please, please, please, please tell me you have something else, because if you don't, I am going to be so disappointed I might just slaughter everyone out there for the fun of it."

"I just needed to know where my friends stood and see if I could sway them back to my side," Gavin said, standing taller. "I figured Isla wouldn't be fooled by you, but I'll agree, she had me going. Excellent work, babe!"

"Can we just kill him and go home?" Isla asked through grit teeth.

"So, you came over here just to check on your friends?" Abraxas-Mon asked. "How sentimental…and stupid."

"No," Gavin said, shaking his head. "'Stupid' was thinking I would be surprised by the Gadabout's betrayal. I've spent the last 17 years working with self-absorbed assholes. You think I wouldn't see that coming? Fralt Randok is a lot of things, but loyal isn't one of them."

"Well played," Abraxas-Mon agreed. "Too bad I can just have you shot right now if I want."

Gavin grinned. "Well, I needed to give some allies a bit of time to get in position too."

He paused dramatically as if waiting for something to happen.

Looking around, Abraxas-Mon bounced on his toes. "Are we waiting for something? Is someone about to make a theatrical entrance?"

"Kind of," Gavin said, eyes looking back and forth. "I thought I had it timed right."

"You'll find when dealing with other people, you always have to be able to adapt," Abraxas-Mon replied. "Things rarely go according to plan unless you're doing it your---"

An explosion rocked the ship, sending a tremor up from the bowls all the way to the command bridge. Gravity throbbed and pushed everyone a few inches off the floor before dropping them again.

Soldiers stumbled and shouted, giving Gavin an opening. He

spun, grabbing a rifle, and turned to fire on the guards closest to Zaire and Ugnol. To his elation, Ugnol already had two sentries in his thick hands, swinging them over his head; while Zaire flipped another combatant over her back and came up firing. Bomb had ripped the helmet off a towering Phylónethese warrior and scratched at the brute's face with merciless abandon.

Chaos erupted as the entire ship shuddered violently. Technicians jumped up from their control panels and shouted. One ran at Seth as he helped Isla to her feet, spinning Gavin's friend around and raising his fist for a punch. Gavin shot the engineer before he could land his blow.

"We need to clear a path to the flight controls," Zaire called to Gavin as she blew a hole in an Athelbrath guard's chest.

Brendant bounded from the elevated control platform and plowed into Zaire from the side. The two women toppled to the ground, rifle skidding away.

"Zaire!" Gavin shouted, raising his gun to shoot Brendant.

"Gavin, watch out!" Isla cried from across the room.

Ducking just in time, Gavin avoided a sword swipe from one of the ceremonial guards. Spinning around, he shot the woman in the hip and backed away as two more blue-clad sentinels approached.

"Gavin Baller is mine!" Abraxas-Mon shouted as he grabbed Bomb's arm and threw her like a ragdoll before she could claw his face.

Gavin fingered the trigger on his rifle, ready to turn Abraxas-Mon's head into nothing more than a pink mist.

The air undulated; gravity spasming once again. This time instead of reasserting itself, the artificial pull dissipated and allowed everyone to float independently like balloons on a breeze.

Abraxas-Mon pushed off from the ground like a superpowered villain and flew at Gavin with a wicked smile. The two men collided in midair and spun around while laser blasts striated the room and exploded against the walls.

"This is more like it!" Abraxas-Mon gloated as he pulled on Gavin's weapon. "Was it Rolatok? Is that who you used to set the explosives?"

"Way worse than that," Gavin grunted, kicking at his attacker.

An angry cry echoed from below as the doors opened and a group of 42 Cádavrite men and women entered wearing white and red military uniforms and large magnetic boots that held them against the flooring. The angry Deadites fired silver rifles, concentrating on the blue and yellow guards as they drifted precariously in the air.

"Death to the tyrant!" they shouted. "To Deadite Hell you'll follow us!"

Several of Abraxas-Mon's sentries tried to swim through the weightless environment to face the new arrivals but found themselves hopelessly outmatched due to their inability to control their movements. More soldiers fell in a barrage of Cádavrite fury. Droplets of blood floated on the air like tufts of cotton in autumn.

Abraxas-Mon let go of the weapon in Gavin's hand and punched him in the face, sending the actor spinning head over heels in the Zero-G atmosphere. He slammed against the glass, losing his grip on the rifle. Abraxas-Mon grabbed one of his soldiers and used the man to thrust forward toward a floating pistol. Grabbing the gun, the warlord twisted and fired on the Cádavrite invaders, hitting six of them in the head with the remaining bullets in the firearm.

More explosions followed, though Gavin could tell whether they came from the outside hull or from within the ship. Looking through the glass, he saw several Gadabout spacecraft and a handful of Commonwealth fighters firing on the Serrated Cleaver.

Gavin could almost make out his Silverback Guard behind the controls of several of the military cruisers.

Thank you, Rolatok, Gavin said to himself. The Cádavrite

soldier had obviously received the message and trusted his commander. If Gavin and his friends could keep things moving inside the ship, and the battle continued in space as well, their plans would be more likely to succeed.

Gravity jerked once more, and Gavin felt himself sliding down the glass toward the battle below. Ugnol landed hard and pushed himself back up to continue his tussle with two Phylónethese soldiers; Bomb bounced with the agility of a tigress and leaped at a guard swinging a sword; Seth and Ashton helped Isla limp over the body of a wounded Cádavrite while pushing off several unarmed bridge techs trying to impede their progress.

Rolling on the ground like a spastic teenager trying to parkour, Gavin scrambled to his feet and ran at Abraxas-Mon, who continued killing Cádavrite with the ease of a man splattering a canvas with red paint.

"Zaire!" Gavin shouted as he ran. "Get to the controls!"

"I am occupied at the moment!" she shouted back as Brendant blocked a right hook and countered Zaire's offensive move with an uppercut.

"I have her," Isla said as she tackled Brendant and threw the pompous Matriarch to the ground.

Gavin blinked in surprise as Isla punched Brendant over and over again, mercilessly turning the woman's face into a slick mass of spaghetti.

"Alright then," he whispered.

Zaire immediately bolted toward one of the flight-control panels. A technician jumped up to stand in her way, finding himself turned around by the expert fighter, face slammed against the glass paneling.

"I am plotting course!" Zaire confirmed as Gavin turned to face Abraxas-Mon.

"Where are you taking us, Gavin?" Abraxas-Mon asked as he

throttled the life from the last remaining Cádavrite. "We going back to Earth? That's a long trip. It will give us time to get to know each other better."

"Not exactly," Gavin said as he charged at the man.

Abraxas-Mon dodged his foe with a smile and swung his arm down on Gavin's shoulder. Using the warlord's momentum, Gavin retaliated with a punishing body blow to the ribs. The two men exchanged hits and blocks as the floor slowly tipped to the left and sent them both faltering toward the windows that now looked directly down on the planet. They tripped and fell before the ship righted itself once more.

Red emergency lights began to flash, filling the bridge with an ominous glow. Alarms sounded, piercing the ears with a squealing that punished the senses.

"Evacuate! Evacuate!" a recorded voice bellowed through the communication system. "Orders have been issued to abandon Bolta'atrox and make your way to designated escape pods."

"Gavin!" Seth shouted as he pushed a fleeing technician aside. "What's happening?"

"Get Ashton and Bomb to the center of the room!" Gavin answered, pushing himself back to his feet as Abraxas-Mon jumped up ready to fight.

Bomb joined Seth and Ashton, ripping through the attacking crewmen like claws against wet paper.

Before Gavin could advance on Abraxas-Mon, one of the Phylónethese soldiers grabbed him from behind and spun him into the air. Reaching back, Gavin plunged his finger into the alien's eye, eliciting a deep scream and spurt of reddish-gray blood.

Gavin dropped back to the ground while the guard raged behind him.

"He's mine!" Abraxas-Mon shouted.

With eyes wide like a wild animal, Abraxas-Mon blitzed,

punching Gavin in the face before the actor could mount a defense. One blow turned into two as Abraxas-Mon pummeled Gavin from his chin to his stomach. Falling back, Gavin did his best to mount a counterattack, but found his feeble attempts laughable at best. He tasted blood, tripping backward, and hitting the floor. Vibrations tingled his fingers as the Serrated Cleaver drew closer to Cartoshi.

Alarm screeching in his ears, Gavin tried to feel the air around him to anticipate Abraxas-Mon's next angle of assault but found himself unable to discern through the pain. Blackness threatened to overcome him when a blurry shape grabbed Abraxas-Mon's arm and stopped his battering.

"You will not touch the man I love again," Isla said as she stabbed Abraxas-Mon in the ribs with one of the dead soldier's six-inch blades.

The warlord backhanded Isla with enough force to send her plummeting to the floor. He pulled out the knife and looked at the crimson-smeared blade. Blood seeped from his wound, but Abraxas-Mon didn't seem to notice or care.

"You think that's the first time I've been stabbed?" he asked, stomping toward Gavin. "I pulled a sword out of my stomach when I was 17! I used it to disembowel the man who had tried to kill me. You're going to have to do better than that."

"Die!" Ugnol shouted as he tossed one of his opponents aside and ran toward Abraxas-Mon.

"Sounds good to me," Abraxas-Mon said as he flipped the knife in his hand and threw it end over end toward the advancing Phylónethese. Before Ugnol could dodge, the blade buried itself between the gray alien's two noses. He stopped in place, arms moving to block the knife in delayed reaction. Tumbling forward, Ugnol hit the ground in a lump of dead muscle and sinew.

Gavin slammed his fist against the floor, spitting blood out of his mouth. He would never get the chance to introduce Ugnol and Brek and see the two Phylónethese jostle for superiority. Someone else had now died trying to protect him.

"They're big and strong, but one well-placed shot will take down a Phylónethese as easily as anything else," Abraxas-Mon chuckled.

A quake ran through every surface on the ship, metal groaning as if under immense strain. The corpse-littered bridge rattled intensely, clouds flying past the windows at terrifying speed.

"We are hitting the atmosphere!" Zaire shouted over the alarm as she fought off three console operators attempting to alter their course.

Pushing himself up once again, Gavin looked at Abraxas-Mon's thoughtful face.

"That's why you wanted the city evacuated," the warlord said with a knowing nod.

Seth ran to Gavin's side along with Bomb and a bleeding Ashton. How the New Zealander had cut his head, Gavin didn't know.

"Are we going to crash?!" Seth asked, shaking Gavin to pull his attention away from Ashton's bloodied forehead.

"Yep," Gavin confirmed, trying to shake the fog from his pummeled brain.

Clouds broke against the window, revealing a vast ocean and an impressive tower rapidly advancing on the horizon.

Abraxas-Mon smiled. "I'm glad this isn't the end for us. I look forward to bashing your brains in using the bricks of my ruined citadel."

"Yes," Isla said as she limped over to Gavin, blood dripping from her mouth. "I look forward to killing you, Abraxas-Mon, at my first opportunity."

"What are they talking about?!" Ashton cried; eyes fixed on the tower now mere seconds away. "We're all going to die!"

A ripple moved through the air like a stone on the surface of a placid pond. Gravity fluctuated and lifted everyone toward the center of the room, forming a translucent film around them as if encased in a giant soap bubble. Zaire kicked against one of the remaining technicians and twirled toward Gavin. Abraxas-Mon hovered twenty feet away, making no move to advance on his enemies.

"Gravity wells have been deployed around the ship, and the call to abandon the vessel has been sent," Zaire informed. "As long as the city has been at least partially evacuated, casualties should be at a minimum."

"Look at you, Zaire," Abraxas-Mon said, grabbing Brendant's unconscious body as it floated toward him. "Still trying to save lives even when you're about to send thousands of soldiers to the hereafter."

"Life is sacred," Zaire snapped. "I believe in sacrifice, and if my life can be traded to save others, I will do so."

Abraxas-Mon smiled and cradled Brendant in his arms. "Keep telling yourself that."

"Isla! Grab my hand!" Gavin said, reaching for her. She strained to bridge the distance between them but found their fingers still eight inches apart. "Everyone huddle together as best you can. The gravity wells should keep us safe, but once power goes out, we're going to drop, so be ready!"

"Who thought this was a good idea?!" Ashton shrieked.

"We're going to survive," Gavin said.

"For a little while, anyway," Abraxas-Mon added.

"Shut up!" Gavin shouted.

The gold marbling of the 30-mile-high tower sparkled through the window. *Four seconds*, Gavin thought.

"Four...three...two..." Abraxas-Mon said, looking at Gavin with an elated grin.

The glass shattered on impact, thick shards flying toward the suspended people before being pushed to the side by the ship's protective singularity. Darkness and smoke blew past them while the sound from the impact pounded Gavin's ears and rattled his bones. Gravity held him in place, shielding him from debris and rock, but did nothing to lessen the sound's onslaught.

"Isla!" he shouted over the deafening roar. He reached for her in the darkness but couldn't find his love.

Unsure if they were still moving forward or if the ship had stopped completely against the Citadel, Gavin focused past the rumble and smell of shattered brick. Heat billowed somewhere behind him, scorching his back as a fire broke out. He imagined for a second what the crash must look like from the city bellow as the Serrated Cleaver slammed into the Citadel base at a thousand miles per hour. He hoped no one on the ground would be killed but knew that expectation to be naïve at best. The evacuation had been ordered. Nothing else could be done at this point.

Almost passing out from the strain, Gavin concentrated on the feeling of weightlessness. Without warning, the gravity bubbles flickered and died, shooting Gavin forward at unknown speed. He had anticipated at least another twenty seconds before their protective bubble burst, and the added variable of their velocity now made his original calculations mute.

They may very well die within a few fractions of a second.

Maybe he'd missed something. Maybe the math was just too complicated to get exactly right. Either way, wind blew through his hair as he rocketed into vapor and shadow.

Gavin hoped they would all survive their impending collision but understood the thought to be nothing more than the musings of an ignorant child.

He hit something hard and stopped thinking about anything.

CHAPTER 14

A KINGDOM OF RUBBLE

A brick clattered loudly next to Gavin's ear while distant sirens carried on the breeze. He sniffed, feeling dust particles tickle his nostrils. Wiggling his fingers, dirt crumbled along the knuckles as if he'd been buried alive. A throbbing pain emanated from the top of his head and tore its way down his back until it met an even worse ache in his left shin.

"What the hell happened?" Gavin groaned. He knew that once the gravity engines on the Cleaver were compromised, all the singularities would fail, but he didn't expect to be thrown with quite as much force as they had been. The thought of getting so far only to have everyone die needlessly made Gavin's heart thump uncomfortably fast.

Coughing, he opened his eyes and rolled over onto his back. Blue sky looked down on him; afternoon sun obscured by brown and gray smoke. Fire burned somewhere; Gavin could smell melting plastic while thunder rolled in the distance.

No, it wasn't thunder; it was pieces of Abraxas-Mon's ship crumbling to the ground.

Gavin stood shakily, feeling his head swim and stomach roil. Leaning on a collection of broken stones, he closed his eyes and breathed deeply until the nausea subsided and the throbbing between his ears dropped from its Death Metal chorus to something a bit more serene, like standard Heavy Metal.

Opening his eyes again, Gavin got his first glimpse of the devastation around him. He stood in a vast field of broken stone and twisted steel. Sections of Abraxas-Mon's warship reached to the sky all around him, belching smoke and screams. In the distance, he could see the ocean frothing like a rabid animal; a broken tower stretching off into the distance like a long peninsula.

They had brought it down.

Judging by his elevation, they had hit the Citadel almost ten thousand feet above the city. Cold winds blew off the coast, bringing a mixture of salty air and thinning oxygen. Their speed coupled with the mass of the ship had been enough to obliterate the ultimate symbol of the Hierarchy's power — and Abraxas-Mon's ego.

Red lights flashed on the roofs of flying spacecraft miles away, circling in dramatic formation as if the Cartoshí police force hesitated to approach the crash site. What was left of the building still seemed to resonate with vibrations from the impact.

"Isla!" Gavin shouted, limping toward the Citadel's edge nearly half a mile away. "Isla! Seth!"

A stiff gust blew his words back at him.

He climbed through the rubble calling his friend's names. Stumbling over a section of wall, Gavin looked down on five dead Athelbrath bodies dressed in Commonwealth military uniforms. Whether they had been in the tower or Abraxas-Mon's ship, he couldn't be sure.

"Isla!" he yelled again.

"Gavin," a voice responded from far away...a man's voice.

"Seth?" Gavin replied, pulse beating quicker at the thought of at least one of his friends being alive.

"I'm over here!" Seth called.

Running as fast as his jumbled brain would allow, Gavin scampered in the direction of the voice. A wave of dizziness forced him to slow, but he wouldn't allow the pain and fog to keep him from his friends. He turned a corner around a contorted steel monolith to see Seth helping lift stones off the chest a trapped Phylónethese. Six other Dubaku men and two Athelbrath lifted along with him.

Bomb ran through a cloud of smoke and waved at Seth. "More, over here!" she cried.

"Are you guys okay?" Gavin asked as he ran beside Seth and helped throw the heavy brick off the Phylónethese man.

"Yeah, we're alright," Seth answered. He dusted his hands and looked over at Bomb. "How many?"

"More," she replied with a shake of her arms.

Seth climbed up a section of rubble, motioning for Gavin to follow. Pain shot from Gavin's injured shin, but he pressed on behind Seth despite the agony. Chunks of wreckage shifted under his feet, making their climb far more precarious than expected.

"Careful," Seth said as they slowly clambered. "The ground isn't as secure is it seems. Bomb and I were almost swallowed when a room collapsed somewhere beneath us, and the floor turned into a rocky whirlpool."

"I'll watch my step."

"After the crash, I couldn't find you," Seth continued.

"I hit my head or something," Gavin said. "I just came to a couple minutes ago."

"Yeah, it looks like some of the gravity generators lost power before others did," Seth said, throwing a brick aside as he climbed. "It was hard to see with all the smoke, but Bomb, Ashton and I all landed a bit slower than the rest of you. It looks like most of the ship broke off and fell to the east side of the tower, while the Citadel itself crumbled to the west, off into the ocean."

"Yeah, I saw that through the smoke. It fell more or less right where Zaire and I plotted it would."

Seth nodded, looking out at the yellowish-brown tower stretching off into the water. "You should have been awake to hear the sound as it fell. I'll never forget that sound."

They reached the top of the debris pile and looked down on a crowd of Athelbrath and Dubaku at least 50 strong. Some bled from headwounds, others stumbled around in confused stupors.

"What the hell happened up there," Seth asked, coughing on the smoke. The two men began their descent toward the injured soldiers.

"We had to do more than just stop Abraxas-Mon," Gavin said. "The entire Hierarchy had to be brought to its knees. The Citadel has always been the symbol of their power. People see it as a physical representation of authority. It was a risky move, but Zaire agreed it would make the biggest impact. If we could bring it down, it would throw everything into chaos and give Zaire a chance to regain control and set things right in the power vacuum left behind by Abraxas-Mon. That's why we threatened the city so we could cause the evacuation. We wanted as few people as possible anywhere near this thing when it fell."

"I can't believe I thought that guy was telling the truth. I feel like an idiot." Seth reached over and helped an injured Athelbrath to stand. "Is Abraxas-Mon still alive, do you think?"

"I'm assuming so. Where's Ashton?"

"Over there." Seth pointed past Bomb toward a blond man covered in dust yelling in English for everyone to sit down and rest.

An energy blast shot through the smoke, hitting a section of

warped steel a foot from Gavin's head. He pushed Seth out of the
way and dove behind a pile of tumbled bricks and twisted gold. The
gathered crowd screamed in unison and darted for cover.

"I didn't have to miss, Gavin!" Abraxas-Mon shouted from
somewhere above. "I could have killed you right then, but I didn't."

"Good for you, asshole!" Gavin shouted back, not moving
his head from its concealed position. Looking through a hole in the
rubble, Gavin saw his counterpart step through the smoke holding a
bent silver rifle. Blood dripped from the man's right ear, a large
bruise forming on his forehead.

"Gavin! Stay behind the rocks so he can't shoot you!" Seth
shouted, waving for Bomb to come alongside him for safety.

"I wanted to say, 'thank you' Gavin," Abraxas-Mon
continued. "You took things so much further than I ever thought you
would. I thought ours would be a calculated game of chess played
over months and years as we tried to outwit each other. No, no, no,
no, no; you came at me with everything you had right out the gate
and risked it all on a single stand-off."

"I'm glad I could impress," Gavin yelled.

Abraxas-Mon pushed one of his wounded soldiers aside and
continued walking toward Gavin. "And you *have* impressed me!
This is what our entire lives have been building toward, don't you
understand? This moment! No one could have done this except you
and me. No one could have brought down this Citadel, hell, the
entire Commonwealth, except us. We're the same!"

"We are not the same!"

"Yes, we are!" Abraxas-Mon threw his rifle aside and stood
arms outstretched. "We are exactly the same. Look at what you did
today. You risked everything, your own life, and the lives of your
friends, just to take me down. You could have found another way to
save all of them and escape without a showdown, but you chose
exactly what I would have chosen. Now here we are in the wreck of
what was once beautiful."

Gavin jumped up, stepping out from behind his barrier. "You were going to take over the Commonwealth like a tyrant!"

"I'd already taken over the Commonwealth, Gavin," Abraxas-Mon laughed. "Whether a tyrant or not, things were still running pretty smoothly."

"You started a war!"

"One that would have happened one way or another within the next 50 years. Just admit that we're the same and you'll be a lot happier."

"You're a liar!" Seth shouted, storming to face the bleeding tyrant. "Everything you've said to me is a lie!"

"Seth, get back," Gavin urged.

"You told me my best friend went crazy, and I believed you!" Seth screamed, saliva flying from his tongue.

"Restrain him, please," Abraxas-Mon said, pointing several of his haggard guards toward Seth. Three dust covered Athelbrath warriors walked over with four Dubaku men and stood like a wall between their leader and the pale human.

Bomb pulled Seth away from the soldiers and any potential danger. She spat in Abraxas-Mon's direction before leading her boyfriend back toward Ashton.

Gavin picked up a brick and threw it at his doppelganger with all his strength. Abraxas-Mon dodged the clumsily lobbed projectile easily.

"Just admit it," the warlord smiled. "Admit we're the exact same person."

"We're not the same!" Gavin screamed. "You deserve to die!"

Abraxas-Mon wiped at the blood on his neck and rubbed it between his fingers. "And what do you deserve, Gavin? How many people are dead right now because of you? What do you think all these soldiers would say, or their families on different planets throughout the Commonwealth? Would they choose you over me, even knowing I destroyed Asha'asethol? I don't think so."

Teeth grinding; Gavin searched for a counterargument that wouldn't materialize. Had this been Abraxas-Mon's plan all along, not to goad Gavin into battle, but to show how they truly were the same person? If so, Gavin had fallen into it without the slightest protest.

"You're starting to see things from my angle, aren't you?" the warlord said. "I told you free will didn't exist, and you didn't believe me. Now you're starting to see that we're nothing but a collection of biological urges and subconscious commands. You responded today like a conqueror; like me. Like us."

"That's not what I wanted," Gavin said weakly.

Abraxas-Mon stepped closer, eyes understanding and calm. "But you did. You did. You're starting to understand that even if you win somehow today and I die, I won't be defeated, and do you know why?"

Gavin didn't answer, instead clenching and unclenching his fists in silent response.

"Because I'll still live on in you. If you kill me, you'll eventually just become me; you'll replace me. You're starting to grasp that now, I think. You will make the same choices I have, for the right reasons at first, but eventually you'll see the universe as I see it. My death is meaningless as long as you still live."

Taking a deep breath, Gavin filled his lungs and let his mind relax. He didn't want to accept Abraxas-Mon's words, but they made too much sense for him not to at least pay them the proper respect. All this time, he thought his plan had been to remove a tyrant from power and stop a war. Maybe those had been his original motivations, but somewhere along the way he had done what he always did: charge forward with only his ego in control. The ruin of the citadel, the damage to the city below, the dead under the bricks at his feet, all of it could have been avoided.

He had gotten his ultimate action hero role, only to discover it every bit as fake as his Hollywood movie personas.

"So, what do we do now?" Gavin asked, defeat clinging to his voice.

"We either work together or kill each other on the ruins of my home."

Gavin scratched his forehead, feeling the dull ache in his spine and lower leg. "Do you think Isla survived the crash?"

Abraxas-Mon shook his head. "It doesn't matter."

"I know," Gavin admitted.

With a speed he didn't know he possessed; Gavin lunged forward. His fist connected with Abraxas-Mon's cheek, followed quickly by an uppercut. A scream tore through the air as Gavin punched his foil again and again, much like he had inside this very Citadel less than two weeks before.

After several more hits, Abraxas-Mon retaliated. A swift jab to the gut sent Gavin stumbling. The warlord followed with a punch to the right kidney and an elbow to the throat. Reeling, Gavin choked and grabbed at a pile of rubble looking for extra support. Abraxas-Mon kicked the back of his knee, forcing Gavin to the uneven ground.

"This is what I wanted, Gavin," Abraxas-Mon said between labored breaths. He wiped his sleeve across his bloodied face. "I wanted you and me, face to face in the world's ruin. You gave it to me. It's like our birthday."

"I'm going…to win," Gavin gasped, massaging his throat.

"It doesn't matter," Abraxas-Mon replied. "None of it matters."

A large yellow brick smashed against the back of Abraxas-Mon's head, sending the warlord falling face-first into the wreck at his feet.

"Then you will not mind if I smash your skull," Isla said, sun shining behind her like an angel of light. Both her sleeves had been torn off; a red stain soaking into the fabric of her pants. Gavin couldn't tell if the blood was hers or someone else's.

Gavin opened his mouth to speak but found no words escaping his bruised larynx. Isla kneeled and hugged him close. Sniffing her sweat and the dust from the crash, Gavin shook uncontrollably with joy. She was alive, and she smelled like salvation and perfection.

"I love you," he croaked.

"And I love you," she answered. "I am so sorry. About everything. I need to explain."

"Just help me up for right now."

Isla stood and pulled Gavin to his feet. Fatigued soldiers looked at each other as if unsure whether they should attack or not. Gavin waved his hand at them as if to say, 'let's all take a breather.'

"Is he dead?" Gavin asked, looking back at the prone Abraxas-Mon.

"No," Isla replied. "We should get a rock and crush his head, though it would feel like murder if we did that with him unconscious like this."

"Give me a second to think of something. He'll be out for a few minutes at least. Is Zaire okay?" Gavin asked.

Isla's face darkened. "My mother is alive, though severely injured. When the singularities dispersed, she and I were thrown toward a vent blowing natural gas from lower in the Citadel. It exploded into flames, collapsing a section of tower on top of us. She pushed me aside and saved my life but was caught in the downfall. I have wrapped her wounds and burns, but it is likely she will need to have her right leg amputated."

Feet suddenly too heavy to lift, Gavin stood blank-faced. Amputated? Had he heard right? Zaire, the strongest and most impressive woman he had ever met, lay on the verge of death somewhere in the ruins. She had warned him about their plan and the possibility for their failure. Now apparently, *she* had paid the price while Gavin moralized with his genetic twin and watched the world crumble around them.

Damn ego. Damn Abraxas-Mon. Damn Gavin Baller.

"Where is she?" he asked.

Tears came to her eyes as Isla pointed toward a column of smoke and fire churning about a quarter mile to the south. "Not far. I spirited Ashton away quickly while you and Abraxas-Mon talked. He is caring for her now. I pray medical personnel will fly in shortly and we can get her–"

A kick pitched Isla forward and into a wounded Dubaku man covered in dirt.

"That hurt, bitch!" Abraxas-Mon cursed as he pulled himself back to his feet. "Once Brendant regains consciousness, I was going to let her flay you alive, but I think I'll do it myself!"

"Bastard!" Gavin shouted as he tackled Abraxas-Mon and threw them both against a pile of corrugated metal. Jagged edges cut into Gavin's arms and sliced along the warlord's back as they rolled along the rough surface.

The two men careened against a wall of crumbling brick and knocked the pile over. The crashing stone shifted a section of ground, revealing the once-polished floor of Abraxas-Mon's command ship. Like an earthquake, the segment of spacecraft quivered and began to slide backward.

Gavin let go of his opponent to try and jump to safety, but a hand grabbed at his belt and heaved him back.

"Gavin!" Isla shouted, reaching for him as he pulled away.

A terrifying rumble accompanied the hunk of spacecraft as it slid down an incline like a fallen hiker on a shale mountainside. Gavin held firm to a damaged doorway, knowing once they reached the Citadel's edge, they would fall ten thousand feet. And that would be it.

Before the section of the craft could tumble over the edge, it slammed into a solid section of masonry and spun around, throwing Gavin and Abraxas-Mon unceremoniously out. Broken stone and bent veins of gold rushed to meet Gavin as he rolled among the wreckage. Something sharp punctured his thigh as he skidded, but Gavin just added the wound to his growing list of traumas.

He watched from his belly as the black hull of the Serrated Cleaver tipped over the edge and disappeared in an unsettling roar. Scraping down the side of the Citadel like a knife against brick, the noise sent chills up Gavin's spine.

Wind slowly swallowed the sound and left behind a dominating silence, save for the occasional siren from a flying ambulance or police cruiser on the horizon.

"I don't know about you, Gavin," Abraxas-Mon mumbled with a quiet laugh, lying among the ruins. "But I am in a lot of pain."

Gavin tried to push himself up, but found his strength failing. "Yeah, me too," he groaned. Rolling onto his back, he sat up slowly and felt his entire body scream at him to lie back down. Thick red liquid dripped from a four-inch piece of rebar sticking out of his left thigh.

"You know," Gavin continued, "I had this fantasy that we would be, like brothers, you know?"

"We are like brothers," Abraxas-Mon agreed. "Brothers fight. Brothers kill each other for dominance. It's a historical fact, illustrated very effectively by Earth history. We're the ultimate brothers, just as we are the ultimate example of our species."

"I don't want you to die," Gavin admitted, again picturing the two men as jovial partners, laughing at a 4th of July barbeque. "Even now, after everything, I want us both to live. I could have killed you back there like Isla said, smash your face with a rock or something, and I couldn't do it."

"Because we give each other meaning." Abraxas-Mon smiled and pulled himself up to a sitting position. "And I wasn't unconscious back there anyway. I wanted to see what you would do. You're surprising me, which is refreshing. I don't want you to die either. I never did. I want our fight to continue for decades, punctuated by times of peace until one of us realizes we can't truly be ourselves so long as there are two of us, and the battles begin anew. And that is what we have to look forward to; a glorious competition that will define an entire galaxy."

Sitting back against a twisted mass of stone blocks and mottled gold, Abraxas-Mon closed his eyes with a joyful expression, as if picturing worlds being crushed between the egos of two men unable to overcome their need to destroy each other.

"Can we go back to when we first met and make none of this happen?" Gavin asked, standing up and patting dust from his thighs.

"Nope. We can only move forward."

Stumbling over, Gavin held his hand out for Abraxas-Mon to take. "We need to figure this out. If we keep fighting, we're just going to destroy everything around us."

Abraxas-Mon took his hand and lifted himself to his feet. "I agree," he said with a nod, tired breaths expelling from his chest. "I think our fight is finished for the day. We've done enough damage. I propose a truce for the time being to allow both of us to recuperate. From there, we can celebrate together until nature forces us to collide once more."

Gavin dropped his twin's hand and stretched his back, looking up at a flock of birds soaring overhead. "I'm not sure what to do, but I think I understand one major difference between us: the women we love."

"How so?"

"I really do love Isla," Gavin said. "Do you love Brendant?"

"No," Abraxas-Mon conceded. "Love and hate are emotions too close together to disentwine."

"*I* love and *you* hate? Is that what you're saying?"

"They're the same emotion, in truth."

Gavin coughed on the dust as it blew into his face. "I don't care. I'm going to choose to act out of love for Isla as opposed to any hate I might have for you. What do we do now?"

"Well," Abraxas-Mon began, "We are what we are. We can't change that. The only thing we can do is—"

Gavin slammed his body into Abraxas-Mon and pushed him toward the Citadel's edge. Wavering, Abraxas-Mon stumbled and stepped out on a ten-thousand-foot drop.

As if in slow motion, the warlord pitched backward, arms clutching for something to grab. A look of happiness spread across his face as he opened his mouth to speak.

"That's what I would have done," Abraxas-Mon whispered with a smile.

He pitched over the edge and plummeted head-first toward a pile of destroyed spacecraft and authoritative tower almost two miles below. No scream left his lips as he fell. Unconsciously, Gavin calculated how long it would take for the warlord to hit the ground.

Thirty-eight seconds.

He waited there the entire time just to make sure his doppelganger met his fate at the exact instant his brain predicted.

And just like that, it was over.

Abraxas-Mon was dead.

Wind blew in Gavin's face with almost hurricane force. For a second, he contemplated joining the despot…jumping out and embracing oblivion.

Had Abraxas-Mon been right? Would Gavin supplant him, slowly coming to the same realizations? Was it fate that genetically perfect men became tyrants? Did free will in fact exist, or was the outcome already determined by genetics and circumstance?

Questions grappled with each other in his mind while the drop called out to him.

Only one choice mattered: to live or to die.

Gavin could make that choice right now and end everything. It would be so simple.

He would never become like Abraxas-Mon. Death would guarantee that.

"Gavin!" Isla shouted from somewhere behind him. "Gavin!"

He turned as his love scrambled down the rocks two hundred feet above him, followed by Seth and Bomb farther up the ridge. A look of worry contorted her beautiful face as she slid down the embankment.

She loved him, of that Gavin had no doubt.

And he loved her.

"I'm here!" he called, waving his hand in the direction of his friends.

"Gavin! You are alive!" Isla gushed as she sprinted toward him. Leaping into his arms, they kissed. His lips lingered on hers, feeling their softness almost violently pressed against his face.

"Wow," he said as she pulled away. "That was some kiss." He laughed, tears coming to his eyes.

"I am sorry I had to deceive you on the ship," she said, a look of worry on her face. "I never believed you had left us for any of the reasons we were told, but I needed to know who the true villain was. The fact that my mother joined you, gave me pause, and her broadcast about Abraxas-Mon made me rethink everything. I did not want to believe the great warlord capable of such atrocities. He and I spoke after my mother's report from the Gadabout, and he seemed truly hurt by her words. It was all very confusing. But when I looked into your eyes and you told me you loved me, I knew the truth and had to act."

Gavin's lips bounced between a smile and emotional frown.

"It doesn't matter. I'm sorry I couldn't let you die. Don't hate me for that, please. I couldn't let you go."

"I love you," Isla stated firmly, touching her forehead to Gavin's. "I would have done the same had our situation been reversed. Once I came to that realization, I could accept myself. I am the same as I always have been, and thus the same can be said of all Cádavrite. You saved my life, and for that I will forever be grateful. You will never leave my side again."

Thoughts of jumping to his death receded, replaced by images of the two of them sitting on a porch swing as an old married couple, sipping lemonade or some other clichéd drink, while grandchildren ran around in the yard.

Any desires for Academy Awards or beachfront property, movie rights or gala premieres retreated in the light of Isla's strong will. As long as he had her, no kingdom, fortune or galactic title could compare.

He would never become like Abraxas-Mon. *Choice* would guarantee that.

Feeling suddenly lightheaded, Gavin stumbled slightly before righting himself again. Pain emanated from his shin all the way up to is beaten face.

"Are you alright?" Isla asked, touching his bruised head and bloodied nose.

"I'll be okay," he replied.

Isla clasped his arm. "You need medical attention."

"Ow! Ow! Ow!" he said as her fingers squeezed his shoulder. Pain surged; his body reminding him of its current damaged state.

"Where's Abraxas-Mon!" Seth asked breathlessly as he ran up to the lovers with Bomb by his side.

Gavin nodded his head toward the drop-off.

"Holy shit," Seth gasped, looking over the edge. "Is he dead?"

"I would think so," Gavin answered.

Bomb spit over the side of the shattered Citadel, saying goodbye to the warlord in her own simple way.

"How do we get down?" Seth asked, still gazing out at the city far below.

Isla held up her wrist; Thought-Mech blinking erratically. "Emergency services are currently relaying messages. I would assume ships will be descending shortly. We need to get them to my mother as soon as we can. I pray she is stable, but even if she is, that will not last for long."

"Have you heard from any of the Silverback Guard?" Gavin asked. "Maybe we can call them and have one of them fly us over to her. It will take us an hour to climb back up."

"Everything is jumbled right now," she answered. "I can only make out snippets of emergency signals."

"Well, let's start climbing," Gavin said, limping toward the rocky incline. His arm absently swatted the rebar in his left leg; pain almost blacking him out. He steadied and looked up at the stones in front of him. "Things haven't exactly gone according to my and Zaire's plan since we hit the atmosphere. We better move as fast as we can."

A high-pitched buzzing met Gavin's ears, pulling his attention away from the long climb in front of him and back toward the city. Smoke danced on air currents as a black craft swooped up and hovered in front of them. Four turbines spun on the automobile-sized craft, as if someone had taken a photography drone and expanded it to carry passengers. In this case, red and yellow lights flashed on the roof telling Gavin everything he needed to know about the vessel's occupants.

"Tell the cops to send an ambulance for Zaire," he said, raising his arms to the sky in surrender. "I have a feeling I'm about to get arrested."

CHAPTER 15

THE TRIAL OF GAVIN BALLER

"What are you thinking about?" Seth asked as he adjusted Gavin's uniform jacket.

"That this whole thing is a farce," he replied. "They dress me up like a military leader so they can have this stupid tribunal. It's a joke. At least I'll be dressed nice for later."

A set of double doors waited at the end of a long hallway with arched ceilings reaching 80 feet overhead. Athelbrath guards in full dark gray armor lined the walls silently. Late afternoon light streamed in from upper windows, giving Gavin his first glimpse of the sun since his arrest two weeks prior.

Seth rubbed his hands along Gavin's shoulder to smooth out any wrinkles. "How have things been in the basement?"

"It's pretty comfortable, all things considered. At least it's not a prison cell." Gavin shrugged. "The waiting has sucked pretty bad, but Isla has been coming to see me every day, so that's nice. I used my time effectively, though. You'd be surprised how many contacts I've accumulated since leaving Earth. Still, it's nice to finally get all this over with."

"Sorry I haven't been by in the last few days. I've had to face accusations of my own, along with Isla and Bomb. It's been crazy."

Gavin stretched his arms over his head and felt a pleasant rush of blood. "Yeah, Isla told me. Don't worry. This will be the last time any of us will have to stand in front of one of these hypocritical Plenipotentiary councils."

"Once this is done, you'll be free. We can put everything behind us," Seth assured. "And if everything goes like you claim it will, tonight we can party like it's 1999. Are you nervous at all?"

"Not for this part of the day," Gavin chuckled. "Tonight? A little, maybe. No, I'm feeling good. Will Zaire be in there, do you know? Isla wasn't sure if those pompous bastards would grant her request to attend."

"I think she will be. I haven't seen her since you were detained after the Citadel fight, but Ogpog told me she's doing much better. She's strong. They wouldn't let anyone but him and Isla near her. There seems to be a lot of political wrangling going on since Abraxas-Mon fell out of the picture…literally."

"Everybody wants to fill the vacuum. Have there been any official announcements yet about his death?"

"Nope," Seth replied. "A lot of rumors swirling but nothing concrete yet. There's so much politics in all of this Hierarchy stuff that it makes the Republicans and Democrats look like Booster Gold and Blue Beetle arguing over the Justice League's new catchphrase."

"Who are Booster Gold and Blue Beetle?"

Seth waved his hand dismissively. "They're comic characters; don't worry about it. They talk about stupid stuff when they're together."

A loud squeak cut off their conversation as the doors on the far end of the hallway opened portentously.

"That's my cue," Gavin said, turning toward his tribunal. "Wish me luck."

"Break a leg," Seth smiled, smacking Gavin on the shoulder. "I'll be waiting with Bomb and Ashton in the courtyard. You give the word, and the Silverbacks will rush in here and break you out, I'm sure."

Gavin chuckled. "I appreciate that. I'll see them soon enough. I did talk to Detrius last week so he could do me a couple favors."

"Brek misses you."

"I miss him. Thanks Seth. And don't worry; I think I'm going to handle this 'trial' alright."

"I have no doubt," Seth smiled.

Boots echoed loudly through the corridor as Gavin walked toward his mockery of a hearing. In the two weeks since his arrest in the rubble of the Cartoshí Citadel, he'd heard whispers of conspiracies and how Abraxas-Mon had been murdered while trying to stop a Hierarchy coup. Others claimed Hierarchy members said it was a terrorist attack ordered by the Rebirth Militia. Misinformation seemed the order of the day, which didn't bode well for the reality of a fair trial.

Stepping through the doors, Gavin entered a large circular room 200 feet in diameter. Blue walls ebbed and flowed with tendrils of white energy not unlike the interior of a Commonwealth spaceship. An elevated purple bench rose ten feet from the floor where 14 judges sat in official robes. Six of the magistrates were Nythensus, four Dubaku, and four Athelbrath. In the center sat Brendant, Commonwealth Matriarch and all-around awful person. Pale bruises still marred her lips, but other than that, she seemed back to her healed and horrible self.

Gavin expected to see Luminaries dancing on the air like

wildflowers, but surprisingly no glowing specks met his gaze. Apparently, the trial would not be televised or recorded.

Good. Gavin thought. *That will make things easier.*

Isla stood to Gavin's left beside the elevated bench dressed in a flowing green gown, thick curly hair tumbling over her shoulders. Ogpog entered from a side door and walked up next to her, nodding to Gavin like a coach before a basketball game. He pushed a floating wheelchair in front of him where Zaire sat wearing formal white robes with red highlights and intricate green designs along the fringes. Burn scars ran up her neck and left cheek, right leg missing below the knee.

Isla had told him about Zaire's injuries, of course, and the surgeries that had saved her life, but seeing the disfigurements for himself left Gavin speechless. He hadn't been there when she got hurt; he hadn't been there afterward to comfort her or take responsibility for his actions. Real consequences had followed his grudge match with Abraxas-Mon; Gavin only wished he could take his mentor's wounds away and carry them himself.

A look of love brightened Zaire's face, giving Gavin courage he didn't realize he needed.

Tears came to his eyes as he approached an illuminated circle of glass on the floor in the center of the room.

"Step forward, Gavin Baller," Brendant said, picking up a metallic ball the size of an orange and tapping it loudly against the counter in front of her. "You have been summoned here from your confinement in the detention quarters to answer grave charges brought before this council. We would like to recognize the former Matriarch, Zaire, along with Prelate Ogpog who have asked to observe this hearing. Due to their years of service, their petition has been granted, despite their uncertain standing with this assembly."

"What about Isla?" Gavin asked.

Brendant's eyes narrowed. "I am sorry?"

"Isla is here, too. Say her name."

"I will not acknowledge a Cádavrite within the precincts of this sacred hall…"

"Say her name!" Gavin shouted. Brendant jumped in surprise.

Blinking, Brendant glanced over at Isla with a look of disdain. "The council acknowledges the presence of Isla'a the Cádavrite, daughter of Zaire."

Gavin smiled at Isla, who returned his grin and mouthed the words, 'thank you.'

"That wasn't so hard now, was it?" he said.

"List the charges," an elderly Athelbrath judge stated with a wave of her wrinkled hand.

A Dubaku warrior with a thick afro dressed in the ceremonial garb of a Praetorian, stepped forward. "It is hereby declared that the Idumean known as Gavin Baller is accused of inciting rebellion against the Asha'andasa and their chosen representatives in the Hierarchy; initiating the unauthorized evacuation of the city Mantatol and the temporary displacement of 12 million citizens; attacking a Commonwealth battle vessel known as the Bolta'atrox; destroying said Bolta'atrox; causing the death of over two thousand soldiers and civilians; finally and most grievously, causing the destruction of the sacred Cartoshí Citadel, whose shadow once fell on this very chamber of justice."

"Of course, breaking the tower would be what would piss you guys off the most," Gavin muttered.

"The accused will remain silent unless formally addressed!" the old Athelbrath ordered.

"What is your answer to the charges leveled against you, Gavin Baller?" Brendant asked.

"Guilty," Gavin stated.

The Plenipotentiary judges murmured, looking at each other in confusion. One of the Nythensus motioned with her hands and blinked rapidly.

"You do not dispute these charges?" a hierarchy gentleman in an oversized yellow hat questioned.

"I do not," Gavin answered. "I did everything that guy said, and all of you know exactly why I did it, so why don't we cut through the bullshit and get this over with."

"What is 'bullshit?'" one of the judges asked.

'It means 'feces,' my lord," Ogpog said with a half-smile.

Gavin gave Ogpog a wink and turned back toward the tribunal. "Look, we all know what actually happened. We all know that at least some of you knew about Abraxas-Mon and what he did to the Perennials."

"You would accuse this council of breaking the laws that have been held sacred for thousands of years?!" an Athelbrath judge in a bright green robe spat, slamming his hand down on the judiciary bench.

"*Did* you break the law?" Gavin asked innocently.

Again, murmurs exploded from the judges as suspicious looks shot from magistrate to magistrate.

Brendant banged her metallic orb against the bench to halt any further squabbling. "It is clear Gavin Baller is going to offer no defense for is actions."

"Please, Brendant, let's not mince words here," Gavin said. "You worked directly with Abraxas-Mon. I'm sure that isn't much of a secret to the rest of you, and I get it; all of you have dirty hands, maybe not because of this but because of something else that got you to where you are. None of you are going to call anyone out for having blood under their fingernails for fear someone will look more closely at yours. So, let's not pretend that all of you are somehow high and mighty. You want all of this to go away so you can go back to planning your next vacation. I don't hear any of you crying out in righteous indignation about the destruction of Asha'asethol."

"The Asha'andasa home world will be rebuilt," a Dubaku judge interrupted.

"Whatever," Gavin said with a dismissive wave. "You have other problems to deal with."

"Such as?" Brendant asked.

"Abraxas-Mon caught all of you with your pants down. He manipulated you into starting a war to deplete your forces. You've slowly been weakened over the past five years. Now, I've gone and destroyed the Citadel and with it, the symbol of the Hierarchy's power. If I didn't know better, I'd say you're going to have a lot of challengers cropping up in the near future."

A loud banging reverberated through the chamber as the towering doors creaked open.

"Speaking of which," Gavin continued. "It looks like I'm getting my timing figured out."

Fralt Randok stormed into the hall, cane rapping against the elegant tiles, followed by a delegation of Gadabout clan lords and their bodyguards. Raymond Halford strode beside him, beaming like a teenager who just escaped from detention. Towering behind the two men walked Brek the Phylónethese, flanked by Detrius, Rolatok, and the rest of the Silverback Guard.

"What is the meaning of this?!" the judge with the yellow hat screeched.

"I don't know if you guys have ever met Fralt Randok, but if not, consider this your introduction," Gavin said.

"Hi there," Fralt said, striding next to Gavin with his entourage in-tow.

Brendant stood and pointed down at the intruders. "Fralt Randok! You are a criminal, as are all citizens of the Gadabout."

"Hell yeah, we are," Fralt replied with a deep bow.

"And I'm sure you all know Raymond Halford," Gavin continued. "After all, wasn't it this very council that secretly ordered him to go get me from Earth in the first place? I think it was."

"It was," Raymond agreed.

Gavin nodded. "It totally was."

"How did you get in here?!" an ancient-looking justice squawked.

"That was easy," Gavin said, pointing his thumb back over his shoulder. "You see the guards out there? They are so well trained that they won't even move unless given a direct order. Any of you judges issue an order for them to stop a delegation from walking in here today? Didn't think so. And if they had decided to raise a fuss, my Silverback Guard would have dispatched them with extreme prejudice."

"I would have killed them all myself," Brek growled, pushing next to Gavin.

"This is a travesty!" an Athebrath magistrate shouted.

"You're damn right it is!" Fralt grinned. "I was promised a tower that's now destroyed and all I'm getting in return is the lifting of some stupid sanctions on the Gadabout."

"We haven't talked about that yet," Gavin said.

The Dubaku judge in the yellow hat shot to his feet and wagged his finger. "We demand all of you leave at once!"

"I second the motion!" another judge yelled as the Nythensus next to her gesticulated their fingers and hands as if shouting in sign language.

"Matriarch Brendant," the Athelbrath continued. "Order these ruffians---"

"Will everybody shut up!" Gavin's voice echoed through the chamber with the power and forcefulness of Abraxas-Mon. All lips went silent at his command; eyes focusing nervously on his face. "Thank you! Now, here's how this is all going to go. This council will make a very public statement saying the war with the Rebirth Militia has ended and troops are being sent home to their families.

Then you are going to tell everyone that rogue militants attacked Asha'asethol and destroyed the Citadel, but they were eventually beaten back by Abraxas-Mon."

"You wish for us to hide the truth?" the Dubaku judge asked with a sneer.

"You've been hiding the truth for the past two weeks, feeding the Commonwealth scraps of information so no one would revolt. The legend of Abraxas-Mon is a powerful one. He will continue to be a symbol of goodness, fairness and hope. As much as I would love for everyone to know the truth, things will be better this way. You'll tell everyone Abraxas-Mon is alive and well and that he has commanded the Hierarchy to cede some of its power back to the people."

A Nythensus judge tapped his head and tugged on the sleeve of the magistrate next to him.

"I agree, Lord Anseltok," the justice said. "Why would we do any of this, Gavin Baller? You are here before us as an all but convicted criminal. You've spent 14 roused-cycles in our detention facility below this very building."

"And I appreciate you guys giving me a bit of downtime, honestly. It took a little while to get calls out to everyone," Gavin admitted. "Fralt here is a busy man; Raymond needed to reestablish some contacts so he could send messages for me, things like that. Plus, I needed to recuperate. I don't know if you knew this, but Abraxas-Mon beat me up pretty good. So, thank you for not arraigning me right away."

"Again," the judge pressed, leaning forward, "why would we do anything you say?"

"Because I am Abraxas-Mon," Gavin answered. "He and I were and are the same person. If you wish for another tyrant to rear his head and stomp you to death, I will happily do so. If pushed, I have the same capacity for violence and deceit as he did. You won't see me coming, even when you're looking right at me."

A hush fell over the council. Brendant sat back, lips pressed together with enough force to turn coal into diamond.

Gavin stretched his neck. "Do I have your attention now? Good. I agree to step aside and allow all of you to do your thing without interference so long as you accept what I say now as law. Anyone want to argue against that?"

The justices looked down with contempt but remained silent.

"Sounds to me like they're not arguing," Fralt said.

Gavin wanted to smile but kept his face a stern facade. "Again, you will issue those statements as I have prescribed. In fact, I had Detrius of my Silverback Guard transcribe exact instructions, which will be telegraphed to your Thought-Mechs as soon as I've called an end to this hearing."

"You don't have the authority to dismiss this gathering," the old Athelbrath woman hissed.

"I am the only authority!" Gavin's eyes blazed with fury, cowing the offended judge with his stern glare. "Now that you're all starting to understand things, let us continue. After you've cancelled the war, you will declare the Gadabout an independent state as opposed to a predator city and open up trade with them so that their economic situation can improve without quite so much piracy."

"I'm still going to raid your ships, just so you know," Fralt interrupted.

"You're not helping me," Gavin said. "And even though I knew you would sell me out to Abraxas-Mon doesn't mean I'm any happier about it. Piss me off again and things will go differently. You understand, Fralt?"

An uncomfortable look stole the smirk from Fralt's face. His neck muscles tightened, and he nodded his understanding.

"Did you make this financial deal with them so they would act as your personal mercenaries today?" Brendant asked, scorn dripping from her words.

"We've all got to make sacrifices, Brendant," Gavin replied. "Yours is going to be opening trade and letting go of some of your power. I'm not a fan of the Gadabout or its leadership, but this is the most public way to show your retreat from controlling everything. If the Plenipotentiary visibly opens economic opportunities, it will signal to the Commonwealth that peace is returning. That perception will be enormously powerful. The clan leaders are more than happy to accept the influx of cash and influence, and you will be more than happy to give it to them. Your stranglehold on the Commonwealth economy is coming to an end, and your management is going to work to guarantee that trade opens up beyond Cartoshí and the central Hierarchy cities.

"Along those lines; and this one is the most important and a non-starter if you refuse; Lady Zaire is to be reinstated as the Dubaku Matriarch and made head of this council."

Zaire's eyes went wide in shock. She looked at Gavin from her wheelchair, mouth open.

One of the Athelbrath scoffed. "Lady Brendant has been rightfully given both of those titles and we will not bend to your demand!"

"Then prepare for war like you've never witnessed," Gavin warned, a cold edge to his voice. "I can walk out of this chamber and claim Abraxas-Mon's army in an instant and we will descend on you like flesh-eating insects. Within half an annular cycle, the Hierarchy will be hunted to extinction."

Fumbling with his robes, the Athelbrath stuttered before speaking. "Then we will vote on this suggestion---"

"There will be no vote!" Gavin cried, stomping forward. "I am not issuing 'suggestions.' You started this! All of you! Now I'm going to finish it. I am not on trial here, you are! I am *your* judge. Brendant will be stripped of her title. You will publicly hand it back over to Zaire with apologies. Raymond Halford will act as Zaire's official advisor and remain in contact with me so I can keep an eye on all you. And finally, a decree will be issued that Cádavrite are to be given full citizenship rights."

"That is blasphemy!" a Dubaku judge bawled like a child who scraped his knee.

"The only blasphemy you need to worry about right now, 'judge', is whether or not you blaspheme my orders by not following them to the very letter. Do I make myself clear?"

The justice slumped back in his seat muttering to himself.

"Good," Gavin said. "All of you stood by as Abraxas-Mon slowly undermined everything the Perennials stood for, and once you had a chance to speak up, you either joined him or turned a blind eye. I have to wonder what you planned for when Perennials returned from missions in deep space in the coming years. Would you have stood by as Abraxas-Mon executed them? This moment is the consequence of all your inaction.

"Abraxas-Mon is going to rule over you, just not the Abraxas-Mon you were expecting."

"I am so glad I'm here for this," Raymond whispered to Fralt.

Gavin turned to Brek, motioning toward Brendant with a headshake. "Brek, would you mind escorting Lady Brendant from her seat and placing Matriarch Zaire in her rightful place?"

"I do not require assistance," Zaire said. "Fralt Randok of the Randok Clan; we have had our differences in the past, but it would not go remiss if you would lend me your cane."

Fralt's grip tightened on his staff. Gavin reached over and squeezed his wrist, eyes boring into the man.

"Fine," Fralt conceded finally, tossing his cane with needless force toward Zaire. She caught it easily and smacked the tip against the polished tile.

"I will be keeping this staff, just so you know, until I am finally fitted with my prosthetic," Zaire said with a wink.

Now every bit as frustrated as the judges, Fralt growled like a dog.

Pushing herself up, Zaire stood on one leg, leaning against the cane. With surprising grace, she moved the walking stick forward followed by her left leg and hobbled to the steps leading toward the raised judges.

Gavin glanced at Isla as if to ask if he should go over and help the Matriarch. Isla smiled and shook her head, turning proudly toward her mother as she limped past the self-important judges and stood towering over Brendant.

"I believe you are in my chair," Zaire said, stepping aside to give room for Brendant to leave.

The now-former Matriarch stood, neck muscles tensing, and looked down at Gavin with an emotion so hate-filled, words lacked the nuance to describe it. She stomped down the steps, turned as if to say something, and then continued toward the door. Gavin hoped he would never see her again.

Zaire took her seat and picked up the silver orb. A smile spread across her face. Rapping the sphere against the counter in front of her, Zaire looked to her fellow Hierarchy judges.

"I, Zaire, Dubaku Matriarch and chair of this high council, call for a vote to ratify the proposals issued by the great Gavin Baller of Idumea. Would anyone second the motion?"

"I second!" Raymond shouted to the laughter of the gathered Gadabout procession.

"And I third!" Brek added.

Faces scrunched in frustration; 14 hands eventually raised in acceptance of Gavin's 'suggestions'.

"Let the eternal record show that the vote was unanimous," Zaire continued with full authority. "Let the eternal record also show that this council will release Gavin Baller and perform all required public announcements immediately upon receiving instructions through our individual Thought-Mechs."

"Thank you, Lady Zaire," Gavin said with a bow. "Now, since all of that is done, I have a very important party to attend this evening and I do not want to be late."

Isla walked over to him, followed by Ogpog. She interlaced her fingers with Gavin's and smiled. "Yes, I would hate for you to miss that."

"Let's get the hell out of here," he said with a grin. "Lady Zaire, with your permission I would like to leave the justice chamber."

"Permission granted," Zaire replied.

Gavin waved his hand toward the justices with a wink. "Once you guys are done making the official statements and everything, you are more than welcome to join us for our wedding at sunset. I'd hate for important people such as yourselves to miss such a momentous occasion."

With that, Gavin turned, Isla on his arm, and strode toward the lengthening shadows of the hallway and a freedom he hadn't felt in years.

CHAPTER 16

LOOKING BACKWARD ON A FORWARD WORLD

Waves crashed against rocky ledges as the setting sun peaked through clouds over the ocean. A salty breeze carried the sounds of strange birds and a kiss of moisture from the curling surf. The wreck of the Citadel stretched out into the sea along the horizon, disappearing behind evening mists. Gavin pictured himself on the beach in Malibu as opposed to an alien coastline, and the thought made him suddenly homesick.

Of course, in that moment Gavin could have been standing in the most decrepit section of Los Angeles and it wouldn't have mattered.

Isla stood in front of him smiling, orange rays of sunlight shining on her cheeks and highlighting her grayish-brown skin. A more beautiful woman had never existed as far as Gavin was concerned. He held her hands tightly, afraid if he let go, they would once again be separated by war, tyranny, or Gavin saying something stupid.

One thousand two hundred forty-seven people sat on the beach, beaming at the couple. Gavin counted every individual person, knowing most of them to be friends and colleagues of Isla and Zaire. He lingered on a handful of his own guests though; Seth, Ashton, Bomb, the Silverback Guard, Bray, Seuss and Merida from the Gadabout zoo; hell, even Raymond Halford in his most expensive suit.

Missing faces tinged the moment in sadness as well; Dan, Folomí, Ātrus, Ugnol, even the debauched Frenchman Malory. Gavin thought about his old Executive Producer Tracy Cummings but figured if he were still alive, Isla never would have wanted the jerk at their wedding; and Gavin definitely wouldn't have fought to have him added to the guestlist.

The biggest void had to be Gavin's father. Even as a teenager Gavin had thought about having his dad by his side at his wedding. Maybe they could do some type of nuptial ceremony when he saw his father again; after all, his space-marriage certainly wouldn't be legal in the United States or Brazil.

Zaire sat in her floating wheelchair at the head of the gathering, while Ogpog stood stoically next to her like a bodyguard ready to die for his charge.

"As Dubaku Matriarch," Zaire said loudly so the crowd could hear her voice over the crashing waves, "it is my honor to bless this union. Isla'a; direct descendent of Efua and Kwame, the great parents of the Dubaku people who followed the Asha'andasa into the stars, leaving their home on Mother Idumea; and Gavin Baller, Commonwealth leader and defender of peace, I welcome you both in the final beams of the setting sun, Oktowe. Isla'a has chosen Gavin Baller as her partner and mate, and he has consented to defend her during life's journey. Now as our wedding customs differ from those of Idumea, I have allowed Gavin Baller to speak on his own behalf prior to the sealing of this union."

Gavin smiled, looking over at Seth and Ashton as they stood in front of the Silverback Guard in suits and ties borrowed from Raymond Halford. They looked positively normal in pinstripes and deep navies.

"First of all, I'd like to thank all of you for coming," Gavin began. One of the Plenipotentiary judges, sitting in the sand next to a group of Cádavrite soldiers, scoffed at the comment. Gavin motioned to Seth and Ashton. "I know it's not really a thing here in the Commonwealth, but on Earth…I mean Idumea, it's customary for the groom to have a Best Man; a friend who stands by him no matter what. I would like to invite my best friend, Seth Kemp, to come forward and stand by my side, and I would also invite Ashton Pingree to share in that honor. I would be dead if not for these two men, and I would be honored for them to be here with me."

Crying without shame, both Seth and Ashton stepped forward and took their place next to Gavin.

"What about me?" Brek said with a snarl. "I've saved your life, too."

"Fine," Gavin chuckled. "Get over here, Brek. You've earned it."

Brek tromped over excitedly, four eyes blinking in happy unison. "That Axelroth would have eaten you if I hadn't been there."

"He probably would have," Gavin agreed.

"Is there anyone else you would like to add to the wedding procession?" Zaire asked with a raised eyebrow.

"No, Matriarch," Gavin replied. "I'm good. Isla, you have anything you want to say?"

"I am fine," Isla smiled.

"Very well," Zaire continued, raising her hands toward the sun as it disappeared behind the ocean horizon. "Let these two be joined as one; chosen and lifted up together. May their journey bring peace and honor, and their children continue an unbroken line of life from universe dawn to the entropy of end times. Honor be on them and their posterity."

"Honor be on them and their posterity!" the crowd repeated.

Zaire grinned; eyes wet with emotion. She nodded her head toward Gavin and Isla. Everyone remained silent, as if waiting for something to happen.

"Is that it?" Gavin asked. "Am I supposed to say something now?"

"You may kiss me, if you wish," Isla said with a grin.

"So, are we married, then?"

"We are," Isla answered.

"You guys need to tell me these things, so I don't look stupid."

Isla pulled him in for their kiss. "You would find a way to look stupid either way, my love."

The gathered throng cheered as the couple kissed. Gavin picked Isla up and spun her around, bare feet sinking into the warm sand.

"Now let us celebrate this union!" Ogpog shouted. "Peace may yet again grace the Commonwealth, and we should drink and dance along with this couple!"

"That sounds pretty damn good," Gavin said, pulling Isla into their second kiss as husband and wife.

A bonfire illuminated the beach, casting shadows in every direction as revelers shouted and jumped in the warm glow. Stars flickered in the sky above like sentinels watching over the party.

Gavin sat in the sand, Isla's head on his shoulder, eating a piece of roasted fruit that tasted like an overripe pineapple. He savored the tang on his tongue and swallowed grudgingly.

"We should get out of here," he said, nudging his wife.

"You are excited for us to be alone, my husband?" she asked.

"Hell yeah, I am," Gavin laughed. "You have no idea how much willpower it's taken for me to keep my hands off you for the past six months, let alone the past hour."

"There is still much we need to discuss prior to us retiring together," Isla said, taking the last bite of fruit from Gavin's hand and tossing it into her mouth.

"Don't tell me we have to have some sort of committee meeting before we get to have sex. That doesn't sound like a great way to celebrate our wedding night."

"My mother wished to discuss a few things, is all. It should not take very long."

Gavin jumped up, pulling a laughing Isla with him. "Then let's get it over with so we can go."

They strolled over to a stone table carved from a rocky outcropping overlooking the beach. The heavenly aroma of roasted beef and vegetables met Gavin's nose, his eyes focusing on a platter full of food spread across the slab. Speculates fluttered on the air, illuminating the faces of Zaire, Ogpog, Seth, Bomb, and Ashton as they ate and talked about the events of the past few weeks.

"Isla said we needed to talk to you before we left," Gavin called as they approached.

"The bride and groom!" Ashton shouted. "Pull up a stone chair and have a bit of this meat with us. I don't know what it is, but it tastes awesome."

"We're only staying for a minute, Ashton," Gavin said. He reached over quickly and peeled off a piece of the unknown beef. "It'd be rude not to try some, though…"

"I can hear the impatience in your voice, Gavin Baller," Ogpog said as he ripped seared flesh from the bone with his teeth. "You have the rest of eternity to spend with my daughter. There is no need to rush."

"That's easy for you to say," Gavin mumbled as he chewed the tender meat.

"I did wish to speak with you both," Zaire said, putting down her fork and folding her hands across the table. "Sit."

"I'll stand so we can leave faster," Gavin replied. Seth chuckled as Isla slugged Gavin in the arm playfully. He grimaced. "Be gentle. I'm still a little bruised."

Zaire rolled her eyes and continued. "The Commonwealth is still in turmoil despite the Hierarchy's announcements this afternoon. The Rebirth Militia did not suddenly relinquish its claims that the Athelbrath are on the path to extinction. The species is indeed threatened as birthrates have dropped over the past few centuries, and this war has also taken its toll. The Hierarchy remains a powerful force as well. They will challenge any authority that seeks to remove their influence. We have taken strides toward ending these conflicts, but it will still require decades of work to fully halt what Abraxas-Mon set into motion."

Gavin stretched over the table and grabbed another piece of meat. "Yeah, we figured that's how it would go. What does that have to do with us?"

"You have taken on a leadership role whether you wanted to or not," Zaire informed. "You now shoulder some of the responsibility to see things to their conclusion."

Sitting down half-heartedly, Gavin pulled Isla next to him. "Look, I don't know how to say this, but Abraxas-Mon was right about a lot of things. He and I were the same person, and I don't want to go down the path he did. I'm afraid if I'm given too much power or responsibility, I will become a mirror image of that guy. I don't want that."

"You'd never become like Abraxas-Mon," Seth assured, arm draped over Bomb's shoulder.

Gavin shook his head. "It's easy to say that Seth, but trust me, I know what I'm capable of now, and if push came to shove, I could become something every bit as bad as Abraxas-Mon."

"So, what do we do, then?" Ashton asked.

Gavin rubbed the back of his neck. "Honestly? I want to go home."

"Back to Earth?" Seth questioned.

"Isla and I have been talking about it since after we took down the tower," Gavin admitted.

"We have," Isla agreed.

"You would retreat back to Earth, and what, return to your old life?" Zaire asked, a look of mild anger on her face.

Gavin held up his hand. "No! Think of it more as a sabbatical than a permanent relocation. Look, I need time to be able to process all this stuff. A year and a half ago I was just a famous actor who thought the entire universe revolved around me. Now I've overthrown an intergalactic dictator that looked exactly like me while learning I could kill people without even thinking about it. I can barely wrap my head around all of this as it is."

Isla reached across and touched Zaire's hand. "Mother, it would be wise for us to step back for a brief time. You are now back in control of the Hierarchy and have loyal advisors. The people of the Commonwealth welcome your return and believe that Abraxas-Mon is watching over them like a dutiful protector. Allow us leave to enjoy ourselves during this window of peace."

"I worry that window of peace will close all too quickly," Ogpog said with a shake of his head.

"Plus, I did tell the Hierarchy Council that I would step back and let them do their thing," Gavin added. "This way, I'll be keeping my promise."

"I can authorize one annular-cycle's leave," Zaire said, looking at Ogpog.

"That would be fair," the Prelate agreed.

Isla frowned like a thirteen-year-old girl told she couldn't go to her best friend's slumber party. "Mother, Earth is a six-month voyage from Cartoshí. If we left tomorrow, we would need to turn right around and return."

"Wait, Earth is only six months away?" Gavin asked, mouth turning upward. "But it took eleven months to get to Kr'thotok and another five to get over here."

Isla patted his face softly. "You need to return to your studies of traveling through three-dimensional space, my dear. Cartoshí is closer to Earth than Kr'thotok."

"Even I knew that," Ashton interjected.

Zaire held up her hands to silence the group. "Very well. I will authorize eighteen Earth months for your 'sabbatical.' And I expect you to remain in contact with me throughout that time. Our grip on the Commonwealth is tenuous at best. I have sent word to Perennial vessels scouring the galaxy regarding our current state and urged them to return to aid in our efforts. Their presence will do more to ensure peace than anything else we could do."

"When will they get back?" Seth asked.

"They are far enough away that it will take months for the message to even reach them," Zaire answered. "I would guess the soonest they would return would be two annular-cycles."

Gavin took another bite of the meat and chewed thoughtfully. "Can you hold everything together long enough for them to get here?"

"Hopefully, we find more survivors on Asha'asethol," Zaire said. "The fake broadcasts have been terminated and some communication has resumed. We are already receiving reports of new message channels being opened and finding pockets of Perennial citizens in remote location throughout the planet. That will help a great deal."

"Alright then, it's settled," Gavin said, clapping his hands together. "As soon as we can get a ship, Isla, Seth, Ashton and I will head home. Sounds good to me." He grabbed Isla's hand and stood to leave.

"I'm not going," Seth replied, squeezing Bomb's hand tightly.

Pausing in place, Gavin's mouth moved before his words came out. "What do you mean, 'you're not going?'"

"I'm not going," Seth repeated. He flicked a round vegetable about the size of a grape off his plate. "There's nothing back there for me."

"What about your sister?" Gavin asked. "What about Amber? She's probably worried sick about you after all this time."

Seth blew out a frustrate breath. "I'll record a message for you to give her, okay?"

"Dude, why don't you want to go back?" Gavin questioned, placing his hand on his best friend's shoulder.

Looking at Bomb, Seth smiled. "Because I have everything I want out here. What would I do, go back to my job at the Arizona Department of Transportation? Run into my ex-wife at the liquor store? No way, man. There's a bigger universe out here, and I'm staying."

Gavin tried to come up with some argument to convince Seth to come with them but realized they all had their own path to walk. They had both grown since leaving Earth, and unfortunately, Gavin had been absent for most of Seth's progress. He had hoped to spend some time on the return trip getting reacquainted with his friend without the stresses of language classes and looming war.

Their time would have to wait.

"Alright," Gavin said in acceptance. "But don't go taking over the galaxy while I'm gone, okay?"

Seth grinned. "I wouldn't think of doing such a thing without the great Gavin Baller by my side."

Isla stood and put her arm around her husband. "If things are settled, we can procure a ship in the morning. For now, I wish to be alone with my love."

"Hell yeah," Gavin said, feet moving before the rest of his body could catch up.

"Hey, wait one second, guys," Ashton said, reaching under the table to a canvas bag at his feet.

"I'm going to kill you, Ashton, if you make me stay here one more second," Gavin said with a pointed finger.

Ashton tossed the bag to his friend. "I just thought you'd like to have this back. It was almost incinerated when that bitch Brendant took over the Silver Hammer and had all the rooms searched. I saved it for you and held onto it."

Gavin reached in the bag and pulled out his signed copy of Dr. Seuss' *Oh the Places You'll Go*.

"Holy crap! I'd forgotten about this thing!" Gavin exclaimed. He rubbed his hand over the cover, touching the bent top corner affectionately. "Thanks Ashton; truly."

"That is a relief. I am sure Gavin would have made us turn around and go back for it once he realized we did not have it with us," Isla joked.

"Listen, this book is an important piece of our history," Gavin said, putting the children's story back in the bag and throwing the cloth handles over his shoulder like a purse.

"And thus, we will keep it with us forever," Isla said, kissing Gavin quickly.

Ashton waved his hand excitedly. "Yeah, and I was thinking of writing a sequel when we got back home: *Oh, the Places We've Been!*"

Laughing, Gavin grabbed Isla by the waist and stepped away from the table. "I'm sure it will be a bestseller. Now if you'll excuse us, we've earned a vacation."

"Yes, you have," Zaire agreed. "And I will expect to see you back here in 18 months."

"Affirmative, my Matriarch," Gavin said with a mock salute.

Stepping down the rocks, Gavin and Isla strolled along the beach, hand-in-hand under the watchful eye of a billion stars. Looking up, Gavin smiled.

"'Oh, the places we've been.' It has a nice ring to it."

He leaned over and kissed his wife, content with life for the first time since he stepped onto a Hollywood movie lot.

END OF BOOK 3

COMING EVENTUALLY:

GAVIN BALLER BOOK 4:

PERILS OF HOME

Enjoyed *Gavin Baller Book 3*?
Show your support and leave an Amazon Review!

OTHER NOVELS BY STEVEN HEUMANN

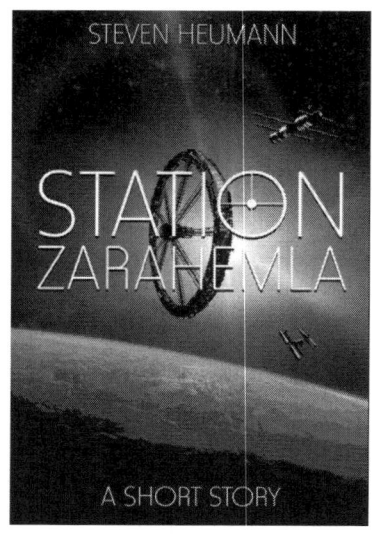

STATION ZARAHEMLA:

Peace is an illusion.

One sneak attack on the very heart of the galaxy turns a space station full of families into ground zero for war.

Veteran-turned-lawyer Helaman must make a stand to save his wife and kids, along with everyone else on the station.

Invading soldiers want him dead.

Local politicians are out to undermine him.

Can he hold things off long enough for the fleet to arrive, or will his efforts just get more people killed?

It's time to stand up for what you believe.

Station Zarahemla takes a historical tale of South American intrigue and gives it a science fiction twist. It's a page-turner that won't disappoint. Pick it up today!

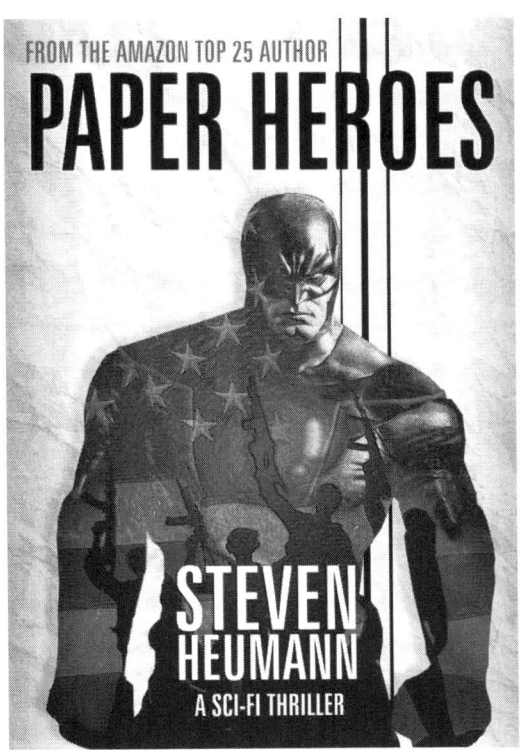

PAPER HEROES:

The bigger the hero, the bigger the lie.

Stewart Mitchell is a nobody, until he witnesses a terrorist attack that changes the world.

Right place right time, or did someone want him in the heat of the explosions?

Who's pulling his strings?

Who wants retribution?

Each choice Stewart makes leads him deeper into a world of fake heroes and villains.

The road to hell? Stewart's paving it as fast as he can. Get ready for superhero thriller where the good guys don't stand a chance. The hunt for Retribution is on! You'll love Paper Heroes.

RETOOLED: SCI-FI TALES OF FAIRIES & FOLK

You only thought you knew the stories!

Jack and the Beanstalk. Bluebeard. The Pied Piper.

Experience them now like never before as you delve into worlds of arcane science, post-war depression, and killer cyborgs!

This collection includes brand new sci-fi retellings and twists, along with several of author Steven Heumann's previously published works that will keep you guessing despite what you think you know about the originals.

It isn't every day you get to experience something again for the first time, but now you can with RETOOLED: Sci-fi Tales of Fairies and Folk!

Check it out now!

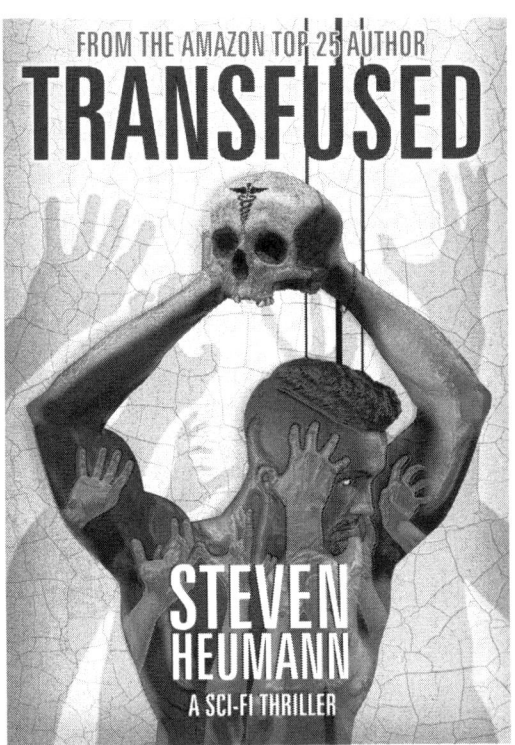

TRANSFUSED

Money. Muscle. Cancer. In the future, they all have one corporation in common.

What if you could receive the benefits of someone else's workout?

That's the promise of TRANSFUSION INC, a trillion-dollar company who offers heath instead of health plans. Anstead Miller is more than happy to get paid to exercise for someone else...until he's pulled into a world of deception, murder, and corporate greed, where even the happiest ending may lead him to an early grave.

TRANSFUSED is a nail-biting sci-fi thriller in the vein of **Andy Weir, Blake Crouch**, and **Michael Crichton**, that tackles the question of what happens when corporate giants start choosing who lives and who dies.

Pick up your copy today!

All of Steven Heumann's novels and short stories
are currently available at

www.stevenheumann.com

Made in the USA
Middletown, DE
26 April 2024

53523793R00170